Advance p
A Field Guide to

"Gabi Coatsworth has hit a home run with this charming story of a small-town library director navigating her recent divorce and new job, not to mention a demanding ghost who pines to be reunited with his true love. A delightful read with a lovable cast of characters. I was rooting for Fiona and George and all the rest!"
  -Linda Rosen, author of *The Emerald Necklace*

"*A Field Guide to Library Ghosts* is a cosily woven romantic mystery, with two storylines that slowly knit together to provide a satisfying and surprising ending."
  -Katherine Williams, author of *The Glovemaker's War*

"*A Field Guide to Library Ghosts* is absolutely delightful. Told from two points of view (one character is not alive but definitely lively), the book explores the depth of love, especially a love that is eternal."
  -Lorraine Norwood, author of *The Margaret Chronicles*

ALSO BY GABI COATSWORTH

A Beginner's Guide to Starting Over – A Brentford Novel

Love's Journey Home (memoir)

Available from your favorite book retailer

A FIELD GUIDE TO LIBRARY GHOSTS

A NOVEL

GABI COATSWORTH

atmosphere press

© 2025 Gabi Coatsworth

Published by Atmosphere Press

Cover design by Felipe Betim

Paperback: 979-8-89132-685-9
eBook: 979-8-89132-686-6

No part of this book may be reproduced without permission from the author except in brief quotations and in reviews. This is a work of fiction, and any resemblance to real places, persons, or events is entirely coincidental.

No generative artificial intelligence (AI) was used in the writing of this work. Without in any way limiting the author's and publisher's exclusive rights under copyright, any use of this publication to "train" generative artificial intelligence (AI) technologies to generate text, or to give away or sell the content, is expressly prohibited. The author reserves all rights to license uses of this work for generative AI training and development of machine learning language models.

Atmospherepress.com

For my friends at the Pequot Library in Southport, Connecticut, who have been my inspiration and support in writing this book.

CHAPTER 1

FIONA

Right now, all Fiona Gordon wanted was to head upstairs, kick off her shoes, pour herself a drink, and forget about the whole evening. In the lobby of her building, she stuffed the mail into an outside pocket of her bag, pushed the button for the old-fashioned elevator, and resigned herself to waiting as it churned its way down from the sixth floor. When it shuddered to a stop and the door opened, she entered, catching sight of herself in the mirror inside. Good grief. She looked every one of her forty-seven years. Her blunt-cut auburn hair was plastered wetly to her head. Her mascara had run, though that might not have been the rain. Thank heaven she hadn't met anyone she knew as she stormed out of the museum.

The evening had started so well. After all, over the years, she'd organized several successful—even perfect—fundraisers at the museum. But tonight's gala had turned into a disaster. Or a tragedy. Or even a farce—at least for Fiona.

All because of Brian and his new young wife, who'd arrived at the event flaunting a baby bump. Something Fiona had never managed. The reason she and Brian were divorced.

How *dare* he ambush her without warning on a night when she couldn't allow herself to react? When she needed everything to run seamlessly.

Fiona wasn't jealous. Absolutely not. Not exactly. But perhaps something akin to it. After years of marriage to this man, trying in vain for children, having to watch Brian's clichéd trophy wife produce one was a step too far.

Their appearance at the gala was the last straw. Now, she would hesitate no longer. She would get out of town, since it was clear her ex and his wife had no intention of leaving her in peace. Fiona pushed aside thoughts of the job search she'd started a year ago, which had still not produced any offers she wanted to accept. To hell with it—she would take the very next thing that came along. So long as it was far away from Philadelphia and the past.

The elevator doors slid open at her floor. Standing in front of her loft apartment, she waited for the customary sense of relief that accompanied her when she reached her safe little corner of the world. Tonight, it seemed elusive.

She entered, kicked the door closed behind her, and threw the mail on the small table nearby before shrugging off her tailored navy trench coat.

This was her own space, decorated the way she liked it. She looked up at the exposed brick walls of the loft that soared to the ceiling, and the tall windows with the view across to Reading Terminal Market and the skyscrapers of the city. She would miss Philadelphia if she moved. *When* she moved, she corrected herself.

She glanced at the now-familiar portrait of the original owner of the building, remembering the day a couple of years before when she'd found it at an antique show. It was a three-quarter profile, about three feet tall by two feet wide, depicting a handsome young nineteenth-century man, likely in his thirties. He wore a tailcoat and carried a top hat, and a small mark near his eye was all that marred the brushstrokes. The paint had probably smudged.

"I can let you have it for twenty percent off, on account of that mark," the youthful stallholder, dressed in boho chic, had said. "He was called George Manchester, and his family was pretty big around here back in the day. And let's face it, he's kinda good-looking if you want a man." She laughed as if this were a hilarious concept.

The person in question wore a confident smile, which appealed to Fiona, so she bought him. She would do a little research to learn more about him when she reached home.

"Hi George," she said aloud, as if the man in the painting could actually hear her.

*

When Fiona and Brian moved into the loft, she'd researched its history. She felt the reverberations of centuries emanating from the walls and wanted to know more. A certain Sebastian Manchester had built it back in the 1830s for warehousing the wool, silk yarn, and cloth he imported from Britain.

Sebastian's son, George, worked there too, but died in his thirties after being thrown from a horse while riding somewhere in the countryside around the city, leaving behind a widow and two small daughters. Fiona was delighted to find that the George in her portrait was indeed the son of the original owner, and that she'd brought him back to his home, as it were.

*

That didn't explain the strange understanding Fiona had with him. It was all nonsense, of course, but it was a welcome distraction when life became difficult. She'd become accustomed to the sensation of his eyes following her around the room. People who knew art said all good portraits did that. Checking him out this evening, she paused—was that a hint of a frown between his brows?

"What's the matter, George? Whatever it is, it can't be as bad as the day I've had." Though she knew he was a figment of her imagination, a bit like an imaginary friend, telling him her woes usually left her feeling better.

First things first, though. She walked into the bedroom to change out of her evening clothes and into something that reflected her frame of mind. Sitting on the side of the bed, she kicked off the new shoes she'd bought the week before, especially for that event. They were killing her.

More relaxed now in her flannel pajamas—the ones Brian always referred to as "passion-killers"—Fiona returned to the open-plan living area. This evening, custom decreed that a shot of something strong was the remedy for a hard day. A gin martini would work.

Maybe she should eat something too. She'd eaten nothing since a hasty protein bar at lunchtime, which had done nothing for her mood. She spread some Saint-André cheese on a few crackers and ate them before walking back into the living room with her drink.

"Since you ask, George, tonight was one of the worst I've had in a very long time. It's bad enough that Brian and I couldn't have children, but to have him show up at work to show off his new wife and..." She trailed off. This wasn't a time to complain. This was a call to action.

"Thanks for listening, George." She knew he wouldn't answer. He never did, because she'd made him up.

Picking up the discarded envelopes and fliers, she settled into the cream-colored sofa and took a sip of her drink as she scanned the letters in her hand. Two requests for donations to cultural institutions, including one from the art museum where she worked. She tossed them both aside.

The next one seemed to have a hand-typed address. She checked the logo in the top left-hand corner. The Wentworth Library, one of the places she'd applied to. Her heart gave a little lurch. So, after all this time, here it was. The yes or no that might change her life. Did she want to open it? Or would she rather not know?

The headhunter she'd contacted after her divorce had been optimistic about finding her something outside Philadelphia, but so far, the only nibble had come from this small library in Brentford, Connecticut. A couple of months ago, she'd traveled up to meet with three members of the board, but her anxiety resulted in a less-than-stellar interview.

The board chair told her the library needed overhauling to bring it into the twenty-first century, which is why they were looking for someone new to run it. This snail-mail letter, a physical example of how out-of-date they were, was probably a quaint way of sending her a polite rejection.

It was unlike her to procrastinate—so why was she delaying now? She turned the envelope over, as if she could absorb the contents through her fingers. Another sip of her drink might help.

Fiona hesitated one more time before she ran her thumb under the flap. One sheet of paper inside, she guessed. A rejection? The only way to find out was to look at it. Slowly, she drew out the single page, unfolded it, and read.

CHAPTER 2
GEORGE

"Thanks for listening, George."

This Fiona person is maddening. Why should I do all the listening? Isn't it time she made an effort to listen to me? After all, I make my attempts to start a conversation with the woman who lives in my warehouse—*my* warehouse, mark you—but she has yet to allow me even one sentence in reply.

Not only maddening, but strange. She must be poor, because she has no maid in the house, no one to cook for her, no one to aid her in maintaining her clothing or helping her dress. Perchance, garments as scant as hers do not require much attention.

In my time, this female's attire would be considered fit only for the boudoir. I have even caught a glimpse of her knees occasionally, no matter how I attempt to avert my gaze! Evidently, she does not realize how much appearances matter. They cement one's first impression of a person.

A point in her favor—she did buy my portrait, though she could not have known that I was trapped within it. I judge it a pretty good likeness. As I recall, it shows a good-looking thirty-four-year-old man in 1874, which is when I—a real gentleman, by the way—sat for it. How I regret having died only a year later. I might have had time to make amends to my beautiful wife Rose before I lost her.

I have been searching for her for a century or more, without success. I have concluded that I need someone in the present day to help me find her, and Fiona is the first person I have found who shows any promise at all as a potential assistant. Except that she doesn't believe my presence is real. Yet.

I have been practicing speaking and even shouting at her—loud enough that any person with a gift for communicating with the supernatural world would surely hear me—but she never reacts. I am becoming desperate.

There was a time when I was certain I detected from her some signs of a gift—a talent for seeing beyond the trappings of this world. Even tonight, I thought she registered my frowning at her. But did she react? No. She simply continued to talk about herself.

No doubt the departure of the man—I cannot call him a gentleman—who lived with her here has rendered her wrapped up in herself and unable to see the plight of anyone around her. Despite that, I cannot find it within myself to pardon her absorption with the one who treated her so ill, which I daresay is the reason for her complete lack of interest in me. Let us face it: one man's poor behavior ought not to taint her view of all men.

I feel the passage of time nipping at my heels, because although I may have eternity to pursue my wife, the woman here, being mortal, does not. I have to make her understand, for Rose's sake.

Poor, dear Rose. How did she fare without me? I am racked with guilt and pain because I abandoned her, albeit not intentionally. Had we not quarreled that day—over some trifle, to be sure—I might not have left the house with my temper so disordered. And perhaps I would have paid more attention to the fences I made my valiant steed attempt to jump, instead of breaking my neck.

I have searched for Rose in this twilight realm, but my efforts have been fruitless. It may be that she does not wish to be reunited with me, but I will not cease in my quest. If I find her, I will apologize for the fight we had and beg her forgiveness. Maybe then we can be happy again for eternity.

There is no point in tormenting myself with these thoughts. I must, I *will*, find Rose so I can make what amends I am able. But I need the help of this woman, Fiona, to do so.

Regardless, she is the best hope I have of finding Rose. Though I find it hard to credit that I am now a figure of history, the evidence of my eyes says it must be so. But the stories of important families such as ours may surely be searched for, and mayhap a perusal of documents or papers will prove instructive. I can only trust in providence.

Could I but appear to Fiona—become audible or visible in some measure—perhaps my fortunes might improve. God knows, I have tried. To no avail. Yet she persists in seeing only the face in my portrait. I cling to the hope that she will recognize my presence as I attempt to connect with her.

I must try harder to manifest before this woman. Perhaps if she sees me, she will recognize her gift for communicating beyond the psychical veil that separates us and provide the aid I seek.

CHAPTER 3
FIONA

"Dear Ms. Gordon,
The Board has not had any response to our communication of the ninth, so in case you didn't receive the email, I am writing this letter. On behalf of the Board of Trustees, I have great pleasure in offering you the position of Executive Director of the Wentworth Library..."

Fiona stopped reading and reached for her phone to find out what had happened to the email. There it was, in the junk folder. She transferred it back to her inbox and, while she was at it, moved Brian's last email into spam and blocked him.

Trying to distract herself from this momentous piece of news was useless. She had to focus on the letter.

So. This was a yes. The opportunity she'd been looking for—and half hoping not to find. Now, she had a tangible prospect of starting over.

She sighed. Her eyes filled with tears. Crying made no sense, because this was what she wanted, wasn't it? The chance to begin again. Maybe to meet someone ready to love her with or without children. And if not, at least to be rid of the feeling that she was second best.

She swirled the remains of her martini around the glass before taking a final gulp. Not a sip. What good would a sip do? This situation demanded that she either celebrate or drown her sorrows, and she couldn't decide which.

She turned back to the letter, scanning the terms of the offer. She wouldn't be paid as much as she was making at the museum. But it might be enough, given that she only had herself to take care of, and her overhead was low. After all, the library was in a small town in Connecticut, where life surely had to be less expensive than in the middle of a big city. In any case, she could negotiate for more.

In her mind's eye, she pictured the town of Brentford. She'd seen it in the early spring, when a late winter storm had left billows of quilted snow masking any ugliness beneath. Later, she'd looked at summer and fall photos of the town on the internet and found it attractive, quaint even.

Calling it a town might have been a stretch. More like an overgrown village with nothing to rival Philadelphia's history, culture, or social life. In fact, it seemed almost too small to support a library of its own. Perhaps the Wentworth drew their patrons from farther afield.

She stood and walked over to one of the floor-to-ceiling windows to look out at the twinkling lights of America's first capital. From the low buildings of the original city to the newer skyscrapers and the gleam of the river a few blocks away, the view was familiar and reassuring. If she moved to Brentford, she'd be unlikely to have anything like this again. The small-town job would be far away from this city's lively cultural scene and the beautiful countryside of Pennsylvania. So why consider it?

Because she couldn't afford the emotional cost of staying

here, and she'd had no other offers. The price of having nothing change, of remaining forever tethered to her past with Brian while watching his perfect future unfold, would kill her eventually—in spirit, if not in body. This might be her last opportunity to make a clean break and start again.

Who knew where this job might lead? When she'd applied for these three positions, her only thought had been to give herself some options. Now she had a choice—a real one—and she'd need to fish or cut bait. Though she wasn't sure she wanted fish.

She returned her attention to the letter.

"...We would be obliged if you would telephone us upon receipt to confirm your acceptance of our offer, since we wish to install the new Executive Director as soon as possible, preferably by the fifteenth of January."

It was signed by Channing Madison, Chairman of the Board of Trustees. She remembered him. A bland, round face, with protuberant eyes that seemed to be appraising not only her words but her appearance. She was accustomed to that, being taller than average and slender. She looked good for a woman in her forties, she knew.

Madison, likely some ten years older than she was, had been a little too full of himself, but, apparently, he'd approved of her interview answers. The man wrote the way he talked, like someone with a mouthful of pebbles. A man who never paused for breath.

Thanksgiving had just passed. They wanted her in place on January fifteenth. Six weeks didn't give her much time. She couldn't possibly get it all together by then, could she?

It was true that when she'd applied, Fiona had been motivated more by the location—not Philly, though not impossibly far away, either—than the position itself. She wanted to stay in touch with her friends and family, and Connecticut wasn't the moon. The Wentworth Library was about a four-hour drive away. Plus, it wasn't as though there were many opportunities in the small world of cultural institutions. Most of their budgets were being slashed these days.

There was housing to consider. Perhaps she could rent out her Philly apartment. That would boost her income. Or she could sell it—that should yield enough for a deposit on something in Brentford. But it would mean she'd burned her bridges completely.

If she decided to move, she'd have to prepare this place to rent or sell, pack up her stuff, find somewhere to live in Connecticut, and...

She pulled herself up short. It was all too easy to become stuck on the obstacles.

Suddenly exhausted, Fiona swung her feet up and stretched out on her beautiful, unblemished white sofa. Pristine, because no child had put a sticky hand on it, and now never would. Sterile, almost, because it had only ever been used by adults—one adult, Brian, mostly—since it had been delivered.

She lay there, too many thoughts racing through her head. If she didn't make a change now, she might be trapped on the sidelines of Brian's life forever, instead of starring in her own. Perhaps she'd manage to sleep if she were in her own bed.

She tried to find a comfortable position between her 600-thread-count Egyptian cotton sheets. Normally, they felt cool against her skin, but tonight she was too hot and thrust a leg outside the duvet to try to cool off. Whoever said that liquor helped you sleep? It didn't seem to be working this evening.

She must stop thinking about all this, or she'd never fall asleep. *Picture something more relaxing,* she told herself.

Connecticut. Pretty, like Pennsylvania. Full of WASPs. Maybe actual wasps too.

This wasn't improving the situation.

Perhaps the library would give her a little more time. She'd need it if she were to tie up the loose ends here in Philadelphia. So many things to arrange.

She rolled over again and punched her pillow a couple of times, trying to get comfortable. Breathe in, breathe out. Count down from a thousand. Should she take an antihistamine? Those generally put her out for seven hours straight, but she had to get up five hours from now.

"What do you think, George?" In spite of his silence, she often found an answer came to her after running things by him.

Worrying about insomnia only made it worse—that's what they said. She switched on the bedside light. How would she pack all her belongings in time? She had to stop this. Maybe if she got it out of her head and onto paper, she'd fall asleep.

She reached for the notepad and pencil on her nightstand and blinked at the almost indecipherable words staring back at her.

Dearest Lady,
Why must you contemplate this move? I do not wish to part from you. You are the only one who may understand me. You cannot, must not, abandon me here. Please stay.
Yours ever, George M

She rubbed her eyes and looked again. The words were still there.

She sat up to make sure she was awake and not dreaming. Could she have written this note herself—in her sleep? She used to sleepwalk as a child—anxiety, the doctor said. But that hadn't happened for years.

She should never have had that second martini. She must have written it while totally out of it. That was the only explanation. Nothing else made sense. Her stress had ratcheted up to such levels since yesterday that now she apparently needed input from her imaginary companion. Of course, this note wasn't an answer to her doubts. This was just the part of her that didn't want to leave Philadelphia talking.

Fiona sighed. Perhaps writing down the pros and cons would clarify her thinking. She tore the top page off the notepad and began to write. She started with the advantages and disadvantages, but by the time she'd finished, she found herself with a list of things she would have to do before she left.

So, more or less unconsciously, she'd made the decision to go. Calling to accept the offer from the Wentworth Library and quitting her job were the most daunting tasks, but she knew if she got them done sooner rather than later, she'd manage the rest. After all, that was why she always cleaned the bathroom first when doing the housework. Not that ditching Philadelphia was equivalent to wielding a toilet brush.

She smiled. She didn't often make jokes, even to herself.

She placed the notepad on the floor next to the bed, the pencil neatly laid across it again. Three o'clock. She should be able to sleep now.

She surprised herself by waking up minutes before the alarm went off at six and, after a huge yawn, rolled out of bed in a positive mood. Picking up the loose sheet of paper, she expected to reread George's note, but the page was blank.

Scanning it under the bedside light in disbelief, she thought she could make out shallow indents where the writing had once existed. It made no sense.

She couldn't think about this now. She needed to clear her head.

After her usual yoga stretches, she pulled on sweats, headed down into the street, and set out for a run near the harbor. At six-thirty, pale pink streaked the morning sky, as though the painter had decided a light blue fading into peach was too blah and added a warmer color before sitting back, satisfied. The smell of the water, sometimes salty, sometimes a little oily from the ships, soothed her.

She felt chilly as she began running, but soon warmed up. There was hardly anyone about, and she let herself fall into the rhythm that encouraged her mind to relax and come up with solutions.

It usually worked. Today, though, her contemplation of the note that purported to be from George crowded more important thoughts out of her head. What *had* happened last night? It was one thing to have doubts about this new chapter and quite another if she was writing notes to herself and pretending they were from him. That would mean...

A twenty-minute run would have to do. She had a lot to accomplish today.

CHAPTER 4
GEORGE

Will this torment never end? Why would this woman Fiona be contemplating a move away from Philadelphia? This is what I gather from her reaction to a certain letter she received tonight. I thought her life here satisfied her.

I suppose, without children, she requires some distraction, but she clearly does not need money. And although she spends every weekday beyond this place, it does not appear that she is entertaining herself with shopping, for I see no tell-tale parcels containing new purchases. Perhaps she is carrying out charitable works, succoring the poor, and so on.

If this is so, why does she need to move elsewhere?

It seems the letter she received made her some kind of proposition. If I have understood her correctly, a town in Connecticut is her goal. A small and unenterprising state, to be sure. I once passed through it on my way to Boston. In the two days it took the stagecoach to make the trip from the town of Greenwich to the border with Rhode Island, I saw precious little to interest me. Certainly nothing to compare to the City of Brotherly Love.

I left a note for her last night—a note that took a great deal of effort on my part, I might add. Creating writing by sheer force of will is extremely difficult. Yet she ignored it.

I must do more to prevent this move. If she leaves me behind or, God forbid, sells my portrait to someone who lives elsewhere, I shall never find Rose. No one else has even begun to understand my attempts at communicating. I need her to listen, before it's too late and she's gone.

Fiona, I forbid you to leave me!

CHAPTER 5
FIONA

Walking into the museum at eight-forty-five the next morning, Fiona made her way to her office, seeing it with fresh eyes. Soon, this view of the sculpture garden, this room, and this desk would be hers no longer. A momentary doubt flashed through her mind, but she suppressed it immediately.

The enormity of the step she was about to take was borne in on her as she pulled out the letter from the Wentworth. Her fingers, clumsy all of a sudden, gripped the page too firmly. She'd bought a cup of coffee from the café en route, and now drank the cooling remains. She hoped it would give her some Dutch courage, which she desperately needed this morning.

First things first. She must speak to Channing Madison about the job and try to negotiate a later start date. When she'd had her interview, he hadn't given her the impression of being particularly flexible, but if the board were desperate enough, they might give her some leeway.

She punched the number on the letter into her cell.

"Madison."

The voice was deep and businesslike. She realized she

knew practically nothing about him, let alone what he did for a living. He struck her as very conventional, and perhaps she should have Googled him before she called. Maybe he didn't need to work—a man of independent means. A wife and five children. She almost smiled. He would fit right into a novel by Jane Austen.

"Good morning, Mr. Madison. Fiona Gordon here."

"Miss Gordon. Delighted to hear from you." His tone was formal, but she detected an answering smile. She let the "Miss" pass. "Positive news, I hope? You've decided to accept our offer?"

"First, I want to thank you for your confidence in me. The Wentworth Library is a wonderful place that anyone would be happy to work for." She chose not to mention that they'd been searching for someone to do just that for months, according to the local paper, *The Brentford Bee*. "And I'd be honored to help make it the best library in Connecticut, as its director."

"So, that's a yes?"

"I hope so, but I do have a dilemma. I cannot come as early as you'd like me to. I have too many things to tie up here before I leave."

She waited for him to answer.

"Well, that's disappointing, of course."

A phone rang in the background and went unanswered. He must have been in his office.

"What's the earliest you could manage?" he went on.

"February fifteenth?" she tried, not expecting him to agree.

He didn't. "How about the end of January? Could you begin then?"

"Let me check my calendar." The last week of January wasn't much of a concession on the library's part, but it might give her just enough time to make arrangements.

But it would be easier to travel over the following Friday and start on Monday, February second. She explained this to her future employer.

"I think we can probably stretch to that. So, we may expect you on the second?"

Had she just made it official? She squeezed her eyes tightly shut and counted to three, as though she were about to bungee jump off a cliff. Something she wouldn't consider in her wildest nightmares.

"I look forward to it." Her words sounded as if they were coming from somewhere far away. Her calm tone belied the flips her stomach was making. *You could always change your mind*, said a treacherous little voice. She decided to ignore it.

Channing Madison broke into her thoughts. "Excellent. We'll send you a contract, and when you've signed and returned it, we'll be all set. I'm confident we've chosen the right person for the post. And welcome to the Wentworth Library." He hung up.

With the call over, she drew a heavy line through the first item on her list. Now to hand in her notice before she lost her moxie. Relief surged through Fiona. She was definitely making the right choice. Things would fall into place now.

She felt a sudden lightness in her chest. A sense of hope and optimism. Her future, whatever it brought, lay in Brentford, Connecticut, now.

CHAPTER 6
FIONA

The rest of the day passed in a blur. Fiona found it harder to concentrate on work than she'd expected. She called a couple of realtors and chose the one who bubbled with enthusiasm at the thought of selling such a desirable property in the heart of the city.

"Your apartment sounds amazing. I'm certain I can find you the perfect buyer if we price it right." She named a sum substantial enough to make Fiona's decision to sell easier. If she ended up with something close to that, she'd be able to buy a house in Brentford.

Which didn't solve the problem of George.

He'd left her a note a couple of days before.

My dear Miss Gordon,
Can it be true that you plan to abandon me here? Shall I never find my heart's desire? Please assure me it is not so.
Yours very sincerely, GM

This was ridiculous. Fiona sighed. It was hard enough leaving Philadelphia without being made to feel guilty by some character who'd died a century ago.

"How does my going to Connecticut change anything for you?" she asked the empty loft.

*

In the event, the sale of the apartment took longer than the realtor had promised. Until a buyer was found and the deal completed, Fiona was left with no choice but to find a place to rent in Brentford.

She checked the listings in the online edition of the town newspaper, *The Brentford Bee*, and experienced sticker shock at the prices. After all, the town wasn't exactly a metropolis, and though within commuting distance of New Haven, it wasn't a particularly desirable location, was it?

On the other hand, the more she scanned the paper's old-fashioned website, the more she began to understand the attractions of a small town and the idea of living life in a slower lane. She speed-read the articles—each with a photo—about the Cherry Blossom Festival to be held in May, the reports of Scout meetings, weddings, PTA, and sports events at the local high school.

The police blotter consisted of one ticket for impeding traffic. The miscreant, a certain Miss Elaine Johanssen, aged eighty-nine, had been driving twenty miles an hour in a thirty-mile-an-hour zone.

It all appeared blissfully uncomplicated, except Fiona found few rentals that might suit her. Too big, too small—the Goldilocks house remained elusive. As for buying, the homes she might be able to afford eventually always had a drawback. "Structurally sound" generally meant decoratively appalling, judging by the photos in the listings. "Cozy" indicated tiny rooms, and "vintage" was the polite way of saying the house had 1890s plumbing. She wouldn't have the time or money to make any improvements to her new home, whatever it turned out to be.

Time was running short, so right now, renting was the only option, and she needed help, if possible, on the ground in Brentford. She emailed Channing Madison to ask if he could recommend a realtor. He called her back.

"Miss Gordon, I fear there's been a misunderstanding. You may have forgotten—the position of Executive Director comes with free lodging. I'm certain we mentioned it in the contract."

Fiona was pretty sure they hadn't. Or had she just spaced it?

"I'm afraid I don't remember. I was so focused on preparing to move."

Now she recalled something about "grace-and-favor" accommodations. She looked it up and discovered it was a leftover from colonial days, meaning rent-free. For once, she was glad the Wentworth was steeped in tradition.

It had never occurred to her that the library would provide somewhere for her to live. She had visions of a room in someone's home as a lodger, or somewhere out of town altogether.

"What...sort of accommodations are we talking about?"

"Perhaps you recall the gatehouse at the beginning of the drive, as you approach the library?"

A gatehouse? There was something archaic about that word, too. She couldn't remember a gate to the Wentworth, never mind a gatehouse. When she'd arrived for her interview, Fiona had vaguely registered some kind of building near the driveway. Evergreens screened most of it, so she hadn't paid much attention. While Channing kept talking, she pulled up Google Maps on her computer and checked the street view.

She found the library. So, the building near the road must have been the home they were offering her. Only part of it was visible because of the shrubbery. If it were up to her, she'd describe it more as a stone cottage rather than a house, but who was she to argue with the original Mr. Wentworth? After all, he must have commissioned it. At least it looked solid. The front porch even had a rocker on it. She wondered how long ago the photo had been taken.

Channing Madison was still explaining. "The Wentworths built it in the nineteenth century for the coachman, and for the last few years, our janitor has occupied the place. He died in October, and the new man already had somewhere to live, so it's been standing empty since then. It's nothing grand. Two bedrooms. But for a single lady…"

Fiona chose to ignore that. Her relief was so palpable that she had to speak. "It sounds perfect. And thank you," she added hastily, before a thought struck her. "Would it be possible to send me the measurements of the rooms, so I can make sure my furniture will fit?"

She pictured her oversized cream sofa and wondered whether it would have to be jettisoned due to its size. Maybe she ought to get rid of it anyway. She'd be better off without reminders of her old life.

"Certainly. I'll have Joanie send them and ensure the house is aired out before you arrive. You'll inform me of your ETA, so we can arrange for someone to meet you and let you in."

It was more of a statement than a question. Fiona tried, and failed, to remember who Joanie was.

"Of course. I can't tell you how grateful I am. I was beginning to think I'd have to sleep between the stacks in the library, to begin with." She attempted a laugh, but her anxiety made it sound more like a cough.

"That's not permitted, Miss Gordon." He must have realized she'd been joking. "I daresay you weren't serious. Nonetheless, I'm glad this solves your problem. Is there something else I can help with?"

"Thank you, no. Housing was my most pressing issue."

"Well, I hope if you think of anything, you'll let me or Joanie know."

After a last round of thanks and a reminder to send the room measurements, they hung up, and Fiona sat back in her chair and released the breath she hadn't realized she'd been holding. One more thing to cross off her list.

And one to add. *Tell George.*

CHAPTER 7
GEORGE

It is clear that my notes are being ignored by the woman Fiona. I see the steps she is taking to prepare for a move of some distance. Packing boxes are to be found all over the apartment. To hear the language when she trips over one is to wonder how a delicately nurtured female ever came by such a vocabulary. She sounds exactly like the dockers who unloaded our goods in the Port of Philadelphia.

I have heard her having one-sided conversations while holding a small cigarette case to her ear. One such appeared to be with a real estate agent. Something to do with selling this apartment, which is out of the question. I am tempted sometimes to answer her, since she must be lonely, or she would not be talking to herself.

But in this regard, my frustration is growing. She talks to me sometimes—I am convinced of it. I answer her, but perceive no recognition in her face. Perhaps if I raised my voice, something I was taught never to do except in the stables or whilst hunting, that might help. It's a pity no one thought to yell and warn me of the gate I tried to jump that ended my life. But I must not dwell on what's done. I will attempt to shout.

"Miss Gordon! Miss Gordon!"

Silence on her part. She simply continues to sort through books from her shelves.

"Fiona! Fiona!"

No response. And then, "What am I going to do with you, George?"

Do with me? The very idea is preposterous. I bellow beyond the volume my ears can tolerate. But needs must. "Stay here! Stay here!"

She stops suddenly, an open book in her hand, her head cocked to one side, as though...could she be...listening? I try harder.

"Do not go! I need you!" If I were still of the earthly sphere, my throat would doubtless be showing signs of strain by now. But she can hear me. I am certain of it.

Fiona runs the back of her hand across her pale brow. I would pass her a handkerchief if I were able. Still, the effect of my voice is something.

"George? Is that you?" Fiona bats a palm against one ear and shakes her head as if to dislodge something inside. "This can't be happening," she says. "But it is rather fun to imagine it might." Then, cautiously, almost in a whisper, she asks, "George, is it really you?"

"Yes!" I shout. I want to keep repeating it, but there's no need.

She says, "You don't want me to leave?"

I attempt a quieter tone. "I cannot live without you here." I have to make her understand me. She is the first person I have been able to communicate with since I expired.

She squares her shoulders, like a woman who's gained confidence from this exchange, though it's clear she misunderstands it.

"I hesitate to point this out," she says, without hesitating at all, "but you don't...*ahem*...actually *live* here. Your portrait is here, but you are, in fact, an illusion." She pauses. "And what's more, you're late."

"Late? For what?"

"Oh dear. Late, in the sense of departed, you know."

"You are mistaken. It is you who are departing," I say.

A sigh of exasperation. "Are you going to make me say it, George? You're..." The next part of the sentence comes out in a rush. "Defunct, pushing up the daisies, in short—dead."

With this, she falls into a chair, her hand over her mouth, as well she might. Such a tactless thing to say. I imagine my remains are buried in the family plot, not amongst the rest of the hoi-polloi with their daisies. I am certainly not going to respond to this kind of abuse. I will never speak to her again.

Yet—I must. She is the only one I have found who has ever succeeded in hearing me, and although the results of our conversation have not been particularly fruitful so far, I must remind myself—we have at least conversed. I need a way, though, to persuade her that I'm real. Perhaps if I tell her something about myself that only I could know, she will believe in me.

In the meantime, it appears we are destined for pastures new—and less interesting.

CHAPTER 8
FIONA

The five-hour drive to Connecticut hadn't exactly raised Fiona's spirits. Driving a rented van and towing her car slowed her up a lot. A damp-inducing drizzle made the highway harder to see, so every time she found herself in the wake of a truck, she was almost blinded by the spray from its wheels. She didn't remember the trip being quite so bleak last time.

George's portrait sat silently next to her, buckled into the seat belt. Perhaps his ghost or whatever it was had decided to stay behind in Philadelphia, after all. He'd stopped talking to her since she'd told him she was leaving.

*

There'd been absolutely no reason for Fiona to feel guilty when she said, "It's final, George. I'm going to Connecticut." Silence greeted this remark. "But I am taking your painting with me."

A faint thud somewhere in the apartment was probably the icemaker dropping cubes. She must remember to clear it out before she left.

"I know you belong here, in a way, but I'm kind of used to seeing you on my wall. In any case, I own you—your picture anyway. *You*, whatever you are, can always remain here, can't you?" Why was she explaining herself to George? Trying to placate him? The truth was, she would miss him if he weren't with her.

Even though George was someone she'd invented, her one-sided conversations with him had proved useful as a sounding board. Sounding portrait, to be more precise. She knew she was just working out the problems in her life by means of imaginary conversations with this Victorian entity. But he made her feel less lonely, and that might stop if she left his portrait behind. She wasn't about to risk that.

The silence made her feel he was sulking, which was ridiculous. He wasn't real. He was an illusion. Wasn't he?

*

The interstate snaked through every built-up area on the East Coast, and the misty gray of the day made it hard to distinguish one town from another. Eventually, an hour after entering Connecticut, her route had taken her off the highway and onto a winding old road that led to her destination.

The skies began to clear as she approached Brentford—otherwise, she might have missed the fork. But her GPS kept her on track, and soon she spotted St. Michael's church, where Channing Madison had told her to turn for the library on her previous visit. Now she recognized the two stone pillars inscribed with "Wentworth" and "Library" and noted a couple of rusted hinges representing the vestiges of a gate.

As she turned the wheel to enter the driveway, the gatehouse appeared on her right, coming into view between some ancient rhododendrons, judging by their height. Glad she'd managed to make it before dusk, she drew up on the grass, alongside a somewhat battered blue Camry parked next to the house.

"Welcome to the Wentworth Library, Ms. Gordon," chirped a voice from the front door. A small woman with a weather-beaten face and a cheerful smile was standing at the top of the front steps. The porch itself seemed to be listing a few degrees to the left, and it needed a coat of paint, but it gave the place the appealing shabby-chic air that Fiona had seen in movies and magazines. She hoped the cottage was one of those structurally sound, decoratively disastrous houses. Decor could be fixed.

"I'm Joanie Yazbeck. Head librarian. I met you briefly when you came to interview."

The woman smiled as Fiona stuck out a hand and said, "Hello. It's so kind of you to give up your afternoon to meet me."

She had been battling fatigue for the last few days as she pulled together everything she needed to do before the move. It was finally getting to her. She trudged up the porch steps, eyeing the flaking paint as she went.

"No worries. I was on duty at the library today, so it was no problem."

"Still, I appreciate it." Fiona shifted from foot to foot. Ms. Yazbeck was standing in front of the door, as if guarding the entrance.

The librarian gave her a sympathetic look. "You must be tired."

Fiona nodded. An understatement. And it was only four in the afternoon. The day wasn't anywhere near over yet.

Joanie indicated the front door with a wave of her hand. "Come inside and I'll show you around."

She ushered Fiona into the house, giving her a first glimpse of her new home. She flipped a switch, and a single bulb in the hallway came to life, casting shadows as much as illuminating the space. Fiona could see no other light fixtures.

"I'm afraid the place still smells a bit musty. I think it should air out in a day or two."

Fiona heard a low rumbling that sounded as though it came from the old-fashioned radiator to her right. She turned to Joanie, an eyebrow raised in a question.

"Oh, that'll be the heating. You'll be warm as toast before you know it. Besides, there's a fireplace in the living room, as a backup."

Fiona nodded. Right now, all she could deal with were the immediate necessities. She'd had the foresight to research the nearest grocery store. Jackson's Pantry was around the corner with Brentford Ironmongers not far beyond it. With a name like that, the establishment must have been in business since before the Revolution. In any case, she'd be okay.

"Can you tell me when the local stores close?"

"As late as five or six, usually, depending on what you're looking for."

Fiona gave a strained smile and thought longingly of the all-night shops in Philadelphia.

"Just wondering. I have a box of groceries in the car," she said. "I expect they'll tide me over until tomorrow."

She sounded more optimistic than she felt. There were some crackers in there, and a jar of olives. Half a jar of peanut butter. Perhaps a can or two of tuna.

"I've left some soup from Jackson's and some milk and fresh eggs in the fridge. Hopefully, that will supplement whatever you have."

How thoughtful. Not only a place to live, but food too. "Thanks so much, Joanie. I appreciate it."

"Shall we take a look upstairs?"

The two bedrooms were hidden beneath the eaves, and, staring into one in the fading daylight, Fiona figured she'd only be able to stand upright in the middle of the room, where a bed would normally fit.

She took two steps across the landing to the second bedroom. The sky was beginning to clear, and she noticed the hazy setting sun through the window. Encouraging. This room had a higher ceiling and would get afternoon light. She wandered over and surveyed the street. A man walked by with an unidentifiable animal of the canine species on a leash. As she watched, a bright yellow Toyota drove past, weaving in a genteel way to give the pedestrians plenty of space.

She turned back to the room.

"This should work nicely," said Fiona, turning to Joanie, who nodded and led the way back downstairs.

"By the way, I asked my son and a friend of his to help you unload your stuff, or at least enough for your first night," Joanie went on. "I texted them and they said they'd be right over. They're nice boys, but you'll need to keep an eye on them, or they'll put things in the wrong place."

"That's wonderful, thank you. If they can give me a hand with the heavier pieces, like the table and chest of drawers—oh, and the armchairs—I think I can manage almost everything else." She'd abandoned the sofa, after all. It would have stuck out like an enormous sore thumb in this compact room, even if she'd managed to squeeze it through the doorway, which she doubted.

At that moment, a knock on the door announced visitors. They went down to answer it, and Fiona came face to face with a couple of teenage boys, who were shuffling from foot to foot, as if they'd prefer to be anywhere but here.

"Come in and introduce yourselves," said Joanie.

The boys shuffled in and flattened themselves against the wall in the narrow hallway.

"Hi, I'm Kyle." This came from a youth who, being shorter than her, couldn't look Fiona in the eye. He bore a startling resemblance to Johnny Depp. Perhaps his acne made him feel awkward. She could relate. At his age, she'd felt like an ugly duckling too.

Kyle's friend was the spitting image of Joanie. Clearly, this was her son. "I'm Tyler." After a nod and a frown from Joanie, he reached out his hand to shake Fiona's.

"Well, you're a welcome sight. Shall I show you what needs to be done?"

Fiona led the boys out to the van and uncoupled the car. She rolled up the truck's back door and assessed the collection of furniture and other possessions inside.

"Do you want to start unloading the lamps first? I'm going to need them. You'll figure out the right place to put stuff. I'll be in the house if you have to ask me anything."

Joanie took charge of the lampshades, while Fiona carried George into the living room and set him on the mantelpiece. She was accustomed to the feeling that his eyes were following her around, but now they were in a dead stare, looking toward the window.

If that's how he was going to be, too bad.

*

She headed upstairs with one of the smaller rugs and laid it on the bedroom floor. She could make this into a home, she was sure.

"Where do you want this?" came a shout from below. Fiona emerged onto the small landing and looked over the banister. The boys were threatening to lose their grip on the dining-table top.

"In the kitchen, please."

"No problem." They disappeared through the doorway, accompanied by a thud.

"It's fine!" one of them shouted. "It won't show."

Fiona winced and closed her eyes. She must be philosophical about it. Her farmhouse-style table was already distressed. Someone had thought to age it by beating it up a little. There was no point in her getting distressed too.

CHAPTER 9
GEORGE

I find it almost impossible to believe that we could have arrived in Connecticut so soon. We made the trip of something over 150 miles in only five hours—without taking any ferries across the Hudson River! This was fortunate, since it rained most of the way, and the crossing would have been rough. Apparently, they have built bridges of extraordinary length since my time.

Still, when I made that trip in the 1870s—what with stopping to change horses, feed and water them as well as the passengers on the stagecoach—it was long and tedious. I was not yet fully recovered from the pneumonia, which came close to finishing me off, but did bring me home from Gettysburg just before that dreadful battle. A mercy, since I survived the lung fever. My survival of that military encounter would have been less certain.

*

On our trip today, we stopped once, and Fiona returned to her motor carriage holding a container made of paper with a beverage inside. I believe it might have been coffee. And a small canister of something called Dingles—seemingly flaked potatoes—she ate as a snack, while driving the vehicle. I imagine this is not approved behavior, but she succeeded in consuming both items without mishap.

I will say one thing for her—if nothing else, she is resourceful.

Now, it appears we have reached our destination. I can only hope that she will treat me with the respect I deserve and hang me in a prominent place where I can be admired. And where I might have a chance of communicating with her. I shall bide my time, of course. It would not do to make friendly overtures again too soon. She needs to learn that I am not to be trifled with.

*

To my dismay, she has propped me up on what appears to be a mantelpiece! I sincerely hope no one lights a fire beneath me—I would hate to be the victim of another accident. If my portrait were to be destroyed, my quest to find Rose would be over. It could be worse, I suppose. At least I am in what is to become the parlor, or living room, as she calls it. Such a vulgar expression.

All the same, I recognize that hanging in the place of honor won't be enough to help me. My mission may already be doomed. I do not believe Fiona can find out anything about Rose from this distance. Everything we need to know, every document or graveyard we need to examine, must be in Philadelphia.

What single lady would choose to move from there to this overgrown hamlet? The woman is unlikely to be much occupied. In fact, without a spouse, what can she possibly hope to gain by living here? She is someone who likes to be busy, and this podunk town can have nothing of substance to offer her.

I must think more hopeful thoughts, or I will become melancholy. It may be that with the city of my birth less than a day away, I can persuade her to return there for a while to keep looking. Or perhaps boredom will cause her to return to our home for good. She must come to her senses, and I will help her do so.

So. I must not despair. We arrived here so swiftly—it will be a bagatelle to return.

CHAPTER 10
FIONA

Fiona shivered. The house was taking too long to heat up.

The boys had carried in her two small easy chairs, seemingly made-to-measure for the gatehouse. She told them to put the old leather armchair with the comfortable hollow in the seat to one side of the fireplace. The other stood across from it, an antique bergère she'd recovered in scarlet damask in a moment of creative abandon. All she needed was the new bed she'd ordered.

Fiona surveyed the room, and her eyes alighted on George, undamaged in his frame. Propped up on the mantel, he appeared quite at home after his trip—almost as if he'd always been in this house. Perhaps moving into a home of the same vintage as the loft hadn't been too much of a shock after all. She shivered as a chilly draft raced over the back of her neck.

Three substantial logs lay ready on the hearth, and Fiona knew she would have a ton of wrapping paper she could use to start a fire, once she'd unpacked a box or two. That would make the place more welcoming. She might even be able to take off her jacket.

Joanie glanced at her. "Are you okay, Fiona? You must be tired."

"I'm a little overwhelmed, to tell the truth."

"I'm sure you are. You'll feel better once your bed arrives. The boys and I were going to go for pizza after we finish up here. Not a very elegant welcome to town, but we'd love to have you join us."

The invitation was surely well-intentioned, but after the long drive earlier, it was too exhausting to contemplate. "I appreciate the offer, but I think I should stay and wait for the bed. These people aren't always on time, and I'd hate to hold you up. Besides, I still have a ton to do here."

Joanie gave her a concerned glance. "Well, just for now, it seems to me you could use a pick-me-up. How about some coffee?"

Fiona nodded.

"Any idea where your coffeemaker is? I'll brew some."

Fiona found the Nespresso machine in the third box she opened, together with some mugs, a couple of teaspoons, and a roll of paper towels. All of a sudden, the strain of the last few days overwhelmed her, and all she managed to do was sit at the farmhouse table and watch Joanie moving efficiently around, putting a pod in the machine, and filling it with water. Each pod only made half a mug, but that was fine.

Fiona slopped in a little of the milk Joanie had provided and stirred before sitting with her hands wrapped around the cup. Her fingers were practically rigid with cold. It had been several hours since she'd eaten. Her teeth chattered involuntarily.

Kyle stuck his head around the door. "Do you want us to bring in the rest of the stuff?"

When they'd finished, with everything in more or less the right place, she gave them twenty dollars each, after protestations from Joanie that it was far too much, and they all piled into her car and drove away.

Six o'clock. The bed would arrive any minute.

*

The bed company's truck drew up a few minutes before seven.

At least the two burly delivery men seemed to know what they were doing. They had the mattress upstairs within minutes. One of them leaned over the banister and shouted down. "Where's the bed, ma'am?"

She began to climb the stairs. "What do you mean? You have it, don't you?"

They stared at her and then at each other.

Fiona broke the silence. "I ordered a base to go with the mattress. You were supposed to deliver it at the same time."

"No one told me nothing 'bout that," said the older of the two. "Did they tell you, Sam?"

They, whoever they were, hadn't told Sam. He checked the delivery note and grumbled at the other man until she interrupted.

"No point in playing the blame game. Where am I going to sleep?"

Neither offered to answer the question, and she was too tired to make a scene now.

She sighed. "It looks as though I'll be spending the night on the floor. But can you guarantee I'll have my new bed tomorrow?"

She hoped it wasn't a shrug they were giving each other. Tomorrow was a Saturday. And out here in the boonies, that might mean no deliveries.

"We'll have the manager call you in the morning."

That would have to do.

*

In the kitchen on her own for the first time in her new home, Fiona heated up the carrot and ginger soup Joanie had dropped off for her and sat down at the table to eat. She hadn't unpacked the dishes yet, so she used one of the coffee mugs. The hearty creamy soup had a touch of some spice she couldn't quite identify. Surprised, she found herself thinking it was at least as good as anything she might have bought in Reading Market.

She mustn't start reminiscing about Philadelphia. She needed to focus on Brentford as home.

A low rumble told her the heating had finally kicked in. With a hint of heat and something inside her, she felt distinctly warmer as she stood to inspect the white kitchen cabinets, with their doors painted blue. They suited the place. And they were spotless inside, so she began to unload some of the non-perishables she'd brought with her. The canned and dry goods resulted from cleaning out her pantry. Packing to leave, she'd had no time to check the sell-by dates. Too bad.

Grimacing, she turned to toss an ancient jar of corn and mango salsa in the trash, then discovered there was no trash can.

Too tired to check any more items, she gave up and made her way upstairs.

*

Lying on her makeshift bed that night, trying not to notice the distinctive smell of the new mattress, Fiona expected to be wide awake, the way she usually was when away from home. She must remember to add curtains to the list of household stuff she needed. In the meantime, the dark green polyester ones left by the previous tenant were enough to block out most of the illumination from the lonely streetlamp outside.

One of just a few along the road, she noted, but, on the whole, she was glad of it.

Philadelphia had been so bright at night that this felt strange, but at least light pollution wouldn't stop her from getting to sleep. No traffic sounds, just the sighing of the trees above her head. As this thought crossed her mind, she fell asleep.

CHAPTER 11

FIONA

Morning was breaking through the sides of the curtain at the eastern window, which faced the library. Fiona checked her watch. Eight o'clock. She hadn't slept this late for ages, and as she came to, the unfamiliar ceiling swam into focus.

She stretched, feeling her shoulders ache after yesterday's drive and the unaccustomed hefting of household effects. She rolled off the mattress, scrambled to her feet, and did a few quick yoga stretches to loosen her muscles and boost her energy.

The water in the tiny bathroom had heated up overnight, so she took a restorative shower. Afterward, feeling refreshed, she wandered down to the kitchen in jeans and a sweatshirt, ready to continue the business of settling in.

First things first. She made herself a mug of coffee and found a paper towel to serve as a plate for the muffin Joanie had provided, before perching at her dining table to eat it. The muffin was delicious, with a crunchy top and a soft inside filled with blueberries and a hint of lemon. She must find out where to buy another.

From where she sat, she had a clear view of the street outside. Not that there was much to see. Across the snow-dusted road stood a Greek Revival house, its tall columns framing the portico. She was definitely in New England.

The street itself remained quiet, and as she watched, someone walked past with their dog. It might have been the same person as yesterday. The dog's owner was wearing a jacket with a hood, making it hard to guess what they looked like, though the height suggested a man. As for the animal, the rising sun, still low in the sky, made it difficult to discern much about it, save that it was black-and-white and medium-sized.

Gazing at it more carefully, Fiona could see it resembled a border collie, though maybe its parentage included traces of other doggy bloodlines. It trotted along in front of its master, seeming to know exactly which route they'd be taking. So, here was a sighting of someone who lived in this very neighborhood. A library patron, perhaps. The animal pranced along at a fair clip, and the two of them soon disappeared around the bend and vanished from sight.

Now she'd eaten, she had to decide what to do next. She would normally go for a run before tackling anything else, but she had no idea which box contained her gear. And there was so much to do. Still, if she checked a few items off, she could reward herself with some exercise. She added "find running stuff" to the end of her to-do list.

Three hours later, she suddenly realized how hungry she was. She'd been opening boxes, sorting through the various possessions, and putting them away. The mattress people had phoned to say they'd drop off the missing base at four. She glanced at her watch. A couple of minutes after twelve. She had time to take a break and walk into town to forage for food.

Soon, she was walking down the road. No sidewalks here, she noted, and hoped people in cars paid attention. At that moment, an old Volvo passed by, and the driver, whom she couldn't see, waved at her. They'd mistaken her for someone else, of course, but at least the natives were friendly.

Rounding the corner onto Main Street, she saw the town green before her. A small bandstand in the middle was draped with a banner proclaiming "Happy New Year!" She couldn't see Barb's Bakery, where her muffin had come from, but on the other side of the green, she spotted a fairly substantial establishment, Brentford Books & Beans. Was every shop here named something beginning with a B?

Taking the pathway that snaked across the grass, she smiled as the window displays came into focus. A combined bookstore and café, by the looks of it.

An old-fashioned bell rang as she swung the door open and walked in. She thought she must be in the bookshop part, although it was hard to tell where the books stopped and the coffee shop began.

"Good morning." The amiable voice contained the faint cadence of England. "You look a little lost. Can I help you find something?"

Fiona turned and found herself looking into the smoky gray eyes of a woman about her own age, with dark blond hair and an attractive smile. Judging by her casual clothes, she might have been a sales assistant.

"I'm looking for some lunch, actually." Fiona could smell coffee in the air.

"Well, you've come to the right place. And if you need something to read after you've eaten, we have books too." The woman waved a hand, first at the stacks, and then toward what appeared to be the café, though it had bookshelves too. "Passing through?"

People were certainly nosy around here. Maybe it had something to do with being in a small town. She hadn't considered this aspect of the situation when she'd decided to take the job. But surely it was a positive thing, on the whole. She didn't have to bare her soul to the locals, but Brentford might be a place where it was easier to make new friends, even though the prospect made her anxious. She forced herself to let her shoulders relax.

"I'm sure the festival will be amazing, but in fact, I've just moved here. Yesterday."

"Well, welcome." The smile was genuine. "I'm Molly Stevenson. I own this place." She indicated the café with a wave of her hand. "Along with Renzo."

"It's lovely. I'm Fiona. Fiona Gordon."

"Oh, right. I know who you are," said Molly, her face registering understanding. "You're the new executive director of the library." She stretched out a hand and Fiona shook it. "Well, this is super. You and I need to work together to put Brentford on the literary map."

It would be reassuring to have someone helping her get the library on its feet again. But the almost audible rumble in her stomach warned Fiona she shouldn't discuss potential projects when she felt so hungry. She might agree to anything.

"Sounds great," she said. "But I have to eat something before I can think straight."

"Of course. Come with me. The café is right this way."

Fiona followed her into the second part of the store, where a man, his back to them, was busy behind the counter. Three women, in line in front of him, were chatting to each other. As Molly and Fiona entered, the customers stopped talking, as if by some unspoken rule, and turned to look at her.

"Renzo, I'd like you to be extra nice to Ms. Gordon. She's the new executive director at the Wentworth."

The man turned around to say hello. She'd seen his photo in the paper, among the other local business owners. He was the handsome one. Roughly her age. About five foot nine. She couldn't help it. She noticed people's heights, particularly men's. Being taller didn't make a difference to her, but it sometimes did to them. She smiled uncertainly.

"Well, I don't start until Monday." She hoped this would be enough to deflect curiosity.

"Wonderful," said Renzo. "Welcome to town. I hope we'll see a lot of you." Not only good-looking, but he spoke with a charming accent—from somewhere in South America, she guessed.

Molly took her by the arm and placed her in the line. "I'll leave you to check out the menu, but if you'd like to eat in the bookshop, I'd be happy to keep you company."

Fiona peered back through the archway to the bookstore. Several cozy armchairs sat in twos with small tables between them. A couple of teenage girls on a Victorian loveseat were showing each other pages of an oversized book on fashion. She didn't think she could cope with a whole conversation with a stranger right now. Once she'd gotten to grips with the library, she'd have a better idea of what she was doing and would know how to speak to people with some authority.

"Unfortunately, I have to get home. I'm expecting a delivery. But someday soon." This was a reply she often used when she wanted to put someone off. The bed wouldn't arrive until four. This meant she had plenty of time once she returned to keep unpacking, especially if they ran late, as they had last night.

"Understood. Well, bon appétit." Molly turned back toward the bookstore.

"Thanks." The clock on the wall told Fiona it was close to one before she left the café, clutching a sandwich—one of her favorites, brie and tomato on ciabatta.

As she strolled back to the house, she took stock of her new neighborhood. Across the green, more cherry trees lined Main Street—no wonder the town made the most of them. When they bloomed in May, the display would be breathtaking.

A FIELD GUIDE TO LIBRARY GHOSTS

She passed the Town Hall, a white clapboard building hardly larger than a private house. A painted board on the wall bore the proud inscription: *Brentford—founded in 1732*. She wondered if there was a historical society somewhere. So much to learn.

St. Michael's marked the turn for the Wentworth. Scaffolding covering the steeple made it hard to see the belfry, and instead of bells ringing, she could hear the sound of hammers. Apparently, the percussion section was playing today. If the congregation could afford to raise the funds for church repairs, perhaps they would support the library financially too. Unless they'd spent all their money on the church. No point in counting her chickens.

She heaved a sigh of relief as she reached her own front door.

"Hello there." On the porch, Joanie seemed to have made herself comfortable on the rocking chair. "Finding your way around town?" She glanced at the paper bag and the coffee cup in Fiona's hand. "Excellent—you found Books & Beans."

Fiona would have liked to scream. Her hunger hadn't diminished since she'd bought the sandwich. If anything, she wasn't hungry any longer—she was ravenous. Now she'd either be forced to wait or would have to eat while Joanie watched her. Neither option appealed.

"Yes. I thought I'd try the local fare."

"Well, you won't go wrong there."

"Would you like to come in?" What she really meant was, *What are you doing here? I need my lunch. Now.*

"I won't, thanks," said Joanie. "But I was looking out of my office window and happened to notice the van from the mattress place. When I saw they weren't having any success knocking at your door, I came over." She rose and pointed behind her. "They told me it was your bed base, so I signed for it."

Remorse swept over Fiona. "That's so kind of you, Joanie. They said they'd be coming at four."

"No problem." She smiled. "I'm glad I was here to let them in. They've assembled it in your bedroom. I imagine you'll be more comfortable tonight."

"Thanks so much. I don't know what I'd have done without you. I'll see you on Monday, if not before."

"No problem," said Joanie and turned to go before pivoting back. "Speaking of seeing you again, Mr. Madison asked me to tell you that we'd like you to come over for drinks tomorrow evening, as a way for you to meet everyone. Five-thirty all right?"

Fiona felt a swarm of butterflies take off just under her heart, but she nodded. She hadn't expected to be dropped in the deep end quite so soon. "Great," she said, her voice a little hoarse. She tried again. "Great."

And terrifying. Like being interviewed all over again.

CHAPTER 12

FIONA

The following morning, the bells of what she felt sure was St. Michael's were finally pealing, reminding Fiona that today was Sunday. By the afternoon, she began to feel she'd broken the back of the moving process. One end of the living room was stacked with boxes of books, files, and clothing, waiting to be discovered, but they would have to wait.

As the evening event drew closer, Fiona's anxiety about this new position mounted, and she glanced out the window to take stock. The sun had set almost completely—she'd left it too late to take a walk to decompress. A shower would have to do instead.

Hot water hit her head and ran down her shoulders and back as she tried to stifle thoughts about the upcoming introductions. Certain members of the board had been on the interview panel, but since her arrival, she'd only met Joanie. She'd been welcoming, but Fiona wondered how the rest of them would treat her.

She shrugged to release the tension and considered the worst-case scenario.

She'd been hired to make major changes, and hoped the board members wouldn't interrogate her about her plans—she hadn't had time to formulate any yet. She'd have to come up with something soon, because if she didn't deliver, she'd be stuck in a strange town with no job and no prospect of finding another quickly. She had to make this work.

She discovered the iron in a box of cleaning materials and started pressing the business suit that had become creased in the move. At least she could present herself as efficient.

*

The Abigail Room, Channing explained, was named after the founder of the library. Fiona, in something of a trance, surveyed the wood-paneled space, wondering which of the small group assembled there was Abigail.

"In 1925," Channing said, seeing her confusion. "When the house became a library."

Fiona's cheeks were burning. She'd researched the library months ago, before her interview, but hadn't had time to review the information. The Wentworth was almost a hundred years old. "Of course. Yes. I'll get the hang of the history soon, I'm sure."

"We've got books on the subject," he said dryly. "And you might look up John LaFarge while you're at it."

Fiona scanned the room again. "Which one is he?"

"That one," said Channing, pointing at a beautiful Art-Nouveau window of a toga-clad woman reading a book. "He made all the stained glass in the building."

"Ah," said Fiona, choosing not to mention that books didn't exist in the classical world except as scrolls. "I look forward to learning more."

"I'll find some information sheets about the history for you." Joanie arrived, like the cavalry, to rescue her. "I should have thought of it before." She handed her a glass of red wine, and Fiona took a grateful sip. Some kind of Malbec, possibly, one of her favorites. Evidently, someone here knew their wines.

"Thanks, Joanie." Maybe this would help her relax. The glass was a large one.

Channing was clearly finished with small talk. "Come and meet the rest of the board," he said. "They're all coming, apart from Andrew Mackenzie. He's a math professor at Carnarvon College and sent regrets. He had something else going on this evening, but you'll run into him soon enough, I daresay."

He grasped Fiona's arm and led her with determination across the room to where an elegant woman stood chatting with a tall, attractive man.

"Let me introduce you to my mother, Acacia Todd."

Fiona found herself looking down at a woman somewhere in her early seventies, with bold, scarlet-framed spectacles and a twinkle in her eye.

"Please, call me Acacia," she said. "'Mrs. Todd' sounds so formal. I've been on the board here forever, and I run a book club for the local bookstore. Have you been there yet? They have a wonderful selection of books—and delicious coffee too."

Fiona barely had time to explain that she'd visited the shop and met Molly and Renzo before Channing interrupted.

"And this is Bill Hawley. Bill's the editor of our town paper, the *Brentford Bee*. I'm going to leave you with them for a minute. I must talk to Mrs. Yazbeck."

As she turned to meet the journalist, Fiona's elbow bumped against Channing's arm, and she watched as, to her horror, a wave of Malbec flew toward him, landing on his shirtfront, blending smoothly with his burgundy-colored tie.

Fiona clapped her other hand to her mouth, her eyes darting around the room, looking for tissues, wishing she hadn't left her purse by the door. That might have some unused but crumpled ones in it. All that met her eyes were the dismayed faces of the other guests. This was why she should never drink at work.

"Oh my God, I'm so sorry. I didn't mean to..." She was babbling. Had to calm down and *do* something. She didn't dare raise her eyes to Channing's face and kept them glued to his chest.

A clean, folded handkerchief appeared in her line of vision. Bill Hawley was handing it to Channing, who, as she glanced up, was looking down with a stupefied expression on his face. His cheeks were turning the same shade as the wine, and his eyes were bulging as though he couldn't believe what he was seeing.

Trance-like, he wiped the tie and began to dab at his shirt. "Of all the..." If the usually verbose Channing was at a loss for words, this had to be a major disaster.

"I don't know what happened. One minute I was..." She ran out of explanations.

"It's my yacht club tie." He said this in a flat voice, as if it explained everything.

"I'll pay for the dry cleaning, of course." Had she seen a dry cleaner in town? "Or replace it."

Channing's face now resembled a pot about to boil over. "It was my grandfather's. It's irreplaceable," he said through gritted teeth.

Someone took a step toward them. "Now then, Channing dear, things could be worse." His mother's voice was calm and soothing. "Why don't you pop home and change? We'll take care of everything here."

Fiona could have kissed Acacia. Though she had a feeling the chances of Channing changing anything other than his clothes were slim. His character appeared to be set in stone.

Now Bill intervened. "Come on, Channing. It was an accident. Could happen to anyone."

A wave of relief swept over Fiona, and she gave him a grateful look.

With one last fulminating frown in her direction, Channing stalked out of the room, still making a show of rubbing at his shirt.

Bill smiled wryly. "Well, I guess I'm kissing that handkerchief goodbye."

"I'll buy you another," said Acacia, with a flirty glance.

"I can't thank you both enough. It was such a dreadful thing to happen—especially to Channing—just when I was trying to make a good impression. It goes without saying, I'll replace your handkerchief, Mr. Hawley."

"Bill, please." He reached out a hand, and Fiona remembered that they had barely been introduced before the incident.

He was a man whose age was hard to decipher. His warm smile and closely cropped hair, with its traces of gray, reminded her of Denzel Washington. He was over six feet, she guessed, and rangy, with a firm handshake she found reassuring.

"Bill, why don't you tell Fiona about the *Bee*? It's a town institution," Acacia said, turning to face her.

Grateful for the change in subject, Fiona said, "I read some of it online. It's clearly a vital community resource."

Bill explained that he'd been the *Bee*'s editor for more than twenty years, and asked if he could interview her for the paper. "And naturally, whenever you have any news to share, I'd be happy to use it. Other than stories about raucous parties that get out of hand." He grinned at her, and Acacia laughed, apparently delighted with this witticism.

It took Fiona a little longer to get it. "Oh, right. Yes, of course I'll keep you updated."

One by one, she met the other guests, about ten in all. Most sympathized over her accident, some commenting that Channing had a rather short fuse. Fiona would have to ensure she didn't give him cause to explode again, and the feeling of walking a tightrope returned, to be firmly squashed down.

It would take time for Fiona to remember the board members individually, but Joanie must have a list. With any luck, the series of photo portraits hanging in the lobby would be of them, and she'd be able to memorize their names.

Channing finally reappeared, though he seemed to be avoiding her. Fiona had long abandoned the wine in favor of sparkling water, just in case. The remainder of the evening was something of a blur.

*

Back in the safety of her cottage, Fiona shucked off her shoes, made herself a stiff gin martini, and flopped in one of the comfortable chairs flanking the fireplace.

"What an evening," she said aloud. "What is it about work events? This is the second one in two months. Damn Channing. I'm going to have to do everything perfectly from now on."

"What do you mean?"

Without thinking, she answered, "Oh, you know. I can't make any more mistakes at work, or he'll send me packing."

"Packing? What's so bad about that?"

Fiona suddenly sat up and looked around. There was the voice again. Even clearer this time. She hadn't heard it for several weeks.

"George? Are you still with me?" She waited, as if for an echo.

The answering voice sounded masculine. "You brought me with you." Of *course* she had. He was in her head, after all.

This was a comforting thought, though Fiona had no idea why it should be. Thank heavens for George. He was always here, ready to listen. Even if she was generating the answers.

It occurred to her that the voice was only audible when she was stressed, which she definitely was this evening. Might as well humor the voice.

"I did. I know you wanted us to stay in Philly, but I needed to get away."

"You did that. Frying pan into the fire. This man—Channing—sounds like your late husband."

"We don't say 'late.' It's 'ex-husband' if you're divorced."

Funny he should get that wrong, if she was only imagining him.

He wasn't incorrect, though. Brian and Channing might be brothers from another mother. Though Channing's mother Acacia appeared to be a delightful person. What had she done to end up with a son like that?

As Fiona lay in her new bed that night, head buzzing with replays of the embarrassing evening, she suddenly broke into a sweat. She had a meeting with Channing scheduled for the next day. How would she ever be able to look him in the eye?

CHAPTER 13
GEORGE

So. This is what comes of a single woman attending a party without an escort. It appears the man Channing made some kind of advances to her, which she has naturally rejected. I can tell it has unnerved her, though. As well it might.

Why does she surround herself with these clowns? Surely there are better men in the offing? Perhaps it is her status as a divorced woman that causes them to take liberties. Or perhaps it is the rather indecent clothes she wears that make men misunderstand.

I find it difficult to come to grips with these new mores. The woman Joanie, who came to aid her in moving into this house, wore trousers! I have seen Fiona in clothing more suited to a gold prospector in the Yukon than polite society. I have had to avert my gaze from time to time, but I confess I noticed that these waist overalls appear to be made of blue canvas and have rivets in them. Rivets! They are only suitable for common laborers.

However, the most important thing is that she heard me when I spoke.

Did she mention a work event? What can she mean? Does she have an occupation after all? If so, it will complicate matters considerably. I find it curious—she did not wear these laborer's garments to go to this place of employment. In fact, she wore an almost respectable ensemble with a skirt and matching blazer. I have become accustomed to the not-unpleasing sight of her knees, but I must not allow myself to become distracted by these frivolous thoughts.

In my day... I have to stop comparing these modern times to my own century. Things have changed, and I must cease criticizing. That's not the way to enlist Fiona's support.

This Channing person must be her supervisor in the enterprise where she has found employment. Otherwise, she would not need to appease him with perfect work. Since she is not wearing laboring clothes, she cannot be employed in a factory but somewhere more elevated. Not a teacher, clearly, for a divorced woman would never be employed to educate the young. Yet she is too respectable to be an "actress."

Which leaves the retail trade. A shop assistant, maybe. There is no disgrace in that. Perhaps she will tell me if I ask her. In the meantime, I must continue to practice materializing. No one told me it would be so difficult.

CHAPTER 14
FIONA

The following morning, Fiona arrived early for her first day of work. She had no commute other than the two hundred yards of driveway leading to the library's front door, located beneath a porte-cochère. Fiona pictured the carriages that would have pulled up under it a century ago to disgorge the Wentworths and their visitors, before driving to the stables behind the house.

While waiting for someone to come and unlock the building, she took a stroll around it, wondering if the stables still existed. Sure enough, a more modern extension incorporating an older structure at the back looked as if it might once have housed horses.

The library itself was small as libraries go, though huge considering it had once been a single-family home. Like the cottage, it was built of Connecticut granite, mellowed to a pale gray over the decades.

Looking up at the turret at one corner and the number of gables, she decided it was an example of Queen-Anne-style Victorian architecture. It was kind of ugly, truth be told. And with so many windows, sloping roofs, and rooms, it must be difficult to organize the contents. But the rising sun reflecting off the glass gave it a silvery shimmer that added a note of beauty.

"Good morning. What a beautiful day for your first one here."

Fiona jumped, not having heard anyone approaching, and turned.

"Hello, Joanie. It certainly is. I don't have a key yet, so I'm glad you're an early bird too."

A few robins, the original early birds, were picking their way across the dew-laden lawn surrounding the library. It might have been a fabulous garden once, but now, apart from a tall tree overshadowing one side of the building, only some of the local cherry trees surrounded by grass remained of its former glory.

"Let me give you the ten-cent tour before we open to the public."

Fiona followed her into the library. The evening before, she'd been struck by the fact that very little seemed to have changed since the place was a private home. Standing in the original lobby of the house, she glanced down at the elaborately tiled floor, and at the arches that led into what she guessed must be the reading room. She imagined the former owners, in long dresses and over-decorated chapeaux, their menfolk in tails and top hats, with a flock of servants ready to do their bidding.

Joanie indicated an arch to the right. "That's the main reading room, and we have extra space with armchairs and a sofa in the circular turret room in the corner. And you know the Abigail Room already. It's where we met last night."

They walked through, passing a couple of heavy oak tables with a few books, some open, lying as if left in a hurry. "Those ought to have been picked up for re-shelving on Saturday evening. I'll have to speak to someone about it."

The corner room was bathed in light, and the somewhat battered leather armchair and sofas conveyed a sense of informality and comfort that had likely been there for a century. A small table with newspapers on it stood near the entrance.

"We replace those every morning," Joanie said. "We have several patrons who like to sit in the sun and read a physical newspaper."

Fiona, who'd long ago abandoned the paper version of the news, and read hers via online apps, could suddenly appreciate why people still liked to read that way.

Leading her back to the lobby, Joanie pointed at the room to the left. "That's the old ballroom, where we hold bigger events, and beyond it is the conservatory, which we rent out for weddings and so forth."

"Do you have many of those?"

"It varies by season, of course, but we have two bookings for June. One of them is Molly's father, Tom Beresford—he's marrying his sweetheart Bonnie, and they're a lovely couple. In their seventies."

"How romantic. It shows it's never too late." Privately, Fiona recalled someone's maxim about a second marriage being a triumph of hope over experience. She was never going to marry again. She'd had enough of romance and was doing much better without Brian. Men were completely unnecessary. Unless they were employing you. Or vice versa.

Joanie broke into her thoughts. "Let me show you the second floor. That's where all the work gets done."

Fiona followed Joanie up the grand staircase, made of highly polished mahogany. On the half-landing, which branched off into opposite directions, the wall held a series of portraits, a woman in late middle age and three smaller ones of girls.

Fiona stopped to study them. "Are those..."

"Abigail Wentworth and her daughters, yes. They were

painted before she gifted us the house, and in her will, she stipulated that they be hung permanently in the library. No one objected, of course, because they're beautiful, aren't they?"

"They certainly are. Abigail looks like a woman with a strong character." Her clothing revealed nothing of her physical charms. In her face, Fiona read a woman who'd suffered, and her eyes had something sad about them. Perhaps the painter was at fault. He'd failed to give them any spark of light.

"Yes, indeed. Had to be, really, after Albert Wentworth, her husband, died. She could have retired into widowhood, but she chose to stay involved in his business and used the profits to benefit the community."

"She sounds like she was ahead of her time." Fiona was about to ask more questions, when Joanie reminded her they were supposed to be checking out the second floor. With curious reluctance, Fiona turned and followed her up the next flight of stairs.

The landing was lined with books in glass cases, with tasseled keys hanging from the doors. They appeared to contain leather-bound volumes of various sizes and in varying states of perfection.

"Those are part of our rare books collection," said Joanie. "There are more stored at the top of the building, in the old servants' quarters. Jane Kennedy's in charge of the rare books, so her office is up there too. She says she likes being under the eaves, although since she's the reference librarian too, it's not always easy for patrons to find her. But that's Jane."

Joanie didn't linger but ushered Fiona into a beautiful, sunny room. It wasn't particularly spacious, but walking past a desk and over to the window, she found herself looking down on the roof of the porte-cochère and the front garden.

"What a lovely room," she said. The morning sun was slanting in through the windows, while outside, the tiny icicles on many of the plants were slowly dissolving in the sun.

"This is yours," said Joanie. "It's old-fashioned, but the computer is more or less modern, so that's something."

By modern, Fiona surmised she meant fewer than ten years old. It was older than the computers she'd used at the museum by several years at least. She'd have to use her own laptop until they upgraded the system. But the light in the room made up for a lot. She'd enjoy working here.

They toured the rest of the floor, where Joanie pointed out her own office and the children's department, with its brightly painted walls. "They say this used to be the Wentworth girls' nursery when they were little, so I guess it's appropriate for children to use it now. It has a small room off it that used to be for the Wentworths' nanny, where Isabel has her office."

A knot formed in Fiona's chest as she contemplated being surrounded by small patrons, none of them hers. She thought she'd stopped envying mothers their little ones, but apparently, the sorrow lingered. Perhaps the only way to expunge it was to use exposure therapy. Face these children despite her feelings of yearning and regret until she was able to truly enjoy being with them.

"I'm here." A slightly disheveled young woman dressed in eye-popping clothes presumably designed to attract children stuck her pink-haired head around the door. "I just arrived." She emerged into the room, her expression interested and welcoming.

"Great to meet you, Isabel," said Fiona, returning to the present. "I'll be coming round to speak to everyone later, to find out what you do, and what I can do to help you do it even better."

"I'll look forward to it."

The library was beginning to show signs of life as various employees turned up for work.

"I'm impressed that everyone starts so early, Joanie," said Fiona, glancing at her watch.

"I have to admit," Joanie said, "they don't usually make an appearance at this hour. I imagine they're curious about their new boss."

Of course. Fiona hoped she was making a positive impression. She'd dressed carefully that morning in a neat navy suit with a soft pink shirt under it. She wore kitten-heeled pumps but was aware she was still taller than average. Some would find that intimidating, as she knew from experience.

By the time the library opened at ten o'clock, Fiona's head was spinning with names and faces. She hoped she'd be able to match them the next time she ran across her employees.

For now, she'd kill for a cup of coffee.

Joanie led her up a narrow staircase labeled "Staff Only." At the top, a long corridor flanked by rows of doors was all there was to be seen. "Here's where the servants slept, originally. Now it's extra storage for the antiquarian books. This is our kitchen. And next door is our staff room."

Fiona eyed the fridge, sink, electric kettle, and microwave. An old-fashioned drip coffeemaker waited to be fired up. She groaned inwardly, but squared her shoulders and braced herself for a terrible cup of coffee. The first thing she would do would be to donate proper brewing equipment. The staff would surely appreciate it.

Taking a couple of mugs from the collection hanging above the sink, Joanie told Fiona where to find everything she needed to brew. "By the way, you have an appointment with Channing Madison at eleven. I believe he wants to discuss the budget with you."

CHAPTER 15
FIONA

Fiona's heart sank. She had just over an hour before Channing showed up. She'd hoped to impress him with her grasp of the facts, but after last night's incident, she thought it unlikely he'd cut her any slack. At the thought of his tie, ruined by her glass of red wine, she shuddered involuntarily, before giving herself a mental shake. She'd have to buy him a new one, and a shirt too, but for now, it was budget time. "Do you know where I can find the numbers, Joanie?"

"They'll be on your computer, and I imagine there are copies in the filing cabinet in your office. However, I think finding everything is likely to be a complicated task."

It couldn't be that bad, surely. The previous incumbent had to have left the financials in some sort of shape.

An hour later, Fiona had managed to at least look at and print out a copy of the budget for the year that had ended in December. It was smaller than she expected, but that was part of the reason she was here. To allocate it efficiently, and to raise more money.

She took a deep breath when Channing approached her

office door and entered without knocking.

*

Going over it in her mind afterward, the meeting had produced some unexpected information, to say the least.

Channing's countenance when he'd entered her office was hardly encouraging. "Good morning," he said.

"Good morning." Fiona wondered how to broach the subject that she thought must be as much on his mind as hers. No point in putting it off. "I'm really sorry about what happened last night. I hope you'll let me replace your shirt and tie." She couldn't replace his lost dignity, of course. He'd have to do that.

"The shirt was hand-made for me in England, and the tie is completely irreplaceable. It's the Yacht Club tie."

Which yacht club? Surely, no matter which one it was, she could purchase a substitute for him. "Could I find another at the club?"

He gave her a look that would have turned a lesser person to stone, but Fiona stared straight back at him. If she showed fear or mortification now, she'd never get his respect back.

"It was my grandfather's. So, no."

"Well, please let me do what I can. Perhaps a specialist dry cleaner could restore it for you." This would cost a fortune, assuming she could find such a person, but she would do it. Before Channing had a chance to answer, she said, "Coffee?" It would be awful, but he was probably used to that. "I'll ask someone to make some."

"Isabel," he said without further comment. He gave her a thin-lipped smile. Better than no smile at all, she supposed.

"Of course." She was saying "of course" much too often.

Fiona made an effort to talk about innocuous subjects while they waited for Isabel to bring cups of coffee for them.

No mugs for visitors. The old-fashioned cup and saucer, covered with crimson roses, looked like the ones her grandmother had owned. A matching pitcher and bowl filled with sugar lumps with a pair of silver sugar tongs increased the illusion that she'd moved back in time.

Isabel set them down and gave Fiona a smile that felt encouraging, somehow. Perhaps she'd heard about the accident at last night's reception.

"Cream?" Fiona asked as she lifted the pitcher. Channing reared back as though expecting her to throw the contents at him. "Perhaps you'd like to serve yourself."

She replaced the pitcher on the tray, its handle toward him. He picked up the delicate china vessel and, as he brought it closer to the cup, knocked it against the rim, spilling cream all over the desk. Fiona clamped her lips together to avert a smile as she mopped up the mess with tissues.

"Please don't worry. Accidents will happen." For a moment, she felt sorry for this man, whose dignity seemed so fragile.

Channing, his gaze averted, harrumphed and evidently decided to get down to business. "Have you had a chance to look at the budget?"

"I have," Fiona said, returning to her professional self. "And it looks as though we're ticking over right now when it comes to day-to-day running expenses, but the Wentworth's endowment is smaller than I anticipated. I'd expected it to be more substantial, given the length of time the library's been in existence."

"A hundred years next year. But running costs have been going up."

"That makes sense. But still, shouldn't the library have a contingency fund somewhere?"

Channing cleared his throat and studied the floor. "The thing is..." He raised his eyes to look at her, his cheeks reddening as he did so. "The last director, for reasons I needn't go into, failed to alert the board that funds were running low."

What was the man talking about? A sudden icy finger traced its way down Fiona's back. This wasn't going to be good news. Oh, well. Better deal with it.

"What do you mean? Didn't he present budgets at every meeting, as I'm expected to?"

Channing shifted in his seat. "He did, but they weren't very detailed. And I'm afraid we took him at his word."

Fiona had a good instinct for people covering things up. Every nerve in her body was telling her now that Channing was hiding something. She needed to find out what. "So, he misrepresented the amount of money available?"

"When we had the annual audit, it turned out to be worse than that. He, um, used some of it for his own purposes."

Fiona found it almost impossible to credit that no one had spotted this. Of course, she knew embezzling happened—she'd learned something about financial misconduct in her MBA classes. But being a scrupulously honest person, she couldn't imagine how someone could steal from under the noses of a board of people who were supposed to keep tabs on them. She fixed Channing with a stare Medusa would have been proud of—one that would have turned most men into stone.

"I can't believe you didn't tell me before. I might not have taken the position if I'd known the mess I was to inherit."

Mess was putting it mildly. This was going to make her task ten times more difficult.

"That's why we...didn't make a point of it." Channing couldn't meet her eyes. "We probably should have disclosed it."

Fiona could barely form a coherent sentence. "Probably? You have to be kidding. You expect me to raise enough to make up the shortfall?"

Channing tried an ingratiating smile, which only served to annoy Fiona further. "Well, the book sale will bring in a reliable seventy-five thousand dollars, and that's happening soon."

Ignoring his attempt to deflect her, she said, "That's already in the budget, I see. But one extraordinary expense and the library will be in real trouble." She could feel her blood pressure rising. She needed time to consider the implications of this for her job and the library. "I'm sorry, I need to give this some thought. I think we should talk about this later." *After I've cooled down*, she added silently.

*

At the end of a day that had started what seemed like a week ago, Fiona was finally able to leave the library behind and walk down the drive to the gatehouse. As she rounded the corner to the front porch, she noticed the dog-walker across the way, and, deciding it might be best to be friendly, lifted a hand to wave.

The movement caught the dog's attention, and it turned its head to bark. Its owner told it to hush, and it did so. In the process, she caught a glimpse of the man's face.

His somewhat stern expression provided no clues about him. Was he a little irritated at this interruption to his solitary walk? Perhaps she'd been wrong to wave. It was impossible to guess at the etiquette that prevailed in a small town like Brentford. Car drivers seemed inclined to acknowledge her existence. This man clearly didn't.

Right now, she was too tired to care.

CHAPTER 16

GEORGE

Fiona has returned. I have to say that she must be fatigued, judging by the way she entered the house. Shoulders slumped—never a good thing. Perfect deportment is vital if a woman is to make a good impression. I surmise she kicked her shoes off at the front door, since she appeared barefoot as she headed into the kitchen.

After a few minutes, she came into the salon to place an attaché case on the desk in the corner. Why she should be carrying such an object is inexplicable. No doubt it belongs to someone else. The man Channing, perhaps.

Ah. She has reappeared from the kitchen with her usual glass of wine. Yet, no. This looks much more like geneva, and neat at that. She may think that disguising gin in a fancy vessel will hide the fact that she's imbibing it undiluted, but she doesn't deceive *me*.

I must get to the bottom of her problem. I cannot have her in a befuddled state, or she won't be useful to me. Besides, I hate to see her cheapening herself this way.

"Fiona?"

She does not reply. I repeat myself louder each time until she raises her head.

"George?"

Success!

"Fiona—why are you drinking that dreadful liquor?"

"None of your business." She is attempting to put me in what she considers my place, but I am not so easily dismissed. In fact, I am permanently in my place.

"I believe something is wrong," I say, my voice sympathetic, I think. "What is it? Can I help?"

She's looking straight at me now. "If you must know, I started my new job today and it's been trying, to say the least. So, when I spotted someone walking along the road, I waved to them, hoping they might at least wave back. Just to be neighborly. But they ignored me, and that was the last straw."

This doesn't strike me as lamentable, as things go. She should try being flung off a horse and... Well, perhaps there's no sense in mentioning that.

"What is this work that causes you so much distress? Are you a sales clerk in a store?"

She actually smiles at this. "Come on, George. I'm making you up, so you know perfectly well that I'm the new executive director of the Wentworth Library."

Making me up? We'll see about that. "They have libraries in towns as small as this one now?"

"Don't mess with me, George. You know they do. They're the backbone of any community."

"And people can afford to pay the subscription fees?"

"What subscriptions? Subscription libraries barely exist anymore."

"So, the hoi-polloi may use them?" I raise my eyebrows in surprise, but of course she cannot see that. "I am shocked."

Her expression changes to one of incredulity. The blood drains from her face. "George, are you...are you *real*?"

"As real as any spirit can be," I tell her, pleased that she believes me at last.

She runs the back of her hand across her brow and says nothing for several minutes.

Then, all of a sudden, as if freed from constraint, she begins to tell me about her employment. Apparently, most women work these days. Some, who have no necessity to support themselves, do so because they like it. She explains about the late—I mean "ex"-husband, and why she fled Philadelphia. At this point, I feel obliged to interrupt.

"Fiona, this is all very well, but I need to tell you why I am still here, in this portrait."

She glances at my picture. "I have to admit, I have no idea what you're talking about, so, okay."

Terrible turn of phrase. So unrefined. I ignore it and proceed.

"I believe you have been informed that I died in 1875. You may or may not be aware that I left behind a wife, Rose, and two daughters, the apples of my eye."

I explain how I found myself in this portrait, hoping to ensure that my little family would be cared for, and how we became separated. "I must find her again, or I shall yearn for her forever. However, I need the help of someone who still lives to accomplish my mission."

"And you think I am that person? I don't see why."

"Well, you're alive, for one thing. Furthermore, you can hear me. I have observed that you are resourceful and independent. I'm persuaded you will be able to check the records that must still exist to search for the answers."

"But..."

"You must appreciate my problem—I am trapped here and I need your help."

She seems not to take this in, but I persevere.

"I understand your reluctance. This place is not near

the archives and registers of births, marriages, and deaths of Philadelphia, but I am certain you could journey back there for a brief time to search on my behalf."

"You're the one who doesn't understand. That's not how we do it these days..." Her voice trails off. She pinches the bridge of her nose and frowns. "Look. I'm exhausted. I have to sleep on it." I think I hear her mutter, "Not that I'll get a wink of shut-eye after this."

"Please," I say. "Don't let me down. I'm relying on you."

Fiona takes a swig (there is no other word for it) of her drink, leans back, and closes her eyes.

"I would love to hear all about your employment later," I say. I'm not certain she hears me.

CHAPTER 17

FIONA

Despite the unnerving events of the evening before, Fiona rose early, as she always had, and decided to go for a run around the streets of Brentford. Arriving back at the cottage—*her* cottage, she reminded herself—she made a cup of coffee and settled down to cool off by the window overlooking the street.

There he was again. The man with the dog. She became distracted for a moment by the unexpected appearance of Channing, barely recognizable in a sweatshirt and matching pants, striding down the road in the opposite direction. He was swinging his arms briskly and was already red in the face from exertion.

He nodded at the man in the hood and kept going. Good riddance.

Before she'd finished her coffee, he returned, at a slower pace now, mopping his brow with a handkerchief. He must have spent all of fifteen minutes on his walk. He'd need to go a lot further if he was aiming for a fitness routine.

She made a mental note to picture him this way the next time she found him intimidating, and smiled as she went upstairs to shower.

In the days that followed, she continued with the same morning pattern, taking a different route each time to familiarize herself with the town. Other early risers became accustomed to seeing her running by in leggings and a sweatshirt, regular as clockwork.

Almost daily, she drank her coffee and surveyed the street from the window, knowing that the man with the dog would soon show up. He appeared to be a creature of habit too, walking past on the dot of 7:05 every day.

She'd taken to thinking of him as Mr. Hood because that's what he'd been wearing the first time she saw him. She thought he might be around her age, though it was hard to tell from that distance. The putative border collie she named Bouncer, because its energy and gait suggested an animal that would bounce at the drop of a hat.

On Sunday morning, she allowed herself to skip her run and remained in her pajamas while she ate breakfast and scanned the day's newspaper, now delivered weekly. As she glanced out of the window, a flash of black caught her eye.

She raised a second cup of coffee to her lips, looked over the rim, and saw Bouncer trotting along the road. Alone. That couldn't be good. Curious, as dogs always were in her experience, Bouncer had seemingly taken this burst of freedom as a license to explore places he didn't usually have access to. Now, he was making his way up to her porch, nose to the ground, following some trail only he could divine.

She grabbed the brie from the fridge and cut off a small corner, hoping that this wandering dog could be tempted by French cheese.

Opening the front door with great care, so as not to scare him, Fiona tiptoed onto the porch, crouched down, and held out the morsel on the flat of her hand. Bouncer caught the smell on the breeze and took a cautious step forward, sniffing as he went. As he put out a tentative tongue to eat the cheese, she managed to catch his collar and hold him steady.

He didn't appear to object to this cavalier behavior from a stranger, so she checked around and discovered an identifying tag with what she needed—Newton, either the name of the dog or its owner, and the address. She couldn't place it. All she had was the general direction.

If she were going to take him home, she'd need to be wearing something more appropriate. Currently, she was sitting on her porch with a strange dog on a Sunday morning in her pajamas. Slowly, she encouraged Newton up the steps and into the house, where she put him in the kitchen for a while, praying he couldn't get into too much trouble there.

When she returned to collect him ten minutes later, she'd dressed and run a brush through her curls. The only cord she could find to use as a leash was the pale peach sash from her robe, but it would have to do. She opened the kitchen door to discover the dog lying in a resigned way on the floor, his head on his front paws. He rose and stretched as she entered.

"Hey, Newton. Come on, boy. We have to take you home. Someone's going to be worried about you."

Newton seemed not to object to this plan and stood docile as she looped the cord through his collar and wound the other end around her hand.

They set off, and although she'd checked the destination on her phone, she needn't have bothered. Newton knew where he lived. Five minutes later, they were walking up the path, the dog straining at his makeshift leash. Fiona felt the nervous tension she often experienced when meeting strangers under unfamiliar circumstances.

She rang the front doorbell. Inside, she heard a voice call out, "I'll get it," as footsteps clacked toward the door. It was opened by a woman of around forty, dressed in jeans and a sloppy mohair sweater in a shade of blue that reflected the eyes behind pink-framed glasses. Long, dark hair hung in waves to her shoulders, and even without makeup, she looked ready for a social event.

Fiona was all too aware that she, too, was makeup-free, though not remotely ready for prime time, and raised a hand to her disheveled head. Newton and she had encountered a stiff breeze on the way over. Oh, well.

"Sorry, my brother's on the phone," the woman began, before her eyes fell on the dog. She grinned and bent down to receive a licking that would have removed all her makeup, had she been wearing any.

"Bad Newton. Where did you get to? Who's a naughty boy?" She said this in such a loving voice that Newton stood there and panted, wagging his tail.

Seeming to remember Fiona's presence, the woman straightened up and took the cord she was holding out.

"I, um, found him walking alone—" Fiona began.

"Thank you so much. Andrew's been worried sick. He's trying to call Animal Rescue, but I told him they wouldn't be open today."

Newton's enthusiastic barking had summoned his owner from the depths of the house, and the man Fiona watched every day appeared behind his sister's shoulder. He tried simultaneously to calm his pet and say hello to Fiona, so neither operation was a complete success. As he straightened up to thank her properly, she took the time to assess him.

As she'd guessed, he was over six feet and a smile turned him from average to attractive, though not exactly handsome. His eyes were the unusually light shade of blue of a sailor who'd been staring at the horizon for years. She wondered whether he was married, then dismissed the thought as being irrelevant.

He wore his thick, evenly graying hair somewhat longer than the men she met in business, and it looked as if he had been running his hands through it.

He frowned. "All right, Newton, that's enough. No need to be quite so effusive. You've been a bad dog." The mutt assumed a remorseful expression that lasted about ten seconds, as Andrew leaned down again and scratched him behind the ears.

"I don't think he got into any trouble. He was walking past my house, and since he generally passes by with you, I thought I ought to intercept him."

"I can't tell you how much I appreciate it. I let him out in the garden and didn't realize he'd managed to escape until I noticed how quiet it was." Andrew wasn't looking at her. He was too busy fiddling with the knot she'd used to tie the sash to Newton's collar. She decided to leave him to it. In her limited experience, men didn't enjoy being helped.

"He didn't travel too far, you'll be happy to know," she said. "I only live a short distance away. At the Wentworth." Their puzzled faces made her add, "I'm the executive director."

The man rose, and his face cleared. "You must be Ms. Gordon. Sorry I wasn't at the library to meet you the other night. I'm Andrew Mackenzie, one of the trustees."

That explained his professorial air. Teaching at Carnarvon College. Mathematics, was it?

"I'm Cece Mackenzie, by the way, Andrew's sister. He sometimes forgets to introduce me." She nudged him, as if to remind him of something else.

"Oh, right. Would you like to come in? We can offer you coffee, and maybe we have a muffin left."

The thought of getting to know these interesting people was tempting, but Fiona was all too aware of her unprofessional appearance. "I must head home," she said. "I have a lot to do. Working on budgets and so forth." She had no idea why she was over-explaining.

Andrew nodded. "Understood. Well, thanks again."

"Perhaps you could let me have my belt back when you've

managed to untie it. I don't really have time to wait now."

"Of course." Andrew's sister nudged him once more. "I must apologize for my brother. He lives alone and his social skills are a little rusty." She laughed affectionately.

So, no wife, then. "It's been nice to meet you both. And I hope to see you," she nodded at Andrew, "at the next board meeting."

CHAPTER 18

FIONA

Back in Philadelphia, Fiona had enjoyed supporting her local bookstore by going to the author events they held. She'd been to afternoon teas, evening events, and simple book signings. The Wentworth should be hosting more events like that—Molly would know.

"Hello, Brentford Books & Beans. How can I help?"

She recognized the faint English accent. "Hello, Molly. It's Fiona—Gordon. From the Wentworth Library."

"Well, hello there. What can I do for you?"

"I'm looking for ideas to increase donations, but also to attract new people to the library—people who might become donors long-term. I'm hoping you might have time to brainstorm some money-making events with me."

"Excellent. I've been pushing for this kind of initiative from the Wentworth for ages, so I'd love to get together with you and talk it over."

*

Molly arrived at the library a couple of days later, bearing homemade cookies, ready to suggest bookish activities. Her first idea was to invite authors, or a series of them, to the library. "They used to have at least one a month, but they seem to have petered out after the volunteer in charge moved away. No one else stepped up. We attracted quite a crowd, and I think we could again—especially if we can recruit best-selling authors."

Fiona couldn't help but absorb some of Molly's enthusiasm as she continued.

"I've been thinking for ages about asking Lucinda Parks if she'd come. She's such a popular author, one of the biggest. She lives somewhere in the Northeast, I believe, so paying her travel expenses shouldn't cost too much." Molly nibbled at one of her own cookies, which, Fiona noted, were delicious, with a hint of orange, chocolate, and hazelnuts.

"Good idea."

Fiona was well aware of the writer's popularity. One of the most prolific and popular authors in the country, Lucinda was largely scorned by sophisticated readers because she wrote romances. *Romances with heart*, it said on the covers.

"Lucinda Parks? I've been reading her books for years. Whenever I want a quick escapist read." She'd read a ton of them over the past year, to distract her from the divorce and the move. She doubted she'd have much time to read anything more substantial for a while.

Molly beamed. "You like Lucinda Parks? Me too." She twinkled as she confessed the author was her "secret vice." She'd begun reading them when her husband died four years earlier. They'd been a comforting escape when she felt overwhelmed by her new life without him. She'd kept reading them because they were well-written and had flashes of humor that sometimes made her laugh out loud.

Fiona wanted to stay focused. "I'd love to get her for a

really big author event. The library centenary is the perfect time to host someone special. We have that lovely ballroom at the library, and I'm sure we'd fill it. I'm told it seats around a hundred and fifty people."

Molly leaned forward. "You're right. The ballroom would be perfect. I'll talk to Lucinda's publisher to find out when she's available." Her face clouded over. "Although she's very hard to get. She's probably booked months in advance."

"All the more reason to start now. That would give her several months' notice before the centenary begins in January."

"Sounds good. I'm on it."

Fiona arrived home that evening with a feeling of having accomplished something. She and Molly had planned one event that, if they could pull it off, was bound to be a success. Time to begin working on the rest.

*

The following day, Channing's mother stuck her head around the door to say hello.

Fiona greeted her warmly. In her early seventies, Acacia Todd's appearance suggested a conventional matron, except for the startling frames of her spectacles—chunky and modern in various bright colors. Today they were scarlet. In fact, she exuded a vitality that belied her years.

"As head of the Friends of the Library committee, I wanted to be sure you know what we do. Essentially, we're here to suggest programming and help with fundraising for the Wentworth, which it desperately needs, I might add."

"I know," said Fiona wryly. "That's to say, I've just found out. So, how is *your* fundraising going?"

"You've seen the budget, so you know there's room for improvement. We spend a lot of time chasing donors, and they're very generous, but we always need more. That's where the new programming comes in." Acacia smiled.

"I'm sure I can rely on you." Fiona wasn't sure at all, but she wanted to be encouraging. "Please keep me updated as you go, and I'll help where I can."

Acacia had more to say. "In the meantime—and this is something volunteers could do at very little cost to us—the grounds could do with sprucing up. For one thing, the trees need pruning. Especially the maple near the building."

She had a point. But a pretty garden wasn't what Fiona would call a priority. "It wouldn't do any harm to have the outside looking good, but I'm not certain it should be top of your list."

"I'd consider it an ongoing project, nothing to interfere with the more important things. Abigail Wentworth loved flowers, as you know." She paused, her head to one side, considering. "I have an idea. Why not plant the gardens here with the flowers of the Wentworth daughters? It would be a kind of tribute to the family."

"Is there anyone left of the Wentworths?"

Acacia chuckled. "I see no one's told you. Abigail was my great-grandmother."

Fiona leaned forward. "So, your grandmother was one of her daughters?"

"Violet, yes. I've got the family tree starting with Albert Wentworth. His family went back a long way. And I've got information about Abigail after they married, but not a great deal about her life before that. Jane, in the rare books department, enjoys dabbling in genealogy, as well as being in charge of the rare books, and knows a lot."

God, there was so much to learn. Fiona wondered if she'd ever get the hang of it all.

"As it happens," Acacia went on, "Jane's been looking for an excuse to start a genealogy group, showing people how to find out about their forebears using the internet and other resources we have here. You'd be surprised at how many people are interested but don't know where to start. I'm one of them."

Fiona considered. She'd never been particularly curious about anyone further back than her grandparents, but it might prove to be a popular project. A thought occurred to her.

"What about using the Wentworths as a kind of sample family? Show people how to do it themselves using the resources we have here and others. We could put on an exhibit that focuses more on Abigail, since she donated her house to be a library. It would be another way to celebrate the centenary."

Acacia beamed. "I love that idea."

"Good. Would you have time to outline the garden project and the genealogy idea in writing—one page, nothing longer—so I can add it to the list of things we'd like to do?"

"Of course, and I'll discuss it with the Friends to see whether they have any further suggestions."

CHAPTER 19
FIONA

Heading downstairs later that day, Fiona stopped by the four portraits on the half-landing.

"I wonder what your story is," she murmured, contemplating the largest of them—Abigail Wentworth. "You're beautiful, but you look sad. Is that because you're a widow?"

A sudden thud behind her made her jump. Spinning around, she saw a book lying open on the parquet. Where had it fallen from? She glanced up, expecting to see someone on the second floor leaning over the banisters, ready to apologize. There was no one there.

Feeling a little guilty for some reason, she bent down, picked up the leather-bound volume, and turned it this way and that, hoping there was no damage. It appeared to be fine, so she flipped to the title page.

The Official Guide to the Great Philadelphia Centennial Exhibition of 1876.

In smaller type beneath, it read, *Being a complete listing with maps*. Intrigued, Fiona riffled through a few of the yellowed pages. A book about Philadelphia. What were the odds? And what was it doing *here*?

She placed it on the desk in her office, intending to focus on the accounts and ask Jane about it later. But as the afternoon wore on, she felt more and more drawn to this book that showed her hometown as it had been a century and a half ago.

Finally, after poring over the accounts for a while and unable to resist, she opened the *Official Guide* and studied the map. She was able to pick out the buildings erected for the World's Fair without any trouble—they took up most of the space. The whole thing must have been built in Fountain Park, across the river from where she used to live.

As Fiona leafed through the other pages, she spotted sponsorship notices from various manufacturers and businesses, some—but not all—local. And then, there it was.

Importation of Finest Wool and Silk
for the manufacturing of excellent fabrics
Sebastian Manchester & Son

It was followed by her former street address and the location of their booth at the exhibition. A shiver ran through her.

Seeing George's father's name in print made her sociable spirit more real. She would take this home and show it to him. Well, obviously, she couldn't *show* it to him. But she would let him know somehow that she had found a little piece of his history.

It was a start.

*

She was about to leave work, one of the last to do so, when she spotted Jane in the front lobby, putting on her bicycle helmet. For a woman of her age, which Fiona guessed was somewhere in her sixties, she seemed remarkably fit, her sinewy arms those of someone who lifted weights.

Perhaps this would be a good moment to ask her about the book. Surreptitiously, she took it out of her messenger bag and removed the scarf she'd wrapped it in.

"Been working late, Jane?"

"Oh, hi, Fiona. Actually, I had a dentist appointment this morning, so I came in late and stayed on to make up the time."

"That's very praiseworthy, but you probably didn't need to. I'm sure we can make allowances for things like that."

Jane looked shocked at this. "You start with allowing an hour here and an hour there, and pretty soon you only have half the staff in the building at any given time. And that wouldn't do at all."

Noted. Fiona decided to ignore the remark. Thank heavens Jane wasn't in charge of HR, or she'd be putting people's backs up. "I'm wondering if, before you leave, I can ask you something. I found this book lying about and assume it's part of our collection." She handed the exhibition catalog to the rare books expert.

Jane looked at the spine and then opened it to the title page, frowning. "Where did you find this?"

"It was lying on the floor." That sounded evasive, but for some reason, Fiona didn't want to reveal that it had crashed down out of nowhere. That sounded ridiculous. "Near the staircase," she added, hoping to divert further questions.

"I must say, I don't recognize it," said Jane. "On the other hand, I'm not familiar with every book we have. But I'll check the catalog and let you know." She glanced up at Fiona. "Be sure to leave it here. We don't allow rare books out of the building."

With that, she headed out the door, shaking her helmeted head.

The building fell silent, and Fiona replaced the guide in her bag. She would bring it back tomorrow. After all, she wouldn't be taking it out of the Wentworth's grounds.

Back at the house, she retrieved the book and ran her fingers over the gilt lettering on the front cover. It was somewhat faded now, but still perfectly legible. What would George make of it?

She switched on the lamp as she walked into the living room. Approaching George's portrait, she waved the book in front of it. "What do you think, George?" she said. "I came across this book with an advertisement for your father's company and thought you might like to see it." She riffled through the pages again, wishing she'd had the foresight to mark the place with a bookmark.

Ah, there it was. She held the open book up to the portrait, wondering whether George could actually see it. He said nothing.

She shook her head and laid the book, open to the relevant pages, on the small table by the fireplace. She'd take a closer look at it later.

In the kitchen, she revived herself with a glass of wine and a handful of rice crackers. She couldn't afford to get any food or drink on this rare book, so she washed her hands before returning to the living room, where she picked up the volume and sat back in the bergère chair to study it in more detail.

While she'd been in the kitchen, some of the pages had flipped, and she was now looking at a diagram of the Philadelphia City Building. Peering at the faded print on the page, now tea-colored, she could make out a list of exhibitors, and there they were: Manchester and Son. Somehow, knowing that this book had been published so long ago, and that someone had valued it enough to keep it safe, made her want to cry for a young man who died too soon, and his lonely widow and children. They'd become real to her now.

Fiona traced the walkways on the map with her finger, picturing the crowds of cheerful revelers enjoying the extraordinary sights, sounds, and smells of the exhibition.

"There seems to be a mistake here. I wonder how the printer came to make it? You told me the accident happened in 1875, didn't you? And you haven't mentioned a brother." For some reason, she was loath to use the word *death* when speaking to George, in case it offended him. "But here you are a year later—'and Son.'"

Silence greeted this remark.

This was ridiculous. Why should a year make a difference anyway? It was all ancient history. Yet it was intriguing. Fiona liked to get things straight. Perhaps she could find out the answers by doing a little more research. No more than that, because her work for the library was more important—though not as much fun.

In the meantime, George was saying nothing.

CHAPTER 20
GEORGE

This is interesting. I have never seen the book that Fiona presented to me this evening. *The Official Guide to the Great Philadelphia Centennial Exhibition of 1876.*

I remember talking with my father about the hundredth anniversary of the founding of this country. I can hear him now.

"My boy, we must make our mark on the world, and this exposition will help us do it!" He talked in exclamation marks. I'd thought he was referring to our wonderful new nation, but it was the business he meant, of course.

He was full of plans to exhibit in one of the halls. We were to have a space draped in our fine textiles, so that visitors would be able to touch as well as see them. My concerns about how the fabrics would stand up to this kind of treatment went unheeded, but perhaps he saw sense before the event opened.

I would have liked to attend the celebration. It was to be a truly splendid affair, and, judging by the few pages Fiona allowed me to see, it was. I wonder if Rose visited. Did she take the girls?

It was a while before I answered Fiona's query this evening. She asked me whether the printer had made an error by including the words "and Son" in the catalog

I helped to draft the text for the advertisement, of course, though I did suggest we say more about the various fabrics and what the company did. But my father wanted only the bare details. Still, so long as people were able to find us, that was the most important thing.

It's only fair that Fiona should have her answer, so I called out to attract her attention.

"George?"

Who else could it be? She has no other man to distract her.

"Yes, it is I. To reply to your question—your information concerning my demise is accurate. Although the fatal fall from my beloved horse occurred in 1875, I daresay my father chose not to alter the name of the company. I suspect he felt it sounded like a larger and more impressive enterprise if he had a son working for him. And you're right—I never had a brother."

"Isn't that rather a cynical take on the matter?"

"Ha! My cynicism is unbounded where my father is concerned. The man who could dislike my gentle wife is not a man who understands emotions. I doubt whether my death was much more than an inconvenience to him."

Fiona's face expresses concern—perhaps even shock. "Oh, George. That can't be true. I'm sure any father would be proud to have you as a son and would grieve sincerely for you."

Indeed. I don't believe leaving "and Son" in the company name was from any sentimental consideration. In any case, preparations for the catalog were well advanced by that time, which doubtless resulted in it being too late for alterations to the content.

I wish to change the subject.

"Have you acquired a dog?" A canine of unknown origin

entered the house with her permission the other day.

This was effective in that Fiona stopped frowning and laughed.

"Oh, Newton? No, he belongs to a man who lives around the corner."

Do I detect a faint pinkness in her cheek? I wait to hear more.

"He was walking along the road, so I simply returned him to his master."

"Really? I hope it wasn't inconvenient." I doubt it was, since she reappeared, sans animal, fairly quickly. I am amused to see Fiona's cheeks becoming even pinker. "Did you know the owner?"

"No. That's to say, he turned out to be someone I'd heard of, a professor at the local college. A trustee of the library. I'd not met him before. He has a sister, but I don't think she lives with him. Neither of them is married. He lives around the corner and walks by the house every morning and evening. With Newton."

I feel obliged to stop this torrent of unasked-for information. "I'm glad you managed to find the dog's owners," I say, maintaining an austere tone. All this talk about herself is irritating.

Now she isn't even listening. She seems to be staring into space.

I must unearth a way to have her focus on the matter at hand. It is Rose who concerns me now, and only Fiona can aid me in finding her. I need to be with her again—to apologize for the argument we had. I have pined for my wife long enough.

CHAPTER 21
FIONA

After a night where her inexplicably vivid dreams of George walking a border collie and of Andrew in a top hat, white jodhpurs, and a scarlet hunting jacket mixed and mingled, Fiona woke feeling groggy and rolled out of bed. She made her way to the bathroom, determined to energize herself, and turned on the shower, gasping as she stood under the cold water. The temptation to turn it up to hot was almost irresistible, but the icy spray on her skin was more effective in waking her up.

And coffee would ensure she stayed alert.

As she filled the coffeemaker with water and beans, she allowed her mind to wander, hoping for some logical rationale for her dreams. She'd heard that people reacted to grief in different ways, and decided she was trying to process her sadness at the loss of her marriage and with it the hope of any children, using a relationship with a much younger, long-dead Victorian. That didn't explain Andrew's presence. Nor the way he'd looked away every time his head turned toward her. Though he did look good in hunting gear. An enigma for another day.

*

On her way to work, she stopped in at Books & Beans on the pretext of finding out how Molly's plans for an event with Lucinda Parks were going. Another attraction was a decent cappuccino, since the coffeemaker she'd ordered for the library hadn't arrived yet. As they sat in the café part of the store, Molly explained that they'd managed to secure a date for the author's visit for the following January.

"It's not ideal, because the weather can cause problems at that time of year, but it's better than nothing," she said, handing Fiona a list of the publisher's requirements. "We have to order a certain number of books to sell at the event, but I don't think that'll be a problem. They'll arrive signed, to save time. But the most fantastic news is," she was on the edge of her seat now, "the publisher has said Lucinda won't be charging for her time because she's got family in Connecticut and can visit them the same day."

"Is that a big deal?"

"Oh, yes! Bestselling authors rarely waive their fees completely. It's a wonderful thing for us."

Fiona was excited about the event now. "I'll include this in the plans I'm presenting at the next board meeting," she said. "I'm sure they'll be thrilled, because this will be a great way to kick off the centenary year. And I'll certainly give you credit for getting the deal done."

"They ought to be pleased. We really lucked out."

*

Twelve days later, Fiona sat in the board meeting, mentally noting the members around the table. So, Andrew Mackenzie had attended, as requested. Not in hunting dress, though, which was a shame. She hadn't seen him face to face except in her dreams since they'd met in his house. Today, she smiled at him, but he only nodded back. Why the reserve? Perhaps being in public made him shy.

At least he'd shown up, though she could have wished he hadn't handed her the silk sash of her robe in full view of the other board members. What kind of a socially inept person did something like that? He'd blushed as he did so, but still. Her own cheeks felt hot too, but she'd thanked him with a forced smile and stuffed it into her attaché case, hoping they wouldn't understand what it was, though Acacia's smile indicated that she might have some idea, albeit the wrong one.

Time to begin. Channing called the meeting to order and then handed it over to Fiona. She scanned the faces in front of her and picked up the file with her notes in it. She began to run through her recommendations both for making the library more efficient and for increasing visitors and donations.

Then she moved on to the celebration of the library's centenary next year. There was an almost palpable feeling of relief at having something to look forward to.

She told them about the proposed genealogy group, giving Acacia the credit she was due. "This was Acacia's suggestion, and she's going to run it with Jane Kennedy's expertise about the various available sources. We plan to mount an exhibit celebrating the Wentworths and the history of the library."

"You mean you'll be researching my family tree?" Trust Channing to make this about him.

She left it to Acacia to explain the concept in more detail.

Fiona held back the information about Lucinda Parks' visit until the end of her presentation, sure of an enthusiastic response. There would be no need to explain to the trustees who this author was. She was known all over the world.

"And finally, I'm delighted to tell you that as the grand finale for next year's anniversary celebrations, we have secured the author Lucinda Parks, who will be coming to do a talk and book signing here at the Wentworth in January."

She beamed at the people assembled around the large mahogany dining table in the Lavender Room. Honoring another Wentworth daughter, it now served as a meeting room for book clubs, knitting circles, and the board.

Acacia was the one talking now. "Lucinda Parks—the romance author? That's incredible. I don't read them much myself, but I have friends who do, and I'll be delighted to buy signed copies for them."

"What's this amount here? It says 'author's stipend.'" Channing's voice sounded aggressive, though he couldn't have meant it to, surely.

"Libraries usually pay bestselling authors a substantial fee for their visits, but in this case, Ms. Parks has said she will forgo it, to allow more money to come to the library. However, we must be prepared to cover some of her expenses. It's standard practice."

"And you're sure the event itself will make a profit?"

"Molly Stevenson is confident that it will. The main purpose is to increase library membership."

"Hear, hear," said Acacia. The other board members murmured their agreement, and finally, Channing nodded. "Well done, Fiona."

High praise from Channing, who wasn't usually generous with it. Her shoulders relaxed, and her hands no longer exhibited white knuckles as she clung to the papers she'd taken so much trouble over.

Apart from Andrew Mackenzie, who'd barely said a word, everyone else expressed their support. Without offering an opinion, he'd voted for the plans.

After the meeting, members lingered in the room, chatting. Andrew was talking to Acacia, without a shred of shyness, so far as she could tell. Before she could walk over to them, Channing came up to her and stood just a little too close. Fiona took a step backward.

"That was fairly satisfactory," he said.

As an opening conversational gambit, it lacked something, but she supposed he wanted to be encouraging. After a few questions about how she was settling in, he left her and went to talk to his mother. He seemed to have forgiven her for the destruction of his grandfather's tie. The specialist dry cleaner had done a commendable job, and the high standard was reflected in the eye-watering price.

By the time she could seek out Andrew again, he'd disappeared. Did he have a problem with her or the ideas she'd presented?

Acacia came up and put a hand on Fiona's arm. "Don't worry about Andrew—he rarely says anything at meetings. But when he does, it's always worth listening to."

"Andrew? I barely noticed he'd gone," said Fiona, aware of the blood rushing to her cheeks.

"Good." Acacia's eyes twinkled as she said this. So, Acacia had noticed her interest. Damn.

CHAPTER 22

FIONA

Thank God for her morning runs. Had it not been for those, and the support of her team at the library, Fiona might have found the job with its problems—and Channing—too daunting. She still didn't have a sense of how she was doing. That wouldn't happen until she solved this financial issue.

Fiona let her mind wander, hoping for inspiration as she ran in Brent Woods, having taken a new route, just for variety's sake. It was a beautiful early summer day, and the air was fresh and light, the morning sun slanting through the trees. She filled her lungs with the crisp tang of early summer, feeling an effortless energy that kept her going.

It wasn't until she stopped on a rise to look for the trail markers that she realized she hadn't seen any for some time. Was this, in fact, a trail? Or was it simply a path worn by the deer that watched her before lifting their white tails and bounding away?

A minute ago, she'd been confident she knew where she was headed—now her irritation rose. Perhaps she'd be able to find out where she was on the map app. She pulled the phone out of her pocket. Then she checked the bars. No signal. Crap. Small-town life had its drawbacks. All she could do was try to retrace her steps.

Turning back, she started down the path, which appeared harder to discern this time. When she reached the brook that ran through the woods, her spirits rose. If she followed the flow in its current direction, it should lead her to the River Brent.

Her optimism restored, she began to walk as close to the stream as possible. Thirty minutes, forty. Still no sign of a bigger river. Had she been going the wrong way all this time?

She stopped again to take stock. As she did so, an enthusiastic barking started up behind her. Thank heavens. A dog must have a person with them. Someone to ask.

"Hello."

Fiona swiveled as she heard the mild voice before she made out who it was, though she'd recognized the animal the minute she'd seen him. Newton.

As Andrew Mackenzie came into view, she heaved a sigh of relief, quickly followed by a flush of embarrassment. To be found, lost, like a little girl in a fairy tale, would not persuade people that she was a person who knew what she was doing. Perhaps if she brazened it out, he'd never guess.

"Hello, there. Taking your morning walk in the woods today?" she said.

He thought about this for a moment. No wonder. What an inane question. Since he was here, walking, then it followed...

"I like the woods on a Sunday. It's peaceful," he said.

Newton was bouncing around the two of them, making encouraging panting noises. So, not entirely peaceful.

"Are you on your way out, or going back?" Fiona sincerely hoped he was headed for home. She'd already been in the woods for an hour and was beginning to feel a little dizzy. She needed water. Her stamina seemed to have leaked out somewhere.

"We're headed home." Andrew's voice was polite, but he didn't offer to walk with her. She'd have to confess she was lost.

"Can you show me the right way? I seem to have wandered off the main track, and I'm not sure of the way back."

"I'd be happy to. It's not too difficult. You can follow the stream until it crosses the trail and turn left onto it."

She indicated the path she'd been on. "I've been following it, but I never get anywhere."

"That's because you're going in the wrong direction. There's a shortcut." He seemed to consider for a moment. "I'm going that way. We can walk together if you like."

His voice betrayed no special enthusiasm for this plan, but Fiona was past caring. "Thank you so much. The thought of backtracking another half an hour along the brook is somewhat daunting at this point."

They turned toward home, and she was grateful he hadn't suggested running—she didn't think she'd be able to at this point. She followed him on the deer path, which ran across the main trail after only ten minutes. The blue flashes painted on the tree trunks were visible now.

"I was so close. I had no idea."

"An easy mistake to make if you're not familiar with the woods."

Not exactly a sparkling conversationalist. But then, neither was she, usually, unless it concerned work.

They walked side by side, their strides well-matched. He must be about six-three or four, she thought, glancing at his profile. No clues there as to his personality. His weekend clothes were well suited for the terrain they were covering. More than well-suited. He was equipped for a trek across some mountain, with expensive hiking boots and a water bottle on a belt around his waist. Newton ran in and out between them and from time to time disappeared into the woods after some unknown quarry.

"Why is he called Newton?" she asked. It seemed an innocuous question.

"After Sir Isaac."

Who? A second later, it clicked. Sir Isaac Newton, of course. "The mathematician."

He looked at her, and for the first time in their acquaintance, she thought he smiled in a way that reached his eyes, though he bent down to pet Newton almost immediately, so she couldn't be quite sure. "I'm glad you described him that way. Most people think of him as the man who had an apple fall on his head, which made him invent *gravity*." He invested the last word with heavy sarcasm.

She laughed, happy she'd gotten it right. "You teach math at Carnarvon College, I'm told, so I guessed that would be your take on him."

"He invented calculus, you know."

Fiona studied the dog. Any animal less like a mathematical genius would be hard to imagine. "Oh, you mean the real Newton." Light-headed from dehydration, she was making no sense. Could she ask him for a drink from his water bottle? No, that seemed too intimate, somehow. Time to focus. "So, he was responsible for those painful hours in high school? Never mind. Your Newton is lovely."

As if hearing this, the dog licked her hand.

By the time they reached the road and turned homeward, Fiona was weary. Andrew regarded her with concern.

"You need some water, I think. Come in and I'll get you some. You'll have to excuse the mess. I wasn't expecting anyone."

She hadn't intended to impose on him any further, but the thought of walking the extra distance to her house without a drink was too much. "Thanks. I'd appreciate it."

Newton bounded through the scarlet front door and ran off to what Fiona assumed was the kitchen. The sound of him slurping water was audible from where she stood in the hall.

"Why don't you take a seat in the living room, and I'll bring you a glass?" Andrew said.

She walked in and scanned the room. A mess? The Sunday papers lay strewn on a pine coffee table, and an empty mug was perched next to them, but apart from that, the place was virtually immaculate. Her eyes were drawn to the bookshelves, where she noted the expected books on math, engineering, and architecture.

The lower shelves caught her eye—they could hardly fail to. The brightly colored spines of ten or more books were unlike any textbooks she'd seen. *When Autumn Comes, Last of the Great Pretenders, Hot Summer Days.* That one sounded familiar. She bent down to check the name of the author. Parks? Lucinda Parks?

She straightened with a start as she heard his footsteps returning along the corridor. Too late. He'd found her examining this extraordinary collection.

He flushed and swallowed. "My sister's," he said, without further explanation. "Here's your water."

He handed it to her, and she accepted gratefully. As she began drinking, the feeling of cool liquid running over her lips and tongue was all she could think about as she chugged it down. She hoped she wasn't making as much noise as Newton had been.

The dog had walked back into the living room and plopped down next to the sofa. To all intents and purposes, he was out cold.

Andrew's face softened as he looked at his border collie, and he seemed to relax.

"I can't thank you enough," Fiona said. Realizing that she might not have been clear, she added, "For the water, and for guiding me out of the woods."

"It's a good job we came across you, or you might have

been there all day." He gave her a small smile, which took the sting out of his remark.

Fiona hated to be thought incompetent. "I would have figured my way out eventually, I'm sure, but you did save me some time," she said, trying to be gracious.

"By the way, there's a map at the other entrance to Brent Woods," he said peaceably. "You could take a photo of it, and then you'd have it with you."

Lowering her half-empty glass, she said, "I'll do that, thanks. So, I won't have to depend on your help next time." She smiled.

His expression was quizzical, and he looked away, then said, "I don't mind rescuing you. Any time."

Fiona frowned. She didn't need to be rescued. Except when she did. "I mustn't stay. I have things to do and I expect you do too." She rose and walked toward the door. "Thanks again."

"You're welcome. Newton enjoyed the diversion. And if there's anything I can do to help, don't hesitate." He glanced at her and smiled again. Twice in one conversation. This was progress. She smiled in return.

Walking home, she thought about the Lucinda Parks collection. Why would his sister keep them in his house?

None of her business, she supposed. She needed to concentrate on the much more urgent issue of raising money.

CHAPTER 23
FIONA

Fiona stopped by the first meeting of the Ancestry Club in the Violet Room, delighted that five people had shown up. They'd hoped for more, but the sunny July weather hadn't worked in their favor. Still, the number was manageable for Jane Kennedy, who was to lead them.

"Let's introduce ourselves," said Jane. "For those of you who haven't met her yet, this is Fiona Gordon, our new executive director." Fiona smiled and said hello. Jane carried on. "You all know me, I think. I'm in charge of the reference department and the rare book collection as well. I've been helping my brother research our family tree, so I have an idea of what works and what doesn't." She turned and nodded at Acacia.

"I'm Acacia Todd, and I believe we're going to be researching my antecedents because they're the ones who donated this house as a library. The library holds many of our family papers, and I'm looking forward to finding out more about them."

A murmur of approval rose and then subsided.

Fiona recognized the next speaker—Elaine Johanssen, the lady who brought fresh eggs from her farm for the library's employees. A hefty book, its binding rather loose, sat in front of her, and her ancient hand rested on top of it. The woman must be stronger than she looked, if she'd carried it here.

"My sister and I didn't have any children," Elaine said when it was her turn, with a tinge of something in her voice. Fiona glanced at her with some sympathy, but no surprise. She'd heard the woman had never married.

Elaine straightened her spine and tugged at the rust-colored mohair sweater that might have been chosen to match her pixie haircut. She smiled. "I'd like to find out more about my Swedish heritage. All I can say for sure is, they arrived from Scandinavia in the late 1800s and settled in Minnesota. With all the other Scandinavians," she announced, and the others chuckled. "That's pretty typical, of course, but I'd love to discover exactly where they came from."

"Do you have access to the resources for international research, Jane?" asked Fiona.

"I think so. If this is your family Bible, Elaine, you should be able to glean quite a bit of information from it as a starting point."

Elaine lifted the heavy cover of her book, and Fiona could make out a list of handwritten names inside the front cover.

"Family bibles can be an excellent way to figure out family origins, Elaine, and we'll be studying how to use these kinds of documents in a couple of weeks." Jane shuffled her notes. "And how about the rest of you?"

One by one, the others introduced themselves, though it seemed to Fiona they almost didn't need to. Brentford was a small town, after all. When Jane asked her what she hoped to learn from the group, Fiona demurred.

"I'm not really here to do research—I wish I could spare the time, but I'd love to stop by when you're studying the

Wentworths. They must have a fascinating history."

And maybe she'd pick up some clues as to how to research George and his kin. Perhaps she'd be able to figure out what had happened to his wife and daughters.

Jane continued. "As Fiona said, I'm planning to begin with the Wentworths. Who knows, if we can go back far enough, we're almost certain to find that Albert and Abigail Wentworth had immigrant forebears. The plan is, you'll be able to use them as examples of ways to uncover information about your own ancestors."

"Must we study that woman's history?" Elaine's voice had an uncharacteristic quaver in it. "After all, the money for the library came from Albert Wentworth, didn't it? We don't need to learn anything more about his widow."

The group turned to Elaine and stared at her.

Only Jane remained her usual unemotional self. "Does this have something to do with your avoiding her portrait?"

"I have no idea what you mean," said Elaine, a slight blush appearing beneath her rouged cheek.

"I think you do. I remember the day you said you felt a little faint when you reached the landing where the portraits are."

Elaine looked flustered. "That was only because I took the stairs too quickly. I was out of breath."

The others nodded. This made sense, so what on earth was Jane talking about?

"You always take the back staircase now. I've seen you." Jane was like a terrier with a rat, not ready to let it go. "I always wondered whether there was something about those paintings that upset you."

Elaine sat up straighter and squared her thin shoulders. "You all know I've long considered the library to be otherworldly. It's just a feeling I have, and I don't need to explain it to you or anyone else."

"Well." Jane paused as if she were ready to argue, but instead said, "It's certainly not going to stop us from finding out more about Abigail Wentworth. So, let's return to the reason we're here."

She opened the file in front of her.

Elaine rose and, picking up her bible with some effort, left the room.

Fiona, with a terse glance at Jane, followed her into the hallway. The Wentworths could wait.

"Miss Johanssen—Elaine—hold up. Let me at least carry the book for you."

Elaine paused, turned to Fiona, and handed it over with evident relief. "That's kind of you, dear. I sometimes find Jane rather...strict."

"I hear you—but she's really good at her job. I wanted to ask you, though. Was she right about the haunting of the library? I mean, that you believe it's haunted."

Elaine sighed, and Fiona, realizing the octogenarian must be tired after her contretemps with Jane, ushered her into a chair in her office.

"Can I get you anything?"

"No, dear. I'm fine." Elaine glanced up at Fiona, who'd seated herself nearby. "I've always had a sort of sixth sense, although I didn't recognize it until a few years ago. I thought I had a vivid imagination that helped me think of things that might happen. But Jane wasn't wrong about the Wentworth paintings. I did feel something as I walked past them. Particularly from Abigail's portrait."

This was fascinating.

"What kind of thing?"

"Well, great sadness, I suppose. It's understandable, of course, if she's a widow, and I thought I might be hallucinating the feeling, if one can do that. But the sensation grew stronger each time I passed, until eventually, I felt so dizzy with it, I avoided using those stairs."

Fiona remained silent while she considered all this. Knowing what she knew about the power of portraits and the supernatural, she found herself inclined to accept Elaine's statement. She glanced at the Philadelphia Exhibition catalog she'd left on her desk. Finding it after it had landed on the floor next to her remained an unexplained occurrence too.

Elaine was regarding her hopefully. "You do believe me, don't you?"

"I do. Stranger things have happened. But I suppose most people might think you were...exaggerating, let's say. So perhaps we should keep this between ourselves for now. I don't want you to miss any meetings because they'll help you figure out your own family history. And you don't need to participate in any of the research into the Wentworths if you don't want to. Just ignore Jane. I'll see she doesn't bother you again."

She would talk to Jane about her attitude.

Elaine held Fiona's gaze. "That would make it a lot easier, if you're sure. I would like to work on it. I don't know how much time I have left."

Fiona opened her mouth to say something reassuring, but the old lady held up a hand like a cop stopping traffic. "No, listen. I'm in good health now, but one never knows. And this is something I've always wanted to do. After all, I might discover some new relations somewhere."

"Yes, indeed. Well, let me know how I can help. And do you think you could come again next week?"

Elaine nodded. "Definitely. I wouldn't miss it."

CHAPTER 24

GEORGE

I am fuming. One is not supposed to experience such extreme emotions in the afterlife, and perchance my anger signifies a lack of eligibility for the state of perfect bliss one is expected to attain here. And yet, how else should I feel?

This evening, Fiona comes home and, as is her custom, pours herself a glass of wine and enters the living room to see me. I confess I often enjoy these chats after work, but not tonight. It may be that I look thoughtful, which she interprets incorrectly. A typical female.

"No need to look like that," she begins, and then changes the subject. "I've decided to learn about your family—your ancestors in particular." She pulls a kind of metallic book onto her lap and opens it sideways.

I cannot believe it. I know as much about them as I care to know. They do not interest me. She must concentrate on my—what is the opposite of ancestors? Well, on Rose, anyway.

Fiona doesn't wait for me to answer this opening remark. "I'm starting with you and your father, because I have your names and the date you died. Jane, who's helping me, tells me that information should enable me to track down your records and then work my way backward." She takes a sip of her wine and replaces the glass on the side table next to her chair, no doubt waiting for a response.

Backward? Why would she need to go backward? She has to go *forward* from the day I left this Earth—to find out what happened to my love.

I try to interrupt her, to no avail.

"Plus, there's the exhibition catalog. The city of Philadelphia might know more about your father's company, which could lead to..." She trails off.

"To what, exactly?"

She looks up. "I can't say for sure. But it all helps to paint a better picture of you and your family."

"I can tell you everything you might want to know about *them*, although it strikes me that your interest is misplaced." She frowns at me, so it seems I need to make myself clear. "You should be looking for information about my widow. Surely her name is on my, um, death certificate. You must travel to the records office in Philadelphia to find out more."

"That's where you're wrong," she says.

Such nerve. Women never used to contradict men in my—more civilized—day. I daresay it's all of a piece with wearing trousers and drinking gin, but it is not becoming in a female. Not at all.

I reply with a degree of icy hauteur in my voice. "Would you care to clarify?"

Apparently, she does not note my sarcastic tone. Either that, or she ignores it.

"I started to tell you the other day, but I was too tired to explain. We do our research on the internet nowadays."

"This is not an explanation. In fact, it makes less sense than a bear in a brewery."

She sighs. "It's almost impossible to describe to a person

who lived before electricity, and cars, and television."

"Try," I say, keeping a firm grip on my annoyance.

"We have machines that contain more information than you can possibly dream of. They're called computers. We can get weather reports for today or any other date in the past. Using this machine, we can order items that are delivered to our houses, check railroad timetables, and, most important of all, so far as you're concerned, find the records of births, marriages, and deaths going back centuries."

I am dumbstruck, so she continues.

"You can send a letter to anyone, anywhere in the world, in seconds and get a reply back as fast as they can type it."

"Type?"

"Yes. Surely you remember typewriters?" She returns her gaze to the metal book on her lap and taps at some buttons as if she were playing the pianoforte. "Okay. The first commercially successful typewriter—a device that created type like that in books—came out just before your demise. And this," she points down at her contraption, "is the modern-day equivalent."

"This is making my head spin—much too complicated for me to understand."

"That's why I didn't explain it earlier. Let's see. Think of the telegraph. That was able to send messages over the electrical wires using Morse code. This is similar, but you don't need code to use it."

"Indeed. But of course, the messages couldn't go everywhere, as you say this information does."

She sighs. "I guess you'll have to trust me on this. Perhaps I can show you how it works by finding some record of you online."

What line? I wonder, but remain silent as Fiona continues to strike the keys. After a few minutes of muttering, she looks up, a somewhat smug expression marring her features.

"Right. I've found the 1870 census for Philadelphia."

Oh. If she has indeed discovered that, maybe she has reason to feel self-satisfied. But she cannot mean all the information contained within those volumes of bound documents, surely. Still. "I remember that. They sent people round to interview us. We had to list everyone who lived in the house. You've discovered it, you say?"

"Give me a minute or two. I'm looking for the Manchester name. Ah, yes. Here you are, living with Rose, at number 15 Spring Street. Is that correct?"

It's uncanny. This small machine has magical properties I will never comprehend, but she is right. I feel a tremor pass through me before I answer.

"I don't know how you discovered this, but the machine's information is accurate. What else does it tell you?"

"It gives your ages, and your employment as an importer. That's also true, isn't it?"

I'm finding it hard to take this in—yet it is exhilarating. I wonder what other traces of my life may be hidden in the—computer, was it? I nod at Fiona, but of course she can't see that.

"Yes," I say, and hesitate. "Is there anything else about me in there? Or about Rose?"

"Let me check the next census—1880." She keeps tapping, and then she frowns. "I've found the census, and I've looked for your last name, but I'm only finding your parents. There's no sign of Rose—or the girls."

"What do you mean? How can that be? They must be there. Surely, she was still alive then—only five years after my demise."

Fiona closes the lid on her magic machine. "Look, there could be several explanations. She might have moved away from Philadelphia. To almost any town, or maybe back to her own parents."

I interrupt her. "They lived near Philadelphia, at least until her father died. Her mother was suffering from consumption before I...left. She may not have survived until 1880." It seems odd to be considering a time I didn't live through, but my family did.

"Okay. Well, then, it's possible she, um, changed her name."

"Why would she have any reason to do that? Manchester is—was—a highly respected name in the city."

If I didn't know better, I'd say Fiona was looking apologetic. I see her shoulders rise as she takes a breath. "She might have...remarried."

I refuse to consider this explanation. I simply cannot. If Rose took a name other than mine, all my dreams of finding her are at an end.

CHAPTER 25
FIONA

Over the succeeding weeks, the Ancestry Club drew up a family tree for the Wentworths, and Jane produced letters, birth and death certificates, tax papers, and even the original plans for the house from the library's archives. Acacia was delighted to learn more about her forebears, as they traced Albert's history back to the late 1700s.

But information about Abigail proved to be thin on the ground.

Fiona felt discouraged as she realized how little documentation she had on the Manchester family by comparison. George's portrait and official records were the only sources. There was no ephemera at all.

Jane popped into Fiona's office one morning to update her on how the project was coming along, since she was already planning the anniversary exhibit about their benefactor.

She didn't bother with small talk. "The trouble is, we don't have much about the distaff side of the family—that's to say, Abigail Wentworth. We know she was a widow with three daughters when she married Albert. But apart from that, we have precious little to go on. You might almost think she was trying to hide her past, with so little evidence of it." Jane looked puzzled, like a cat after a mouse who had suddenly disappeared down a mousehole.

"Acacia won't be happy about that. After all, Albert was Violet's stepfather, so not related at all. All this research doesn't really apply to her."

"You're right. So, we need some piece of information to start the ball rolling."

Fiona considered the issue. This problem was similar to hers, so perhaps finding a solution here would help her too.

"It's odd that there's so little to go on. What about their marriage certificate? Doesn't it include her previous name?"

Jane shook her head. "It gives us her last name as Prewitt and that isn't much help without knowing which city she came from. It's very frustrating."

Fiona didn't need to be told that. The normally unruffled Jane sat with her legs firmly crossed at the ankle, tapping her pen on the notepad in front of her.

A thought occurred to Fiona. "What about the daughters' birth certificates? Are they in the collection somewhere? Surely, they'd have the information about where they were born, including their father's name?"

Jane raised her head, a new light in her eye. "You're right. I ought to have thought of that. I'll definitely give it a shot. Their given names are all flowers, of course, which might assist in narrowing the search. I'll get on it right away." She was rising from her chair as she spoke—a hound catching the scent of a fox on a distant breeze.

"Happy to be of help," said Fiona, but Jane was halfway out the door before she'd finished.

*

A few weeks later, a brief email from Jane alerted Fiona to the fact that she'd made a discovery.

"Please be sure to attend tomorrow's Ancestry Club meeting. I've got something exciting to share."

If Jane, a stranger to hyperbole, went so far as to use the word "exciting," it must be truly momentous.

Fiona wandered into the Violet Room the next morning with a mug of coffee and stood gazing around at the assembled members of the club. Some reflected impatience at the delay in continuing their own research. Jane appeared positively animated as she took a deep breath and began.

"It has taken a while, but I finally managed to track down where Abigail came from with her daughters." She glanced over at Fiona. "Fiona suggested looking for the daughters' birth certificates, but I found no trace of them. Perhaps Acacia might have them among her papers." She paused to give Acacia a meaningful look.

"Spit it out," came the unapologetic voice of Elaine, who was tapping her fingers on the table, irritation visible on her face.

Jane frowned at the octogenarian, who was unabashed. "I don't have too much time left, and I want to get this done."

Good point. At Elaine's age, no doubt every hour counted.

"If people wouldn't interrupt..."

It was Fiona's turn to frown. A patron was a patron and deserved respect. "All right, Jane. Tell us what you've discovered." She hoped her calm delivery would help ease the tension in the room.

"Well, as I was saying, the lack of the girls' adoption papers was something of a setback, but what I found instead were letters to Mrs. Wentworth from friends in her former hometown." She picked up a file and waved it around, though it might have contained shopping lists for all anyone could see of the contents. "These suggest Mrs. Prewitt arrived from Philadelphia, where we assume her three daughters were born. Of course, we don't have any information about where she came from originally—it might have been anywhere." She glanced at her audience as if expecting applause.

Fiona felt a shiver run up her spine and arms. Philadelphia? And the catalog that had appeared from nowhere was from Philly too.

As if she'd read her mind, Jane carried on. "It occurred to me that a book Fiona found—the guide to the 1876 exhibition in Philadelphia—might have belonged to her. I'll bring it in next time to show you all."

That made sense. What was Abigail's attachment to it? Did it have some sentimental value for her?

Jane was still talking. "Abigail and her three daughters came to Brentford two years after that exhibition, and she married Albert in 1879."

So, Abigail might have visited the exhibition. Perhaps she'd even known the Manchester family. It wasn't beyond the bounds of probability. But how to find out?

*

"Well, that was fascinating," Acacia said. She and Fiona were in the small library kitchen, waiting for the coffee to brew. Acacia's special status as a descendant of the Wentworths allowed her certain privileges. "There was a little too much theory—but that's just Jane. I'm going to leave the internet information to her. Apparently, there's a lot of it, and it's scattered all over." Her face glowed with enthusiasm.

"I expect she'll be able to advise you on the best way to handle your documents. Sifting through the relevant papers and photos without getting distracted is an art in itself."

Fiona smiled at her. "It occurs to me that your grandmother Violet was born a Prewitt, not a Wentworth, so we ought to pursue the Prewitt line."

Acacia stepped back, eyebrows raised. "You're right. I've always thought of those girls as Wentworths, but of course, they had a different father. Anyway, she asked me to look through my family photos to see if any of them predate the Wentworth marriage. They might identify people from Abigail's past in them, and possibly have the location recorded on the back."

"Do you think you might find photographs from her time in Philadelphia?"

"It's just possible. Wouldn't it be great to find one from Abigail's first wedding?" Acacia's face clouded over. "Although I don't think that was a thing in the 1870s."

Fiona smiled at her. "Photography was widely used in the Civil War, wasn't it? So, you never know. Did Jane have any other ideas?"

"Well, she made us take a look at Abigail's portrait, and those of her daughters, because they're all dated. I'm not sure how much help they are. They were done after Abigail and Albert were married."

Acacia interrupted her thoughts. "Which reminds me. Elaine had one of her spells as we were standing looking at the paintings."

"Spells?" Best to pretend that this was news to Fiona.

"She felt faint. I think it's happened before. She recovered quickly, but it was obvious she didn't enjoy it. I've suggested she see her doctor, but she insists she's fine."

Not too surprising. "Older people can be quite stubborn, in my experience," said Fiona.

Acacia shot her a look but apparently decided this wasn't aimed at her. "She said a funny thing, though. She asked if we could move from the Violet Room to another one, and when

Jane asked her why, I could tell she didn't really want to say."

"So, did she explain?"

"Well, eventually, she said she felt the spirits of the departed—that's how she put it—in the room. Which is hardly likely, is it?"

Fiona thought about George and the almost visceral experience she had when with him—they even conversed out loud. Who was to say what was possible? Not that she was about to confess any of this to Acacia or anyone else. "Didn't Elaine once say she thought the library was haunted?"

"You're right, but no one believed her, of course."

"What did the others think?"

"You know Jane. She's not one to take things like that seriously. She made a dismissive remark about it. Something like 'Maybe you're carrying these ghosts around with you, and if so, even if we change rooms, they'll come too.'" Acacia's tone made it clear she didn't think much of that comment.

"I don't suppose she meant anything by it. But you're right—Elaine should see someone about the dizziness."

The question was—did the old lady need a doctor or a psychic?

*

Two weeks later, aware she was a few minutes late, Fiona tiptoed into the Violet Room, where the Ancestry Club was already assembled. She'd wanted to enter unnoticed, but her hopes were thwarted by Jane's eagle eye.

"Welcome, Fiona. We're glad you could make it," she said, emphasizing a point. She addressed the group. "Fiona's suggestion that we take a look at the book she found was a helpful one. If you remember, she mentioned she'd come across it in the library, and here it is." Jane picked up the guidebook. "It's unlikely to have any direct bearing on Abigail Wentworth's history, but it should make for excellent background."

She handed the book to Elaine to pass around. The second she touched it, the old lady dropped it as though it were burning her fingers.

"S-sorry," she stammered. "I didn't mean to. Only..."

"Please be careful with it." Jane's irritation was evident in her voice.

"Don't worry about it," said Fiona, leaning over to pick the catalog up and inspect it. She glared at Jane. "No harm done. It's of historical interest to the library, because of Mrs. Wentworth's origins, so we don't want it damaged." Its fall from somewhere above the library staircase hadn't damaged it, but it was best to be careful.

"I'm sorry about that. I didn't mean to drop it—but...never mind." Elaine avoided Fiona's eyes.

Curious, Fiona looked at her. The old lady's face was drained of color beneath her makeup. "Are you feeling okay? Why don't you come and sit in my office for a while? Perhaps we can get you a cup of coffee."

Elaine grasped her arm as they left the group staring after them and made their way step by step along the hall to the office, where the old lady sank into a chair. Fiona asked Isabel to bring some coffee. "Maybe decaf?" she murmured. "We don't want to do any harm. And at her age... Oh, and a cookie or two as well. She might have low blood sugar."

After a few moments, the color began to return to Elaine's cheeks. "I'm better now. There's no need to make a fuss."

Fiona eyed her with concern. "Are you sure? Should we call for an ambulance?"

"No, no. Please don't bother. It was just a passing thing. I'm fine."

Isabel entered with two cups of coffee and some crackers on a tray. "Sorry," she apologized, setting it down on Fiona's desk, careful not to spill anything. "We didn't have any cookies, so I brought these. And these." She handed Elaine a couple of pieces of hard candy.

"Thanks, Isabel." Fiona watched the children's librarian as she left, then turned to Elaine.

"So, what happened there? Did you feel dizzy?"

Elaine sipped at her coffee, then put the cup and saucer down, her veined hand shaking a little with the effort. "I'm not usually this frail. And I wasn't dizzy exactly." She glanced up at Fiona as if deciding something. Then she said, "It was the book. I felt something as I picked it up."

"Like a muscle spasm or a shock?" Fiona had no idea what symptoms might afflict people of that age—her mother was only in her seventies and in decent health.

Elaine took a breath. "It was as if...I sensed a person nearby. I don't think it was anyone in the room. But I became aware of someone in the vicinity...with links to the book."

Strange. Although it *was* about Philadelphia, and Fiona had a connection to that city. Still, being able to detect some kind of emanation by handling it seemed extremely far-fetched, if not impossible. She decided to act as if what Elaine was saying made perfect sense. "As it happens, I took the book home the other day, so maybe it was something to do with me."

Elaine remained silent as she took another sip of her coffee. Her hand had stopped shaking. Wrapping her fingers around the cup, she looked up and said, "It's called psychometry." Seeing Fiona's puzzled countenance, she added, "It's when a sensitive or a psychic gets a strong feeling about the owner of an object if they handle it."

It was clear Elaine thought what she was saying was true, though Fiona was still skeptical. A sensitive? She'd never believed in psychics. But who knew? There were more things in heaven and earth, as the Bard said.

"So, you're one of these clairvoyant people? And this has happened to you before?"

"Not as strongly as it did just now. Not for a long time. That's why I dropped it. The surprise. The shock, even. I don't know what the book was trying to tell me, only that it had to do with a soul—I mean a person—close by." She looked at Fiona. "I have a feeling you might understand what I'm talking about."

The hairs stood up on the back of Fiona's neck. She'd have to do some research on this extrasensory perception, if that's what it was. After all, perhaps her interactions with George proved *she* was a sensitive too. And Elaine had recognized her gift.

CHAPTER 26

GEORGE

So much for using the small machine to find out more about me and my family. After recounting the events of her day, Fiona apologized for having found nothing.

It seems the Ancestry Club—and what kind of inane name is that?—met today, and one of the members confessed to experiencing an unusual reaction to certain things in the library, including the centennial exhibition catalog. Mind you, this member is female, and somewhere near ninety, according to Fiona, so I imagine her word is unreliable, to say the least. I make this point.

"You're almost two hundred years old yourself, so I'd stop criticizing if I were you."

I do not appreciate her crisp tone. Fiona can be quite critical too, though I don't choose to mention this. I'd like to keep the channels of our communications open, no matter what happens. For one thing, I must admit I'm not so lonely when she's around.

"I remain forever thirty-five, if you must know. At least, I think I remain the same as at my passing. So, I am only pointing out the problems with an unreliable witness," I say. "You could test out her so-called gift by bringing her here, I suppose." Although, frankly, I see no reason why my existence should be the object of an experiment.

"Why would I do that?"

I consider. It might be interesting to meet this woman—if indeed she is a sensitive. "Well, you might be able to see whether she detects my presence here. I presume, if she is psychic, she'd know I was in the room."

Fiona appears to be thinking this over because she says nothing for a while.

I give her a verbal nudge. "What do you think?"

"I suppose I could ask her for coffee when she delivers my eggs."

Another completely incomprehensible comment from my companion. "You want her to deliver coffee as well as eggs?"

Fiona snorts—I do wish she wouldn't. It is yet more evidence that her upbringing was sorely lacking. Based on what she says next, I imagine she is trying to convey exasperation.

"Elaine Johanssen drops off half a dozen eggs for me once a week or so, on her way to help out at the library. I believe she lives on her own. She might welcome a chance to sit and chat over a cup of coffee when she makes a delivery. I must ask her."

"I see. And you believe she would accept?"

"I do. At her age, she might be happy to relax for a while."

"Very well. I agree."

Fiona purses her lips. "Of course you do—it was your idea. Although I'm not sure I'm ready to share you yet."

"Do I detect a hint of the green-eyed monster?" I would not be surprised. Women always found it hard to share me.

"George—you do talk nonsense at times. I'm going to have some dinner."

"Don't forget the cake."

She pauses in the doorway and turns to me, a frown of

incomprehension creasing her forehead. "Cake? I don't have any cake. When have you ever seen me eat cake?"

I have certainly observed her partaking of delicacies of that type, but this is unlikely to be the moment to mention it. As I recall, women can be thrown off balance by remarks about food.

"I meant for when you entertain the ancient psychic, nothing more."

*

This proves to be an odd but entertaining encounter. At least, *I* think so.

The aged person turns out to be even more eccentric than I'd imagined from Fiona's description. Her hair! Hennaed, that much is clear—were it not for her venerable age, one might think she was a woman of ill repute, though perhaps an elf would be more apposite.

Diminutive, with small bones, she wears a garment even shorter than Fiona's. It resembles a jerkin, and depends for decency on the leg coverings, which are close-fitting and sport some kind of stars woven into them. Clearly not silk, for they cling to the legs in a way silk never could. Her face is a mass of wrinkles, but beneath them I detect high cheekbones and a stubborn jaw.

She trips into the living room and pauses in the doorway, looking suddenly uncertain. Then she squares her shoulders and walks in.

I hear Fiona's voice behind her. "Have a seat. Make yourself at home. I'm just preparing some coffee."

The sprite remains where she is, head tilted to one side, as though listening. Finally, she says, "I think there's someone here. Am I correct?"

I am not about to reveal myself to her, but I must admit

her comment occasions some surprise. Has Fiona told her to check for a supernatural spirit?

The elf speaks again. "I'm right, I'm sure. Where are you, you naughty person?"

I believe this is addressed directly to me, in what might be considered a flirtatious tone.

Even so—naughty person? What on earth would make her deduce that I am naughty? I take pride in being as upright a man as could be found anywhere—most of the time.

"Don't hide—I know you're here somewhere." She pauses for a moment. "Oh, there you are, dear."

She has spotted Fiona walking in with a tray on which are balanced cups and saucers and a plate of small pastries—not cake, but a reasonable substitute. Fiona places them on the side table and urges the pixie to sit.

"Cream and sugar?" she asks as she pours some coffee.

"Yes, please, dear. I need all the energy I can get." A tinkling laugh accompanies this remark, followed by a clearing of the throat. "I like this room—you've decorated it very nicely."

Why do people feel obliged to comment on decor? I consider it a commonplace conversational topic.

Fiona, meanwhile, appears unsurprised. "Thank you so much," she replies. "It's mostly things I brought from Pennsylvania with me."

"And the portrait?" The elf indicates my visage. "A relative, perhaps?"

"Goodness, no."

I can't help but feel that Fiona rejects any relationship between us rather too firmly. She continues. "He's a nineteenth-century merchant who lived in Philadelphia and used to work in my apartment."

Her guest's eyebrows shoot up, seeing which, Fiona explains, "They converted the warehouse his business owned into loft apartments. I happened to come across his portrait in a flea market, so I bought it and took it home. Perhaps I should have left him in the flat, but I've grown fond of him."

Well, this is nice to hear, and it makes a pleasant change. She's never mentioned that she has such cordial feelings toward me.

The faerie is staring intently at me now. "I don't suppose... you haven't by any chance...you've never *seen* him, have you?"

Fiona manages to retain her composure. "What on earth do you mean? I see him every time I enter this room."

The old lady clicks her tongue behind her teeth. "Tsk, tsk. I think you understand me perfectly. That portrait hides a spirit, if I'm not much mistaken, and I know you have certain powers. So, I'm wondering how far they extend in his case."

I find it offensive to be talked about as if I weren't here. I direct my next remark at Fiona. "This woman you have introduced into our house is extremely annoying. Can't you get rid of her?"

The elf sits up straighter, her head tilted to one side, concentration apparent on her face. "I believe I almost heard something—or someone," she announces. "Surely you can hear him, too."

"Fiona—say nothing. Admit nothing, or she will not stop." We need to nip this in the bud.

"There. There it is again. Definitely something."

"It's only the wind in the trees outside, I'm sure," says Fiona. "And now, if you'll excuse me, I have some work to catch up on."

"I understand. You want to keep him under wraps. Well, I sympathize. After all, he's rather handsome, isn't he?" She gives me a piercing stare as she says this. At least the woman has good taste in men.

A nervous giggle escapes Fiona. I deduce it's nervous, since a faint color is rising in her cheeks.

"You're so funny, Elaine. And now, I really must..."

"Got it." The tiny woman levers herself up from the chair with obvious effort and gives me one last look. Then she winks at me! What am I to make of that? "Goodbye, dear. I'll see you again soon," she says.

Is she talking to me? Great heavens. Let us hope not.

CHAPTER 27
FIONA

Fiona put her pen down and stared into space, searching for inspiration that refused to come. Looking for funds to pay for the centenary events was difficult, since the only way to do it fast would be to let someone go—and there was no one she could afford to lose.

Joanie came charging into her office without knocking, startling her.

"You'll never believe it!" She panted as though she'd been running. Her color was high, her eyes overly bright, and Fiona wondered for a second whether she had a fever.

She kept her tone soothing. "I won't be able to believe it if you don't tell me."

"I'm fit to burst. It's Leo Alterman." Joanie plopped down in the chair opposite Fiona's desk and leaned forward, one foot tapping, her hands clasped so tightly that the knuckles were white.

"Who?" The name meant nothing to Fiona, who still couldn't tell whether Joanie was bringing good news or bad.

"He's a regular at our book sales—one of the antiquarian

dealers. The handsome one. And guess what?"

Was Joanie in love? "Joanie, there's nothing I hate more than guessing games. Spit it out for heaven's sake." Despite her irritation, Fiona began to find the librarian's enthusiasm infectious. She smiled.

Joanie relaxed a bit. "He just emailed me. One of the books he bought at our book sale—it's turned out to be really valuable."

So, positive news, presumably. For the dealer, at least. "Well, good for him. Did we sell it for a decent price?"

"You don't get it. It was a first edition of *Tender is the Night* signed by F. Scott Fitzgerald, valued at about eight thousand on the open market. It was in exceptional condition, complete with its dust jacket," she explained, seeing Fiona's raised eyebrows. "He bought it for six from us."

"And it was donated to us, so we both did well out of it." Fiona was having trouble understanding why this was so exciting.

"Well, yes. But it wasn't the book."

Fiona might as well have been trying to draw a cork out of a champagne bottle without spilling the fizz. "Sorry? Not the book?"

Joanie gave a little huff of impatience. "No. When Leo inspected it more closely after he got back to New York, what he'd thought was just an old envelope tucked between the pages contained a letter that was even more important. It was written by Scott to Zelda while they were both in different hospitals in the 1930s."

She scarcely paused for breath. "He was in one because of his drinking, and she in another because of her mental illness. That's all I know. No one can figure out how the letter got there. It might have been used as a bookmark and forgotten."

Fiona hoped Joanie would get to the point soon. So far, this sounded like a lost opportunity for the library. She only remembered the bare sketches of Fitzgerald's life—alcoholism, Hollywood screenwriting, an early death, the films of *The Great Gatsby*, and a mentally ill wife. Perhaps if Joanie calmed down a bit, she'd clarify things.

"Well, that's interesting, and Mr. Alterman must be pleased, but I don't see—"

Joanie interrupted her. "I haven't finished. He couldn't be sure the letter was genuine because it was so unexpected, and he thought he'd better have it appraised by an expert. So, he took it to Sotheby's, and it turns out the book and letter together are worth a mint."

"Yes, and—"

Joanie was unable to restrain herself. "Here's the thing. Leo says—and this is amazing—he says it should fetch something in the hundreds of thousands." She sat back in her chair with a smile that reflected her satisfaction at silencing Fiona with this piece of news. She beamed, looking like a puppy that had succeeded in returning a ball when told to retrieve it.

"As I said, it's wonderful for him. Disappointing for us, though. How did we come to miss it?"

"That's not so important now. Because—did I forget to mention?—he's said he'll split the proceeds of the sale with us. He would have talked to you first, obviously, but you were out when he called."

Joanie's hands relaxed, and Fiona took a swig of her coffee, now cold. A small seedling of hope started to sprout. "Has it sold already?"

"No—the auction is sometime next month in New York. I think we should go."

Fiona was still taking this in. If true, the sale might raise enough to cover the costs of the centenary without cutting back on library services.

"How much did you say the reserve was set at?"

"I didn't, but he mentioned a hundred and fifty thousand.

Can you believe it? If it achieves that, he'll give us half of the net, after the auctioneers' commission."

The figure made Fiona gasp. A sum like that would get them out of the hole. "Wow. That would help cover the cost of the centenary celebrations, and maybe leave us with a little change."

"Exactly."

As the facts began to sink in, Fiona sprang to her feet. "So, Leo Alterman turns out to be our guardian angel. Who would've guessed? Joanie—you're a star." She walked around the desk and hugged her. "Wait until the board hears about this."

CHAPTER 28
GEORGE

Fiona announces herself before she even enters my room, her voice reaching me from the hallway.

"George! Listen to this."

As if I had any say in the matter. "Fiona?" I enquire, my tone patient rather than irritated, I hope. A gentleman should always be polite, even in the most trying of circumstances.

She rushes in, drops her attaché case on the sofa, throws herself alongside it, and kicks off her shoes with the ridiculous heels. This is a woman who is keyed up about something, I can tell.

"I'm going to have a party!"

This is unexpected. Fiona does not strike me as a person who enjoys large gatherings. In fact, the old psychic she introduced to the house a few weeks ago was the first person she'd attempted to entertain—and one could hardly consider that event a complete success. She forgot the cake, for one thing.

"Oh, really? Is there some particular reason for this sudden urge to mingle?"

She looks a little deflated. Perhaps I should show more enthusiasm.

"I mean, it sounds delightful."

She revives. "It is, George. It is. We've raised the funds to pay for the centenary events."

"Very satisfactory, I'm sure. And the connection to your proposed party?"

She interrupts me. "Listen, George. This means I can relax a bit and celebrate."

I open my mouth to speak, but she continues regardless.

"I'm going to invite Molly Stevenson, the local bookstore owner, and her friend Nick, a teacher at Carnarvon College. I'm not sure what their exact relationship is, but at the very least, they're close friends."

Hmmm. This doesn't sound quite proper to me.

"And I'm hoping Andrew Mackenzie and Cece can come too."

"And who are they?"

"He's a member of the library board. You might have caught sight of him walking his dog past here in the mornings. His sister Cece is often at his place on weekends. She's beautiful, and a lovely person too. I'm hoping things will go well because Andrew's a math professor, and he and Nick know each other, I think. They teach at the same college."

So tedious. I wish I'd never asked.

"Are you going to invite the elf, perchance?" She might be diverting. And I might have someone else to talk to. I could practice materializing—I'd wager she'd love that.

Fiona appears to consider this, then shakes her head. "I don't think so. The numbers are already off, with more women than men, and adding her would make it worse."

"Is there no other gentleman you could ask? The one you spilled wine on? To make amends for that unfortunate blunder?"

"Who? Oh, Channing Madison? Not in a million years. He'd ruin it. Anyway, I think four plus me is plenty."

Her voice sinks to a murmur as she takes a notepad out of her attaché case and begins making lists.

Four strangers in the house. And all of them taking attention away from me and my hopes for a rapprochement with Rose. Such a maddening delay—and all for some trifling and doubtless tiresome meal.

Let's hope Fiona can get it over with soon. Although, thinking back to the dinner parties Rose and I hosted, it took some time to send out the invitations, confer with the cook about the menu, and prepare and decorate the house—all before the dinner could take place.

CHAPTER 29

FIONA

The morning of the dinner party welcomed Fiona with a brilliant blue sky and a distinct nip in the air, like a typical early fall day. Cool enough to allow her to light a fire in the living room.

She ran over the tasks that still needed doing—setting the table, checking the homemade mango sorbet was freezing, and opening a bottle of red wine so it could breathe. Checking things off her list, she remembered how much she used to enjoy entertaining. She'd dug up one of the menus from her days in Philadelphia—including several of Brian's favorites because she could cook them blindfolded—roast duck stuffed with apples, served with wild rice and roasted onions. Followed by the sorbet for dessert.

Funny. She rarely thought about her ex-husband these days, after marking his emails as spam and blocking them. She smiled—she was definitely on the mend.

As she descended the stairs, having dressed for the evening, she heard the crunch of gravel announcing a car pulling up outside. It was only six-fifteen, and her guests weren't supposed to show up until seven. She walked to the living room window and saw a man stepping out of a bright blue Porsche. As he turned toward the house, she gasped and stepped back from the window in an instinctive effort to hide from him.

Brian.

He looked ridiculous—because of *course* he wore clothes that gave the impression he was trying too hard to be younger than he was. The midlife-crisis car no doubt served the same purpose. What the hell was he doing here? Her first thought was that he'd come to break some bad news to her. She dismissed that thought. More important was the fact that she had just forty-five minutes to get rid of him before her guests arrived.

Her lips pressed together, Fiona took a breath in through her nostrils and opened the front door. She hustled him inside, not wanting anyone to see him and draw the wrong conclusions. She faced him, blocking the small hallway. Without preamble, she said flatly, "I'm expecting company, so you can't stay."

"But I've come all this way to see you." He stood in her hall, sniffing. "Roast duck?" he inquired with a smile she knew all too well. The one he used when he had done something that required an apology he wasn't going to give.

"Not for you. I'm busy. If you'd contacted me to let me know beforehand, I'd have told you not to bother." Fiona clenched her fists in an effort to remain calm. She wanted to step back, to retreat from his too-strong aftershave and his too-close presence, crowding her in her own house.

"Aren't you pleased to see me?"

The arrogance of the man. She needed to squash any such idea immediately. "No. I already told you I'd be happy never to see you again. And your arrival is a damn nuisance, if you must know. I need you to leave. Right now."

"But, Fi, I have to talk to you." He gazed at her soulfully, leaving Fiona unimpressed. So typical of him to see the world from his point of view. How had she not realized that earlier? Before she could reply, he went on, "I've left Melanie."

Fiona backed away in shock. "What do you mean?" He couldn't be saying that he'd parted from his new wife. Two divorces in two years? Impossible—even for someone as feckless as Brian.

"Look, can I come in for a minute? We can't talk here."

She allowed him to walk through to the living room but didn't offer him anything to eat or drink. Which didn't stop him from asking, "Where do you keep the booze? I could use a whiskey."

Fiona had no bourbon, and she wasn't about to waste the wine she was planning to serve her guests. There was the no-name brand of pinot noir she'd brought with her from Philadelphia because she didn't know what else to do with it. Brian had probably bought it long ago. Perhaps if she gave him a glass, he'd leave.

"I've got some red wine somewhere."

"Really? Given up booze, have you?"

Fiona bristled. "My drinking habits have nothing to do with you. Take it or leave it." She would willingly take half a glass herself at this point, but not if it meant Brian would stay.

"No problem. I have a bottle of the best with me. It's in the car. I'll be right back."

A bell jangled in her head. Who traveled with their favorite liquor?

He was back minutes later, letting the front door slam behind him. She shuddered.

"Where do you keep the glasses?" He walked into her kitchen as if he owned the place and scanned the cabinets as though hoping to see inside. His eye fell upon the table, where Fiona had put out stemware but also some tumblers, intended for water. Brian picked one up without commenting on the rest.

"This will do." He headed over to the sink, where he poured a couple of fingers of Widow Jane and waved it in Fiona's direction. The bottle had already been opened, so he hadn't brought it as a gift for her. Just as well. Watching him pour the liquor out raised unpleasant memories of evenings when she drank to keep him company. The faintest hint of it gave her a sick feeling.

"No thanks. I'll stick with water." She took some ice cubes from the old-fashioned fridge and poured water over them, listening to the crackle they made. "Want some ice?" It might dilute the effect. She pulled herself up short. It wasn't for her to try and manage his drinking. It was none of her business.

"I'm fine—thanks."

Slowly, she cut a slice of the lemon that had been sitting on the counter, ready for her guests' drinks, and dropped it into her glass. Damn Brian.

The smell of roasting duck was now pervading the kitchen. Because of his intrusion, the meal would be spoiled. She wasn't about to let him join her friends—he could fend for himself.

Without a word, she switched off the oven and turned to face him. "You still haven't answered my question. What do you mean, you've left Melanie?"

"Can't we sit down somewhere to talk for five minutes? Maybe in the living room? Come on, Fi."

This was going to take longer than she'd hoped. She needed him to leave as soon as possible, and an acrimonious confrontation was unlikely to achieve that. "I suppose so. Just for a minute."

He strolled past her and made himself at home in the living room, where he sprawled on the sofa as if it were his and took a sip of his bourbon. "You have to hear me out first."

She'd had regrets about the end of her marriage when it first broke down. And she still had the occasional pang when she saw a program or film with an actor with the same Irish good looks. Now, in person, he wasn't as handsome as she remembered. He'd missed a spot on his chin when he'd shaved this morning. The warm feeling it used to give her to witness these small imperfections was replaced with a detached sense that this man wasn't doing as well as he wanted her to think.

"Please, Fi, sit. Please. I need you to listen to me."

As he always had. She wondered whether listening was, in fact, the main reason he wanted her.

Watching him drink, she considered giving him some of the white bean dip she'd made as an appetizer. The last thing she needed was to have to cope with a fifty-something man who'd imbibed too much. Someone who wouldn't be fit to drive away.

She rose and went to the kitchen, returning with the dip. Without the parsley she'd intended to use for garnish. She wouldn't waste parsley on this man. She found the carrot sticks and rice crackers and put those out too. He didn't like raw carrots.

Sitting, she took a sip of water and gazed at him. "Fine. Go ahead."

His eyes took on a somewhat puzzled air, as though this wasn't the reaction he'd been expecting. "I made a terrible mistake, leaving you for Melanie. I realize that now."

Fiona had imagined a scene very similar to this after they first separated. Not until Brian and Melanie finally married had she managed to let go of that dream. Now that her fantasy was playing out in front of her, she found herself feeling almost nauseated.

"It's a little late for that, isn't it? You got what you wanted. The younger wife, the baby. How is it, by the way? You had a boy, didn't you?" She'd heard this from her mother, who'd always had a soft spot for her ex-husband, and had, no doubt, kept tabs on him. The child's birth had been the *coup de grâce* to their relationship, but now she could think of Brian's happy little family with only the tiniest pang of envy.

What looked like an unexpectedly genuine flash of pain crossed Brian's face. "That's it. That's why I left."

"But…"

"Hear me out. I found out…" He turned his head away as if not willing to risk eye contact. "I discovered…the baby wasn't mine."

CHAPTER 30
GEORGE

Well. This was unexpected. Sometimes, I almost wish I couldn't overhear things being said in the house. This announcement about his paternity—or lack of it—comes as no real surprise to me.

Having come across this so-called gentleman—her former husband—when Fiona lived in the company warehouse, I judge this is just par for the course, as the golfers say, for a man who mismanages his life to such an extent. His first mistake was to abandon Fiona. Had they still been together, we might all have been in Philadelphia, and she might be making progress in finding Rose.

She was well rid of him until he reappeared tonight. This late—or, rather, ex-husband of hers was always unsatisfactory, to say the least.

When he used to invite himself to her apartment in Philadelphia, she managed not to give vent to her feelings, but once he left, she was inevitably either reduced to tears or would pace up and down in a rage—sometimes both. Her anger was easy to infer from the uttered imprecations that should never cross a lady's lips. I should hate to see her in that state tonight, when she's expecting her friends.

The man is a menace. I grant you, in appearance, he presents himself as well-dressed, clean-shaven, and groomed. But an athlete he is not, as is evidenced by the paunch which he attempts to disguise by the clever tailoring of his suit. Ram dressed as lamb, I'd say. That may not be quite correct—it sounds odd, although a similar idiom is used of women who try too hard to look younger than they are.

In any case, none of that is really to the point. What remains is his cavalier attitude to Fiona. What a boor—storming in here, throwing his weight around. Demanding alcohol and her ear. It's at times like this that I wish I had the capacity to do something to help her.

How I wish I could plant a punch on that smug visage of his. I used to be accounted a fair boxer in my time, and I'd like to see him with a black eye. I used to practice sparring with professional boxers at my gentlemen's club, so one quick hit to the nose should take care of his nonsense.

She would, of course, deny me that pleasure.

"I can stand up for myself." Her voice is as strong as if she'd said this aloud. She hasn't, though. She has no need to. I wonder whether I am able to read her thoughts, or whether I have imagined this comment because I know her so well by now. Either way, I believe her.

This blackguard, who has arrived to boast of his infidelity and then whine about his just desserts, would make me nauseated, were I still capable of such a thing.

Apropos. I find it interesting that I am free to experience emotions in this life, yet I can no longer suffer physical symptoms. So, although nausea is something I remember in a vague way, it no longer exists in any real form for me. I wonder, should I manage to manifest, could I hit the man and sustain no pain? Would *he* feel anything?

Perhaps the shock of seeing me would be sufficient punishment. It's possible, though, he would not even know I was there. My situation is perplexing indeed.

Onward. I can only hope she throws him out soon. He has spent enough time in her home.

Yet, this news of the child's parentage has clearly thrown Fiona. The child, I might add, will be the loser in this, because bearing the stigma of illegitimacy must surely mean its life is blighted forever. Mind you, I have known immigrants of uncertain, shall we say, origins, who made a good living for themselves in our great country, where no proof exists of their family's history.

Back to Fiona. This brave woman is now allowing her shock at this revelation to show in her face. This is not ideal. One never wants to show one's hand to the opposing player.

Will she ask him for more information? I, too, would be interested in knowing who the father is. His name would mean nothing to me, it goes without saying. But I would be delighted on Fiona's behalf to discover he was a tall, handsome, much younger man. It would serve this scoundrel right.

Another point occurs to me. I know from conversations I overheard while the painful separation was happening that Fiona believes herself incapable of bearing children—a tragedy indeed. Now it seems that it might be this cad who has the problem. This man who blamed her for years.

My urge to inflict some physical pain on him is well-nigh overwhelming. I could find it in myself to applaud if Fiona raised her hand to him. There is no man who cannot benefit from a slapped cheek from time to time. Particularly after delivering this kind of psychic blow to his wife. Or, I suppose, ex-wife. Her response, though, is disappointing.

"I'm sorry to hear that," she says. "Genuinely."

I almost believe she means it.

The man cares nothing for her sympathy, I can tell,

because this is his reply: "I've set divorce proceedings in motion. I should be free by the end of the year." He glances up at her with an expression he no doubt regards as appealing, but which, for my part, makes my bile rise. "So, I hope... I miss you," he finishes.

She stares at him. "But you can't possibly imagine..."

Exactly. It is imperative Fiona makes it clear to him that there is no possibility of her changing her mind.

Since we arrived here from Philadelphia, I have seen her become her own woman—she has no use for him now. After all, she needs no one but me for company, and I need her to help me find Rose, so his presence would certainly be *de trop*. She must tell him so.

"Wait. I'm here to ask you..." He is much too persistent. Has he no shame?

If he hopes she will return to him, he is mightily mistaken. I know Fiona, and she has long since made up her mind.

He can still barely look her in the eye. No wonder. This is not an individual accustomed to humility, and asking for anything, rather than demanding it, must be costing him dearly. "Please come back to me. I've changed. I know we can make it work."

As I surmised, a blatant plea for her mercy. What a dolt. However, I must credit him with putting on an adequate show. A more gullible person might believe he was contrite—almost on the verge of weeping. Melodramatic fool. Notwithstanding, he hasn't offered her even a hint of an apology. She must ignore his threatened tears—a performer's tears.

"Say something," he prompts with a frown. "Say yes."

Don't say yes, Fiona! Say no! I wonder if she can hear me.

She takes a breath and raises her eyes to his. I am confident she will take the high road, no matter what.

"This is the last thing I expected, Brian."

Say no! Yet I fear that response will not be enough to make him go.

Hope appears on his countenance, wiping away the faint trace of anxiety, and he smiles, doubtless certain of her answer.

"And?" he says.

"And the answer is—no. Not now. Not ever."

As they say these days, if I'm not mistaken, "Way to go, Fiona!"

CHAPTER 31
FIONA

Brian stood, too fast. Fiona's refusal seemed to have lit a fuse under him. The side table she'd inherited from her grandmother teetered once before coming to rest upright again. The glass with his drink didn't. He paused to dab at the antique rug with his handkerchief, then straightened up and moved toward Fiona.

"Don't you understand, Fi?" He appeared perplexed, like a cat presenting their owner with a dead rat and not understanding why they reacted with revulsion. "I'm offering you a chance to try again. And my undying devotion, of course. I still love you, Fi."

She regarded him as if he were a character in a badly written melodrama. "I used to love *you*. Or I thought I did. But you must accept that whatever we had is gone."

He took a step back. "What? How can you say that? We were wonderful together."

"To begin with. But..." How to explain this so he'd realize she would never change her mind? "Look—I've become accustomed to life without you—I'm happy for the first time in ages. Living on my own suits me, I like my job here, and I've met new people."

"Not like the friends we had in Philadelphia."

"You're right. It's not the same. But those people still keep in touch, and making new friends who've never met *you* is a relief, frankly."

"They're not aware you're divorced?"

"That's not what I said. It may surprise you to know I don't spend any time talking about you. You're part of my past."

He pasted on an ingratiating smile. "Oh, come on. You know that's not true. You still love me."

"I'm not even going to bother answering that." She glanced at her watch.

Brian took a pace backward, his fists clenched. "So—there's someone else." It wasn't a question.

Fiona thought fleetingly of George and almost laughed. "Don't be ridiculous. I've told you—though you appear to be finding it difficult to believe—I like living alone. And now go. Immediately. And don't *think* of coming back."

The vehemence in her voice must have persuaded him she meant business, but he wasn't going to let her have the last word. "I'll leave you to think this over. Sleep on it. I'm sure you love me, deep down. I'll be back tomorrow to talk to you again. We can sort this out." He was almost pleading now. It didn't suit him.

"I'm not interested, so don't bother. I won't be here." She'd been planning to do nothing on Sunday except some work she'd brought home. Now, she decided to take a short trip down to the coast, to run along the beaches at Sandy Point. Brian's threat of returning made taking a day off even more appealing. "So, there's no need to come back. Ever."

Turning on his heel, Brian stalked out of the kitchen, into the hall, and out the front door. She heard it slam behind him, making the walls shudder. Looking out the window, she could see his retreating back as he headed down the porch steps toward his Porsche. As she watched, a figure walked through the gateposts.

Fiona glanced at her watch. What time was it?

Crap. Five past seven, and dinner wasn't ready. A guest who arrived early was inconvenient. Even if it *was* Andrew.

Her eyes widened as she saw Brian veer away from his midlife-crisis car and step forward to throw a punch straight at Andrew's face, sending him sprawling on the drive.

Not pausing to think, Fiona grabbed a box of tissues and sped down the steps.

Andrew sat on the ground, one hand over his nose, from which blood was streaming. The only signs of Brian and his Porsche were his taillights disappearing through the gate as he swerved into the road.

She hurried over to Andrew and handed him a wad of tissues. "Are you okay? I mean, obviously, you're not, but did he hurt you?"

Andrew ran a hand over the back of his head. "I don't think so. I didn't land very hard. But as for my nose..." He fingered it gingerly. "I don't *think* it's broken." He sounded like a man with a heavy cold.

A conflicting rush of fury aimed at Brian and relief that Andrew wasn't too badly injured made her dizzy for a moment, but she pulled herself together.

"Thank heavens. Do you need help getting up?" she said, extending a hand. He grasped it, and she felt the small pieces of gravel stuck to his palm as he did so. "Let me," she said, and brushed them off. His hand was surprisingly strong for someone who didn't do manual labor for a living.

Andrew heaved himself up, putting barely any pressure on her hand, but not letting go of it right away, either.

She pointed at his pants. "I'm so sorry," she said again. "I'll pay for the dry cleaning, of course." Her life was becoming a series of mishaps with men that required her to have their clothes dry-cleaned. Perhaps she could negotiate a discount with the cleaners.

Andrew interrupted her thoughts with a more practical question. "Do you have any frozen peas?"

"I'm sure I do. I have some inside. I should have thought of that. You're sure you're not hurt otherwise?"

"Only my pride. I used to box at school, but I just wasn't expecting... Who the hell was that, anyway?"

Embarrassment took over. She'd have to admit to having married a man without any self-control. "It was my ex-husband. And I'm so mortified he did that."

He stared at her, confused. "I don't suppose it's your fault. But why would he have any beef with me, for Chrissakes?" In trying to frown, he winced, and Fiona realized he needed ice sooner rather than later, if it was to be effective.

With no idea how to answer, Fiona hesitated, and then with relief spotted Cece coming around the corner.

"What's going on?" Cece said as she came toward them. Then she registered Andrew's face, mostly hidden under a bouquet of tissues. "What happened to you?"

Her brother paused to move his hand away from his face. "Saturday night parties in Brentford—you know what they're like. This one got out of control." He gave a wry grin.

"Sorry—*who* did you say was coming?" she asked Fiona with a puzzled frown.

"Molly and Nick. But this was done by someone I never invited. Would never invite."

To Fiona's relief, Cece did not pursue this evasive answer, merely saying, "I can see why you wouldn't. Shall we get Andrew inside?"

Fiona hadn't planned to entertain people in the kitchen, at least not before dinner. The living room was a more traditional place for pre-dinner drinks and hors d'oeuvres. The dip she'd put out for Brian remained there, untouched, no doubt changing color as it dried. Meanwhile, Andrew was sitting at the dining table, a bag of frozen corn melting against his face—she'd defrosted the peas to serve with the duck.

No matter what she did to make amends, this scenario was unlikely to result in an elegant dinner party. Andrew was right. It more closely resembled the aftermath of an illicit teenage rave that had ended badly.

The front doorbell rang again, and Molly entered without waiting for Fiona to open it. She was accompanied by Nick. He was holding a bottle of red wine, and after handing it to Fiona, he surveyed the kitchen.

When he spotted his fellow professor, Nick's face broke into a grin. "I didn't have you figured for a party animal, Andrew," he said.

Molly scanned Andrew's face, and her look of concern subsided. "You're okay, though?"

Andrew nodded. "I'm fine, though I expect I'll look worse tomorrow."

Oh, dear. Fiona was saved from further comments by Molly, who piped up unexpectedly. "Looks like you have someone to keep an eye on you," she said to Andrew before she turned to his sister with a smile. "Hi, Cece."

"You two have met?"

Molly smiled. "Didn't you know? Cece works for one of the big publishers, and she's always got suggestions for books I should stock. Not to mention—she's the person who helped us snag Lucinda Parks for the centenary event."

"Wow. I had no idea. Thanks so much for persuading her to agree, Cece."

She ought to have asked about this before now.

"I was happy to help. Working in publishing is fun most of the time, though there are some authors," she looked around at the assembled crowd, "who can be a royal pain."

"I hope you're not talking about me," said Nick, unexpectedly, leaving Fiona more confused than she was before.

"Nick has published a number of books, including a fabulous one about butterflies, illustrated by Sonya Morten. But it was a different publisher," said Molly.

Fiona was reminded of the evening when Brian had bought one of Sonya's paintings for Melanie. "Small world. I know her, and I love her paintings. She was the star of a gala event at the Philadelphia museum where I worked."

This revelation encouraged enough general conversation that Fiona decided it was safe to start serving her guests.

Molly turned to her. "How can I help?" she said.

"I was going to offer people a drink," Fiona said. "Thank you for the wine, by the way." She had some chilled rosé in the fridge, so Nick's Shiraz joined a bottle of Merlot on the counter. Brian had taken his bourbon with him—and good riddance.

Molly struck a practical note. "Hey, Nick—stop teasing Andrew and open these bottles, will you?"

The meal was a little late, but her friends enjoyed it, so far as she could tell. Even Andrew, struggling to balance a fork and a bag of crushed ice, and who she suspected couldn't taste much, praised the duck. He wasn't effusive, exactly, but with any luck, the comment signaled a rapprochement between them. Fiona relaxed somewhat, and as her guests rose to leave, he lingered, and she hoped he'd forgiven her.

"I'll catch you up, Cece. I just want to…"

"Got it," said his sister, smiling at him. "You want to thank Fiona for saving your nose from disaster."

"Something like that."

It was her fault his nose had needed saving, and Fiona became aware of the heat rising in her face. Perhaps it was the two glasses of wine she'd drunk over dinner. Thank goodness she hadn't drunk anything with Brian. Thinking of Brian made her clench her fists.

"So. What was that all about? You never explained. Your ex-husband, you said."

Crap. How much of an explanation did she owe him? "Well, yes. He drove up here without telling me he was coming. I'd have told him not to bother, if he'd asked."

"Okay, but why *hit* me?" Cautiously, he fingered his nose.

What could she say to that? She assumed Brian thought she and Andrew were an item, but if she said so she'd embarrass him, as well as herself. Because nothing could be further from the truth and, after this, likely never would be. And if she said it was because she'd just insisted Brian leave—would that seem like enough of a reason for him to punch a stranger?

"He'd had too much to drink." It was true, at least.

"I see," Andrew said.

Though it was clear to Fiona that he didn't. His voice was chilly now. Her hopes for forgiveness receded. "I really don't want to explain to anyone why I have two black eyes." He sounded irritated now.

She glanced at him. "But you don't. You look fine, honestly."

"Okay, but tomorrow the bruises will begin to show."

With that, he turned away and stomped down the porch. She wondered whether his injuries were only physical or due to something else.

"Can I give you a ride home?" she said as he began to walk away.

He barely turned his head. "No need. I prefer to walk."

CHAPTER 32
FIONA

For a week following Andrew's fateful encounter with Brian, a mortified Fiona drank her coffee at the table by the window, hoping to catch sight of him. But he seemed to have abandoned the route he used to take in the mornings, and she missed seeing him go by with Newton more than she cared to admit, even to herself.

If she couldn't even wave to him as he passed by, what hope would she have of being able to apologize face-to-face? She'd have to wait until the next board meeting and hope he'd forgiven her for that disastrous evening.

She tried to write him to thank him for connecting them with Cece to help secure Lucinda Parks' presence for the centenary, using the letter as a way to segue into an apology.

Writing it proved more difficult than she expected. She drafted several unsatisfactory versions and eventually sent something that never mentioned that evening.

She'd had no response.

Sitting at her window that weekend, a hideous thought struck her. What if Cece persuaded Lucinda to retract her offer to visit the library after her brother's injury? If she did, Fiona would be the only person responsible for wrecking their main centenary event. She needed to know whether he'd forgiven her for Brian's behavior.

She knew where he lived. Did she have the nerve to go and face him at home? It was an intimidating idea, to be sure.

Before she could talk herself out of it, Fiona set off down the street toward his house, but every time she reached the corner of the lane where he lived, she stopped, her heart pounding, her breath shallow, her palms damp.

She had no reason to be scared, she reassured herself. He was a business connection, after all, and had given his help freely for the good of the library. All she wanted to do was apologize. And ensure that she hadn't wrecked the chances of getting Lucinda to come.

The third time she arrived at the corner, she looked at her watch. Three o'clock. A beautiful early fall day. He'd probably be out. No one would be inside on a day like this. Oh well—if he weren't there, she could tell herself she'd tried.

Inhaling a lungful of clean air, she turned her feet toward his house. She liked the fact that it was a small place, not much larger than hers. Professors of math at private Connecticut colleges probably couldn't afford anything bigger. In fact, perhaps he didn't own the house. Perhaps he only rented.

Either way, it was none of her business. Good relations with Andrew and the centenary celebrations at the library *were* her business, obviously. She rang the bell and stood back, so as not to crowd whoever answered.

A burst of cheerful barking announced her presence. So, Andrew was home, she suspected. A few moments later, she heard someone unlocking the door, and it opened to reveal a harassed Andrew standing there, a sheaf of papers in his hand.

His black eyes had now reached the purplish-yellow phase of healing. This was worse than she'd feared. Still, there was no going back now.

"I'm sorry to disturb you." Judging by his demeanor, she was interrupting something important.

He looked down at the pages in his hand, as though surprised to see them there. A blue ink stain was visible on his left hand.

"Oh, no problem," he said, returning his glance to her. "Is there something I can do for you?"

He could stop making this so hard for her, to begin with. He didn't need to be quite so formal. It appeared he wasn't going to ask her in.

"It's about the other night. About Brian. About him hitting you."

Andrew's face began to turn pink, as though he were the one who should be apologizing, not her.

"I wasn't expecting to see him—" she began to explain.

He spoke simultaneously. "That's okay—"

They fell silent. Then he said, "There's no need to tell me. What you do on your own time is your business. Nothing to do with me."

Now what? How much should she tell him? Did she need to explain in detail?

"Do you want to come in?"

This was better. "Thanks." She followed him into the living room and watched him lay his papers on an antique side table. He indicated the sofa, and she sat. Taking a breath, she began to explain.

"As I mentioned before, Brian is my ex-husband. My very ex-husband. He drove up to see me without telling me."

"Uh-huh."

"I wanted to apologize again for his behavior. I hope you'll forgive me."

"It wasn't your fault. But I was disconcerted, I have to admit." He smiled awkwardly, and she smiled back, relieved.

Time to move on to making amends.

"Anyway, the other reason I came was because I wanted to thank you."

A fleeting inquiry lit up his face. "For what?"

"For your help, and your sister's, of course, in getting Lucinda Parks to come to the library. It was incredibly kind of you both."

"Well..."

She carried on. "I know now that Cece put us in touch with Lucinda's publisher. She's quite reclusive, and I'm sure we couldn't have persuaded her without your help."

"Well, it's my sister who deserves the thanks, if anyone does."

"I know, but I figured if you hadn't encouraged Cece, it might not have happened. As a library trustee..." She trailed off, wondering what to say next. "By the way, I also wanted to thank you properly for rescuing me in the woods." She'd already thanked him, but it never hurt to do so again. What else? Oh, right. "And to tell you it's been fun running with you sometimes."

She hoped she hadn't overdone it. Whatever else she said, she absolutely must not mention that she missed seeing him and Newton walking down the road in the mornings. "And I've missed seeing you and Newton walking past my house in the mornings."

For heaven's sake. Had she no self-control? Hearing his name, Newton stood, shook himself, and wandered over to her. He laid his head on her knee, and she stroked it, feeling the soft fur beneath her fingers. He was a very relaxing dog. So far, there'd been no response from Andrew to her last remark. She avoided looking at him.

"Uh-huh."

He wasn't being exactly encouraging, so she still had no idea where they stood on a personal level. At least she'd tried to tell him she liked him. "Well. I mustn't take up any more of your time. I can see you're busy."

Relief flooded his face. "I am. School starts next week, so I'm on a deadline. I have classes to prepare."

She looked at the papers he'd laid on a side table. From where she sat, they looked more like an essay than anything to do with math. But what did she know? "Of course. Well, good luck. I hope you get a good bunch of students this year."

A good bunch of students? When would she learn to have a regular conversation with him? "Will we see you at the board meeting next week?"

"If I can make it, I will."

So, that would have to do. She gave Newton one more scratch behind the ears before standing and walking to the front door. Andrew didn't move. He sat there, looking a little stunned, she thought. She had no idea why that might be. Maybe he had something else on his mind.

A rumble of far-away thunder reminded her to check the weather forecast.

CHAPTER 33
FIONA

The meteorologists—the weather divas, as Fiona called them—were telling people to expect a major storm overnight. Always cynical about the exaggerations of TV weathermen, she decided it wouldn't be as bad as the predictions. It never was.

She'd always been fascinated—rather than frightened—by storms. Looking out the window, she could see twigs and small branches being blown around the drive—surely that would be the worst of it. At least so far, apart from the occasional lightning flash, this tempest was turning out to be more of a lamb than a lion.

Overcome by a sudden need for sleep, she took a last look around the kitchen. It would do. She turned and headed upstairs to prepare for bed.

The warm and fuzzy feeling when she slipped into pajamas and a cozy robe only lasted until the power went out as she was brushing her teeth. Outside, she could barely discern the outline of the lightless streetlamp. The wind had picked up from brisk to what might even be gale force.

Several old trees stood by the library, and she'd not considered the potential danger they posed before. The beech by her front door looked sturdy, but the maple behind the library itself was probably a century old, and who knew how it would fare in this weather.

Clutching her robe around her and using her phone as a flashlight, she felt her way downstairs, thankful the house was small enough that by now she was familiar with every tread of the stairs.

She reached the bottom as the lights flickered on again and went to retrieve the headlamp her mother had sent her in case of emergencies. Fiona had pooh-poohed the idea at first, but her mother remained adamant.

"You wait until you have a power failure—you'll be glad of it. They happen all the time in the country."

"Brentford's not the end of the world, you know. Not even rural Connecticut," Fiona had said, but she'd taken the gift and hung it up in the hall closet next to her car keys. She'd been in Brentford for several months and had never needed to use it, but tonight she took it out and hung it around her neck—just as the electricity went off again.

After she'd switched on the lamp, she pushed it up to her forehead so its surprisingly strong beam shone on the space in front of her. For once, she was glad her mother had been right.

The lights blinked back on. No point in waiting for the power to stabilize. She might as well try to sleep—there was nothing she could do tonight. With the noise of the storm, she didn't expect to fall asleep with so little trouble. It might have been the rain pelting the roof above her head that soothed her until she drifted off—she liked that about her attic bedroom.

Something—a sudden draft, perhaps—woke her. Fiona lay rigid for a minute, her eyes adjusting to the gloom. She raised herself on one elbow, just before a bolt of lightning outside illuminated an indistinct shape at the foot of the bed, revealing an unfamiliar shape she couldn't make out.

It must be a shadow—maybe the curtains had moved.

Except, there was no reason for them to. The window was shut, the air in the room still. As Fiona sat up and pulled her bedclothes around her, she stared at the silent figure—if that's what it was.

Was it an intruder? It couldn't be. She was certain she'd locked all the doors and windows as she always did. And the outline wasn't clear. Why didn't it speak?

Fiona strained to focus her eyes, hoping an explanation would present itself. Now she couldn't even take a breath—she felt a prickle of sweat under her arms and all over her scalp. This was a man in what looked like a top hat—she was almost certain. A top hat? A man who had no need of doors and windows to get into the house, because he was already inside? She shook her head as if to dislodge the idea. But she had to know.

"George?" she said, her voice coming out in a hoarse whisper. "Is that you?"

The silence mocked her fear. She must pull herself together. Turn on the light. That would prove the room was empty. Yet her arm refused to reach for the bedside lamp or her phone. She couldn't recall what she'd done with the headlamp. In any case—her hands were gripping the coverlet so hard she didn't think she could loosen them.

The figure remained mute, only staring in the direction of its arm, which pointed toward the bedroom window. The outline was becoming less distinct now. Minute by minute, it was melting away.

As her eyes became accustomed to the gloom, she managed to make out the bedside lamp and flipped it on. The bedroom was devoid of any other person—or spirit.

Another shiver ran through her. She hadn't imagined it, surely. If the shadow was a manifestation of George, why had he appeared now? Why hadn't he answered her?

Perhaps the apparition had something to do with the storm. At that moment, a lightning strike outside seemed to run through her too, with what felt like an electric charge, and she leaped out of bed, poised to deal with whatever emergency this might be. A second later, the headlamp was around her head again, and she grabbed her robe and phone. Stiffening her resolve, she walked out to the landing, where she stopped and listened.

"Is there anyone there?"

Nothing.

"George?" She heard only silence, until a roll of thunder heralded a lightning strike so huge that an unmistakable creak came from the front of the house.

She tiptoed down the stairs and cracked open the front door to check the porch. The far end of its roof was listing, giving her the impression the world had shifted on its axis. The bent post that should have been supporting it showed a long split that didn't bode well for its future.

At that moment, a sudden gust of wind almost blew her inside. Safely in the house again, she stood, her back to the door, out of breath—as though she'd run a mile. Her heart was racing.

"Slow down, Fi—it's all right. Everything's going to be okay." It was all she could think of saying to comfort herself.

CHAPTER 34
GEORGE

Finally. At last, I have succeeded in materializing in Fiona's presence, after weeks of practicing whenever she was out. The concentration required to make this happen is immense, and not easy to sustain, as I soon discovered. The storm was becoming stronger and I was certain more dangerous by the minute, so I felt obliged to try and rouse her, and I could only do that by leaving my portrait.

The first time I manifested as a wraith, Fiona was out, working in the library, so I took the opportunity to inspect this cottage. It didn't take many minutes, being about one-third of the size of my townhouse in Philadelphia. Just as well, since I was not able to maintain my form for long. Still, it was a start.

This time, I managed to convey a stronger impression, though not as well-defined as I'd hoped. So, I do not count my appearance a complete success in terms of presentation and vocal contact. To be blunt, although I tried to speak to her, I don't believe she heard me—at least, she registered nothing except alarm. This was disappointing, because when she cannot see me, she can definitely hear me. Perhaps to be seen *and* heard requires more effort than I currently possess. I must keep practicing.

Still, I am convinced that somehow she sensed my presence, because she woke and left her bed before, as luck would have it, an enormous branch fell on her porch, breaking one of the supports. It might have landed on the roof above her, after all.

I should note in passing that I would not have needed to do this had she not chosen to have her bedroom on the upper floor. But my recent cursory inspection of the house indicates that there's nowhere else for Fiona's repose but upstairs, though she really ought not to sleep under the eaves.

I imagine this dwelling was constructed for the servants who worked at the big house, which I'm told is now the library. I suppose this makes sense, because Fiona is in their employ, so she is one of the hired help.

Now I have returned downstairs, the noise outside is deafening, the lightning making electric light unnecessary when it strikes from the sky. As the thunder pounds overhead, I sense something even worse coming. I hear a terrifying crack beyond the window. It seems farther away from this vicinity, but I still worry about Fiona. I hear her opening the front door. I wish she would come back inside. Ah, finally, here she is.

At first sight, her forehead seems to be spreading a white fire in front of her. As she moves her head, I see the rays move with her, illuminating the space before her. As she turns to face the window, I notice a strap of some sort that is holding this light source onto her head—a relief, since I'd thought it might be something supernatural. I dislike unexplained phenomena.

Returning her gaze to me, she speaks, with no preamble. "George, did you wake me a few minutes ago? Was it you I saw, or did I imagine you were in my bedroom?"

I'm no longer visible to her, I can tell. She is looking at my portrait, where I find myself stuck again.

"It was I. I've been practicing," I tell her modestly. "Manifesting in the house."

I'd call her expression skeptical. "Really? So, why didn't you say something? Seeing whatever that was frightened me half to death."

"I tried, believe me. I practically shouted myself hoarse. But for some reason, my voice didn't reach you."

"I suppose it doesn't matter. I don't know what made me wake up, but it's lucky I did. I believe this storm is going to prove even more dangerous than I imagined."

"Luck had nothing to do with it." I aim for a crisp tone. "I willed you to open your eyes, so as to warn you." Well, I stood there and tried to communicate with her. I pointed outside, after all, but she couldn't hear me.

She considers this before she speaks. "You don't mean you can influence me without my knowledge?"

I am not sure how to respond. *Something* caused her to return to consciousness, and if not I, by what means did that happen? After some deliberation, I tell her, "All I can say is, I entered your boudoir intending to alert you to possible danger, and that is what transpired." After all, I practically saved her life. I would have if that branch had landed just a foot or so closer.

"I suppose I should be grateful to you."

Talk about damning a person with faint praise. Is this the best she can come up with? Being a gentleman, I maintain my manners and say, "You might try sounding a little less reluctant. If you would prefer I not help you in the future, you have only to say so."

I will ignore any such request, of course. If her life is threatened, I must intervene if I can. I cannot lose her, or I will never find Rose.

A second lightning flash of powerful proportions hits the ground somewhere close by. Fiona runs to the side window—the one facing the library—and stares out into the inky night. The rolls of thunder are followed by another sound—as of hell's door grinding open—accompanied by a crash that makes the frame of my painting rattle against the wall. A most unnerving occurrence I can only hear, not feel.

Perhaps her eyes are becoming accustomed to the dark outside. She seems agitated.

"What is it? Can you see something?"

"Oh my God." She claps a hand over her mouth.

Another lightning bolt illuminates the grounds for an instant.

"It's the maple—it's leaning toward the building."

The maple, the building, mean nothing to me—I cannot see them. Another almighty reverberation causes Fiona to start—I can see her, despite the gloom.

Her voice is barely a whisper. "It's gone, George. Vanished. I think it's fallen behind the building. Where the conservatory is."

The thunder is faint by comparison. And then all is black and silent once more.

CHAPTER 35
FIONA

Thank God the ancient maple hadn't fallen on her house. If Fiona had been asleep in her bedroom and it had landed on the roof—it didn't bear thinking about. And thank God the library was closed today. She couldn't imagine how bad this might have been if it had happened when the place was open. With a shudder, she contemplated what to do next.

"Are you all right?" George said.

"I think so." As she spoke, Fiona's hands began to tremble, and she wrapped her arms around herself.

"Looks like you're in shock, my dear. You could use a brandy right now. For medicinal purposes."

An old-fashioned remedy, but the idea had some appeal. There might have been a miniature among the collection of small bottles in the kitchen cabinet where she kept the gin. Brian used to bring them back from business trips. She found a tiny bottle of cognac and swallowed it in two gulps, placing the empty container on the side table as she sank onto the sofa.

"Do you think I should go outside to check on the damage?" She pondered the question—her brain seemed to be working slower than usual. No. She wouldn't go out. No matter how serious the devastation, she could do nothing about it right now.

"I wouldn't. It might still be dangerous," George said.

Another shiver engulfed her. She rose and half-heartedly took the poker to stir the ashes in the fireplace, surprised and relieved at the sight of a few stray scarlet sparks flying up the chimney. If she relit the fire and brought down a pillow and her duvet, she'd be able to sleep down here. The idea cheered her. A distant memory from her childhood, of being soothed by her mother after a bad dream, helped her decide— she would make a cup of hot chocolate. She must have some cocoa somewhere.

The cocoa tin informed her that the product had expired two years ago, but she knew better. Cocoa's sell-by date was a myth. She heated some milk and returned to the living room with a steaming mug. The simple kitchen tasks had calmed her somewhat.

Crouching down, she pulled out some old newspaper, some pieces of fatwood, and a few logs. Something drew her gaze to George's portrait, and in an instant, her mind flashed back to the misty figure that had woken her right before the storm started wreaking its havoc over the house.

"I think I'll be safe down here, don't you?" she inquired of George's portrait.

He said nothing.

Ensconced on the sofa, she pulled the duvet over her and snuggled in. A warm sensation began to steal through her— out of all proportion to the heat from the fire.

"Night, George." Fiona's shoulders relaxed.

*

She awoke not because of any noise, but because some ancient bit of her brain became aware of the unnatural silence around her. The fire had died out. She glanced at her phone. Five-thirty. And no sign of George except in his picture.

She slithered off the sofa, clutching the duvet around her, and went to look out the window. In the dim light of the pre-dawn hours, the world remained as still as if it had been covered with a layer of snow, except it was branches, leaves, and twigs that lay strewn around. She couldn't make out much of the fallen tree—only the skeletal outline that rose from behind the roof.

There was no way to know, from this vantage point, how badly the library had been ravaged. Perhaps, she prayed, the tree had missed the building and was lying on the lawn. That would be messy enough. But if it had landed on the roof, the destruction might be considerable.

Standing at her window, she checked for any kind of light flickering in town. Nothing. The power must still be out.

She switched on the headlamp and made a quick check of the house to make sure nothing was leaking upstairs. Everything appeared secure, and she heaved a sigh of relief.

Outdoors, the rain had become a steady drizzle. The wind had died away. A river of water was running down the driveway to the road, carrying a load of gravel with it. Lightning continued to illuminate the scene from time to time. It would be rank stupidity to leave the house in weather like this. She would have to wait until the storm passed. The app on her phone estimated it would end by eight. Another couple of hours.

She tried to settle on the sofa again but found sleep difficult. What would this mean for the library? Her job? The jobs of all the staff, come to that?

Restless, she dozed off and woke at eight-thirty to brilliant sunshine and a clear blue sky. She rolled off the couch and walked into the kitchen, stretched her arms to loosen the tight muscles in her back and shoulders, and flipped on the light. It worked, and she became aware of the ambient sounds that she took for granted as a rule. The hum of the fridge, the crackle of ice cubes falling into the dispenser, the click of the heating as it came on. She shivered, conscious of the chill around her.

She dressed in jeans and a sweatshirt, grabbed a jacket and her tablet to use as a camera, and strode up the driveway. Behind the house, she paused to assess the fallen tree. The size of the thing. Standing, it had been imposing, but seeing it at her level, it was immense. Its roots were perpendicular to the earth now, a tangled mess that should have held the maple in place.

Her first thought was that while the tree had hit the side of the library, it had come to rest on the conservatory. It was a popular setting for wedding photographs, and even as a venue for informal marriage ceremonies. Where the guests would have sat lay the remains of the brilliant scarlet tree, and beneath it, the glass roof had been turned into shards. Broken terracotta tiles were strewn like fallen leaves around it.

Craning her neck to check out the building more clearly, she stepped back as another small avalanche of tiles began its descent in front of her.

"Glad to see you're okay."

She whirled around to find Andrew standing there. The bruising around his eyes now had a faint yellow tinge, but his expression was one of concern rather than that of a man still annoyed with her.

For no apparent reason, a feeling of relief flooded through Fiona, and the tension she'd been carrying drained away, leaving her eyes filled, inexplicably, with tears. "I'm fine," she lied. In truth, she thought she might be in shock. A sudden shiver at the realization of how close she'd come to injury traveled through her, and her legs felt as though they might buckle at any second.

Andrew flung his arm around her shoulders. "Come on, let's get you back to the house."

A sense of relief and reassurance, immediately followed by anxiety, coursed through her. She didn't want to depend on any man for support, but she had to admit, this felt good. It was a friendly gesture, a neighborly response to a natural disaster.

She'd recovered a little by now but allowed herself to be led back home. They maneuvered the porch steps with caution, though the roof appeared to have settled in its damaged state. He sat Fiona down in the kitchen.

Sitting by the window where she'd so often watched him walking by, she stared at the road, seeing it illuminated bit by bit by the rising sun.

"Got any brandy anywhere?" he said.

She managed a smile. Andrew was suggesting the same old-school remedy as George.

"I drank the last of it in the wee hours." Seeing his surprise, she added, "A friend recommended it, and I only had a miniature. But some caffeine would be great."

"A friend?" His gaze slid away from her.

"Yes. She always recommends it as a remedy for shock." Deliberately misleading, but she wasn't prepared to explain further. "I can make some coffee."

"Let me," said Andrew. "Where do you keep it?"

She pointed at a jar full of pods. "The machine's next to it." Stupid thing to say. He couldn't miss the machine. Her brain wasn't firing on all cylinders yet. She strove to maintain an everyday conversation. "Where's Newton?"

"I left him at home."

"Don't you need to take him for his walk? You usually do around now." Did that sound like she was keeping him under surveillance?

"No." He raised an eyebrow but seemed disinclined to say anything more.

"But..."

"I thought I'd better come and check...um...the library was okay."

"That was kind of you. And what about your house? Everything in one piece?"

"More or less. Just twigs and leaves to clear up."

A knock on the front door made them both jump.

"I'll get it," said Andrew.

"Let me do it. Don't want any gossip, do we?" Had she just made a joke? Because she wanted to laugh. Surely nobody would ever think that she—the well-behaved director of the Wentworth—had been entertaining a member of the opposite sex all night.

She opened the door. On the porch stood Channing Madison.

"Just came to determine how you were doing. This looks unsafe."

"That was kind of you."

He pointed at the broken support at one end. "I imagine the whole thing will have to come down."

Before she had a chance to answer, he sniffed and said, "You have power, I take it?"

How could he tell?

Seeing her unspoken query, he said, with a deliberate air, "I can smell coffee."

She was afraid that was a heavy-handed hint, just when she'd been hoping he'd leave before he and Andrew came face to face. Channing was the type to jump to conclusions. Oh, well. Too bad. "Would you like a cup?"

"Maybe in a while. I should check outside and evaluate how bad things are around the main building."

Her relief at this response didn't last long, as Andrew wandered into the hall. "Is that you, Channing?" His face gave nothing away.

Channing, caught unawares by this sudden appearance, took a step back. "Andrew? Been in a fight?" He chuckled, evidently thinking there was no chance of that.

Fiona had no idea how Andrew would explain.

"Cece and I had a minor disagreement." He said this with a disarming smile.

Channing's confusion was clear. "So, what are you doing here?"

"I was passing and saw the downed tree and the branch on Fiona's porch roof, so I came to see if I could help."

Somewhat deflated, Channing's ruffled feathers smoothed themselves down. "And what's the verdict?"

Andrew said nothing. He looked in Fiona's direction as if to let her know this was her job, not Channing's, and she was able to handle it.

And she could. One by one, her mental faculties had returned with each sip of coffee. "The conservatory roof has gone, I'm afraid, and parts of the main roof will need substantial repairs, but the rest of the structure appears sound enough. On the other hand, I haven't looked inside. There might well be rain coming through."

"I don't want anyone going inside until an expert takes a look. But it's clear this isn't good."

To put it mildly. She'd expected something more dramatic from Channing. Maybe in the face of a true disaster, he was restraining himself.

Andrew spoke up. "No, it's not. So, I expect we'll require an occupancy certificate before we can reopen the library. And possibly this cottage too."

"If we can reopen," said Channing.

And there it was. The Eeyore factor. The three of them stared at each other. Would this blow finally end the library's existence, and her job and home with it? She couldn't visualize a life beyond Brentford now.

In the distance, somewhere along the road, the buzz of a saw made itself heard as the cleanup began.

CHAPTER 36
GEORGE

Fiona has been looking discouraged in the weeks since that biblical storm, and, furthermore, has been making no effort to help me find my wife. She barely has time to speak to me, and I need to attract her attention somehow. I have continued to practice manifesting when she is out and believe I have made progress. It seems easier to appear when there is no one else around. It's hard to be sure, of course, because when I stand in front of a looking glass to inspect myself, there's nothing to see. It is disconcerting, but it makes a kind of sense. We are not supposed to exist on Earth anymore.

However, when I look down at my feet, I note that, although I still have a somewhat hazy appearance, my outline is becoming clearer. I appear to be dressed in the clothes I am wearing in my portrait—not surprising, I suppose. Better than the clothes I died in. Having to wear a hunting jacket and riding hat through eternity would be a constant reminder of my foolishness. At least this way, I am respectable in a morning coat and top hat. Although my nether regions are not clearly defined in the painting, I see that when I materialize, I am sporting the appropriate garments and shoes.

I have been practicing making myself heard when I manifest. I failed when I warned Fiona of the storm, and I will not know how much progress I've made until I test my materialization on her, but I am optimistic.

I have decided to sit in one of her armchairs to wait for her. At least that way, I will see her coming, and if I'm right, she will spot me too. This should be fun—seeing her reaction, I mean.

*

All this waiting is boring. I have no real sense of time, so I have delayed my appearance until the evening, so as not to waste my psychic energy. I believe it is fall outside, so she should return when the sun goes down, or shortly thereafter. Yet she is taking her time.

I hear her key in the front door lock. Excellent. There is the hall light. A flick of a switch causes a lamp to illuminate the hall all the way down to the living room door. A truly useful invention. And here come her footsteps. I shall arrange myself in this chair and affect a nonchalant air, as if my being here were perfectly normal. I cross my legs, lean back, and pray she will notice me. I do not want to waste my strength by speaking before I need to.

Here she comes.

What follows doesn't go quite as I envisage it. Fiona seems to stagger slightly when she enters the room—even before she switches on a lamp. Staring in my direction, wide-eyed, she clutches at the back of the sofa for support and flings her attaché case onto it—with unnecessary force, in my opinion.

One thing is clear. She can see me—I am sure of it. I am not surprised at her response. I am an impressive person in real life. Taller than most men at five feet nine inches and well built, due to my athletic pursuits. I am told I am well-favored. Some have even judged me handsome, though modesty prevents me from pointing this out. And I always dress impeccably.

With one hand on the sofa, she comes around it and collapses in a heap, still gaping at me.

"Fiona?" I venture to reassure her. "It is only I."

Now I know she can hear me, because she raises her head and stares. "I...I...never expected to actually see you," she whispers. "Not like this."

I smile at her. My smile used to be irresistible. "Well, here I am," I reply.

The effect of my smile is only to cause some consternation. I suppose Fiona has only ever seen my face as motionless, and of course, the portrait painters always insist that one remain immobile. They never paint a real smile, in my opinion. I have clearly dazzled her. I shall give her a few moments to recover.

"I hope you don't mind that I've come," I say. It's only good manners to apologize for an unscheduled visit.

"I'm still stunned. I'm finding it hard to...to believe you're here. In person." A question occurs to her. "Have you always been able to do this? Can you go anywhere you want? Are you going to follow me around?" She leans back, shakes her head, and, looking away from me, says, "I'm imagining all this. I must be." She closes her eyes.

"I assure you, I am here. And I think I deserve some credit for having worked so hard to appear."

She raises a skeptical eyebrow. If she weren't so essential to my quest, I would leave right now, but I persevere.

"I'm not sure I can answer your questions exactly, but I will try. I have not always been able to manifest this way. As you know, I have practiced, and have come a long way since I appeared in your bedroom only days ago."

"Almost three weeks, actually," she interrupts.

"Whatever you say." This woman irritates me to no end. Why can't she just listen? I decide to carry on. "I find I can move around this house, but I have no idea whether I can move beyond it."

"Okay. What about—"

Another interruption. I grit my teeth and continue. "Am I going to follow you around, dogging your footsteps? I would not be so improper. I gave up following beautiful women when I was fourteen, since I had no trouble finding females to talk to without resorting to stalking them like some exotic prey."

"I'm sorry, George. I didn't mean to offend you. Or hurt your feelings. Please forgive me."

I consider this. While my feathers have been ruffled, I am not immune to the charms of a genuine apology. "Very well," I say magnanimously. "Now perhaps we can converse like civilized people."

"Of course. Yes. I hope you won't object if I keep staring at you. You're fascinating."

At last, she recognizes my charm. And about time too.

I open the conversation by asking about her day. After all, she has seen the results of *mine*.

Fiona frowns, then sighs and opens the attaché case. She pulls out a sheaf of papers. "It's going to cost a fortune, and take a long time to repair everything."

"Please elaborate." I hope I do not come to regret this request.

"You know that the library has been closed to patrons for the last two weeks, and I've been in touch with the insurance company so they can assess the damage and figure out what we'll need to make things whole again."

"I don't see the problem."

"The point is, that we're planning all kinds of celebrations for the library centenary, and we won't be able to carry them out unless we can make the building structurally sound." Now I detect irritation in her voice.

"Has anyone mentioned a timetable?"

"Well, the events begin in January, and it's September now, which isn't long. And we'll have to reschedule all kinds of events, including weddings in the conservatory, or we'll lose that income."

"Is there any way to speed up the repairs?"

"We won't know until we hear from the contractors. And there are other things I need to deal with, like funding the centenary celebrations. It's all too much."

I must keep her focused on the practical. "How much money are you talking about?"

"A hundred thousand dollars would help in the short term. But the endowment could use half a million. That's the goal, anyway."

That's a conversation-stopper, for sure. "The only people with that kind of money are the railway barons, and even they wouldn't be able to raise it easily."

Fiona laughs. She actually laughs. I suppose I should rejoice that I've made her do so, however inadvertently.

"We don't have railway barons anymore. Super-rich people make their money from technology these days." She takes a breath as if planning to explain. The explanation promises to be long-drawn-out and tedious, so I carry on.

"In that case, what options do you have?"

"That's the problem. Remember the firm that took care of the fallen tree a couple of weeks ago? Just cutting it up took three days, as you know, and getting rid of the branches and leaves another three."

"You need not remind me. Had I been alive, the constant chewing of the machine that shredded and pulped the tree into tiny pieces would have made me want to quit this Earth again. I saw it through the window. I quite envy the men who drive such machinery. They are Titans!"

"We're getting side-tracked."

"As trains may do when shunted off the main track."

"What? Oh, yes. Anyway. The emergency board meeting to discuss all this is tomorrow, and I need some ideas before then."

I confess I know of no easy answer. "It appears you have no friendly philanthropist willing to donate money to speed things along."

She shakes her head.

"Do you have no Charles Dickens? No Victor Hugo? No Harriet Beecher Stowe? Surely, they could be persuaded to help. Their living must depend on libraries."

"You forget, George. Those authors were some of the richest in the world when they were alive, but that was over a century ago."

"Well, surely, there must be other authors as successful as they were. You've given me the impression that almost everyone is literate these days, and there are more libraries than ever. So, it follows that there must be more readers, more authors, and more popular books. If they won't give money, perhaps they'll give their books."

"Well, yes. But I don't know any of them personally."

"Don't be such a wet blanket. Find someone who knows someone. That's how we always got things done. Via the old boys' network."

"It may have escaped your attention, but I am not an old boy."

"Nonsense, Fiona. I'm willing to bet that you know people who know people."

Her face lights up. "I might, at that," she says. "Thanks, George."

CHAPTER 37
FIONA

The day of the board meeting was one of those perfect fall days that poets revel in. After a night of heavy wind, every cloud in the sky had moved on somewhere else, and nothing impeded the sun as it cast its rays onto the trees and through Fiona's bedroom window.

She rose early—she needed a run this morning because today would decide whether the board would place their trust in her to bring the town's beloved institution back to its former glory. She stuck to the roads because the woods were still littered with leaves and branches.

By the time she reached her office after a shower and two cups of coffee, some of her anxiety had abated, and she felt ready to tackle the issues. After an inspection by the claims adjuster, it appeared most of the building had escaped relatively unscathed, and those parts were open to the public again, so they were able to meet in the Lavender Room.

Jane brought in coffee for the eight people present and laid it out on the old sideboard, with china cups and saucers, a matching cream jug, sugar, and spoons. "We mustn't let standards drop because of an old tree," she remarked to Fiona as she left the room to check on the rare books collection. As she did so, Molly, who'd been appointed an advisor to the board on public events, arrived with a plate piled high with cookies wafting the gentle aroma of ginger.

"Molly's famous for her baking," said Acacia in Fiona's ear. "Take a couple. One is never enough."

Still somewhat nervous about the forthcoming meeting, Fiona hadn't eaten anything for breakfast, so she did as she was told. Taking a small bite of the crisp cookie, she tasted the chewy pieces of crystallized ginger inside. Heaven.

Then, it was down to business. Channing, in charge as always, rapped on the table with a pen.

"It's time to call the meeting to order."

Fiona looked at the assembled crowd, who were exchanging greetings. The familiar faces included Molly and Joanie, who acted as secretary and took the minutes. Channing was there, of course, and as chair would chuck his weight about and make everyone toe his line. Acacia was a steadying force when her son got out of hand.

Andrew sat quietly at the other end of the table, his eyes now in better shape. Only someone who knew what had happened might notice the fading shadows, and Channing didn't mention it. Andrew glanced at him, and she thought his jaw tightened, but no reciprocal look was forthcoming, and he dropped his gaze to his notepad and began twiddling a pen around his fingers.

Fiona had always wanted to learn how to do that. She'd tried several times, but the pen tended to land on the floor. She had a talent for shuffling cards, though. Long nights of playing solitaire as a child had seen to it that she could do a riffle shuffle blindfolded.

Channing's imperious presence interrupted her thoughts. "Order," he barked.

She snapped her attention back to the matter at hand. She'd prepared an agenda that would cover the most important topics, to facilitate their working together to find a path going forward. The centenary celebrations and the increase in donations were at stake.

Channing fixed his gaze on her. "Fiona? Could you give us a rundown of where we are in terms of our current difficulties? So far, this is turning out to be one of the worst years in the Wentworth's history, if you count the mess left by our former director and this act of nature."

Knowing none of these were problems she'd caused, Fiona felt her hackles rise. The crooked previous director had nothing to do with her. In fact, Channing should be taking the blame, but she would have to let it go. Let him contemplate the mess he'd made by ignoring the signs of embezzlement. Meanwhile, she'd show him how an honest director handled things.

She took a deep breath and began. "Thank you for pointing that out, Mr. Chairman. However, it's not *that* disasters occur, it's how they're dealt with that counts."

"As you see from the agendas I've just handed out, we have a number of pressing issues. First, the good news. We've been able to reopen most of the building after the storm, except for the ballroom and conservatory."

"So far as the current damage goes, what about the insurance? What does that cover?" Acacia said, looking at her son.

"Our insurance should pay for most of the reconstruction," said Fiona. "So, it will cover the cost of repairing the gatehouse porch and the main building, as well as the conservatory."

"At least that's something," said Channing, his words countering any concession he might be making.

"Yes indeed. We must be grateful for that." Acacia sounded like a nanny reprimanding her charge.

"That doesn't mean, though, that we're out of the woods," continued Fiona. "Since the ballroom hosts large gatherings, and the conservatory is used for weddings, we're certain to lose some profitable reservations before it's rebuilt. We have several bookings, including Tom Beresford, Molly's father, and his lovely fiancée, Bonnie Angelini. So we may have to sacrifice that income, which the library budget depends on, if the couples don't want to be rescheduled and decide to go elsewhere."

Molly spoke up. "I'm sure my father will understand the delay. On the other hand, at his time of life, I imagine he'd like to tie the knot sooner rather than later."

"Naturally. But if there's any way they could give us some time, that would be wonderful."

"I'll ask him next time I see him, and who knows, he might find living in sin with Bonnie in the meantime to be somewhat risqué, but fun." Molly grinned as she looked around the room.

Fiona, grateful for this support, smiled back.

"Is there any other urgent business?" Channing seemed keen to end the meeting.

"There is one thing, and it's important to our patrons. We mustn't forget that the maple and the rain that accompanied it soaked the romance collection—housed above the ballroom. The amount the insurance will pay on those isn't nearly enough to replace them with new books. We'll need to find funds to do that."

Channing stretched out a chubby hand and grabbed another cookie. His irritable voice interrupted Fiona before she could continue. "Can we stick to the point?"

"Of course." She would not be intimidated by the likes of Channing. Her eyes bored into him, though he made a point of ignoring her.

"It's hardly important to restock that kind of novel," he

said. "We can do that over time. After all, it's not as though the rare books department suffered."

Acacia, Molly, and Joanie spoke at once. Fiona, scanning the room, recognized her fellow romance lovers. They would expect some satisfying escapist reads and would not be happy if their needs were ignored.

"This is probably our most popular section, Channing." An image of Elaine checking out the latest hot romance flashed through Fiona's mind. "So, it's essential we replace those books as soon as possible. Inter-library loans might tide us over for a while, but not permanently, and we don't want patrons going elsewhere for their books. Sorry, Molly. I didn't mean you—I meant to other libraries."

"No offense taken," said Molly.

"A friend suggested we try to get some of the authors to donate their books to us." Fiona saw no need to mention this was George's idea.

Andrew raised his eyes from his notepad. "Fiona's friend has come up with a creative solution, if you ask me," he said, glancing at her. She was grateful for his support. "I'm sure you'll find the authors are only too happy to help."

Channing snorted. "And what would you know about it?"

"There's no need to be quite so...blunt," Acacia said, frowning. "Andrew's entitled to his opinion."

Channing ignored her. "You're a fan, Andrew?" He chuckled at his witticism.

Another man might have been rattled by this aggressive form of questioning, but Andrew was hard to read. For all intents and purposes, though, he remained unfazed and replied without answering the question. "My sister's in publishing, if you remember, and she knows several authors. It can't hurt to get in touch."

"That's right. Cece is great—she helped us book Lucinda Parks as our star attraction in January. That's another reason why we need to have an extensive selection of romance novels. Although, her visit might be in jeopardy if the ballroom isn't ready." Fiona's gaze landed on each person as she spoke, reinforcing her point.

"And Ms. Parks is one of the most successful authors in the country. Internationally, too," said Molly. "I agree with Andrew—Lucinda might be willing to help us, in principle. She's always supported libraries, as well as independent bookstores. It would be incredible if she could help us again." She fell silent.

"I imagine the same company publishes other writers in that genre too, so we might be able to kill several birds with one stone," Acacia added.

"True," said Molly. "I'll check in with Cece and some of the publishers' sales reps and see what we can acquire that way."

Joanie, who had been silent until now, spoke up. "That sounds like an excellent start."

"Here's hoping," said Molly. "Cookie, anyone?"

Channing reached out again.

CHAPTER 38
GEORGE

I do believe Fiona is feeling more cheerful. She returned from yesterday's board meeting in a much better frame of mind. Today, being Saturday, should have been a day of rest for her, but it didn't last too long. No sooner had she settled herself with a cup of coffee and one of those French pastries they call a croissant than a knock at the door indicated someone had come to disturb her peace.

Mind you, trying to eat a croissant in the living room is a fool's game. Those flaky crumbs fall everywhere. But since she was holding a book, I imagine she was planning to read.

The visitor turned out to be the red-haired sprite who believes, without evidence, in my existence. It is unlikely that she, too, has Fiona's gift of communicating with spirits. On her previous visit, she claimed she could hear faint sounds—as if someone were speaking far away. It may be that all speech sounds like that to her. At her venerable age, she is probably becoming deaf.

In this town, Fiona tells me, people knock at a front door and feel comfortable walking straight into other people's homes—a provincial custom better suited to country folk, who have no locks. However, as I have mentioned, modern mores are inexplicable.

"Hello, dear," says the pixie as Fiona struggles to rise and simultaneously stop her breakfast from sliding off its plate.

Caught off guard, as I can tell from her reaction, Fiona brushes crumbs off her chest and attempts to be polite. "Good morning, Miss Johanssen—Elaine. What brings you here?"

In Fiona's shoes, I should be wishing the woman at the devil, but, though small, this Elaine person has a determined manner and a chin to match.

"I'm sorry to interrupt your...breakfast, is it? I thought at this hour you'd be preparing lunch, if anything."

I see by the clock on the adjacent wall that it is not yet eleven. Surely, Fiona is allowed to partake of a late breakfast from time to time. I say as much. A mistake.

"Oh, there he is!" The elf gives a little squeal of delight. "I can hear him. I can definitely hear him now."

Fiona attempts to dissemble. "Sorry? Hear whom? I can't hear anyone."

Elaine gives her an arch glance. "I'm sure you can, dear. If I can, surely you must be able to."

Fiona's blush gives her away every time. In some respects, it is a charming trait, but not at all useful in a situation like this one. She tries again to deflect this person. "Would you like some coffee? It's freshly made. Or I could make you a cappuccino."

"No thanks, Fiona. There's only so much excitement I can manage in one day." She smiles—rather a sweet smile, as it happens.

"How can I help you?"

"What's his name? I'd like to see whether he can hear me too."

We are in treacherous waters now. Will Fiona decide to

share me? Should I remain silent? Why does this miniature witch want to interrogate me?

"Are you talking about the man in the portrait? He's—he was—called George Manchester. I found this picture at an antiques fair."

More or less correct, I suppose.

"Hello, George."

Such impertinence. We haven't even been introduced, and she is addressing me by my first name. I shall not deign to reply.

"My name is Elaine."

I know this already, from eavesdropping on their conversation. Fiona appears overcome, her lips parted as if about to speak but uttering no word.

"George, I'm wondering whether you can tell me something about how you operate."

Operate? The woman does not have all her wits, clearly. I do not operate—I exist. I'm almost inclined to tell her.

"Elaine, what are you doing?"

"I'm talking to George. I have the same feeling in his presence as I do with the portraits in the library, but he doesn't make me feel dizzy. On the contrary—I feel fizzy, if anything, which is delightful."

Interesting. The fairy appreciates my charm much more swiftly than Fiona did.

Damn. I must have spoken aloud without meaning to. So, the secret is out.

"Oh, George—I knew you were real. Now I'm truly excited."

And why not? "Delighted to make your acquaintance, I'm sure."

I can almost discern a thrill going through her tiny frame. She turns to Fiona. "He can hear you too? You can converse?"

Fiona, in the meantime, has returned to the sofa and is sitting there, fingers massaging her temples, a defeated air about her. I have the distinct impression that she expects trouble to result from this encounter. She may be right. A lot will depend on whether this little woman is discreet.

I wonder how she will answer this question. I don't think distracting the elf will work now.

"We can. Occasionally."

This is untrue, of course. We talk almost every day, but I believe Fiona is trying to discourage further inquiry. Yet she goes on to relate our history.

"It started, I think, because I was living in the building that housed the warehouse belonging to George's family over a century ago. It began with notes he left me, and eventually his voice became audible."

I wonder whether she will admit that she can see me.

"When I moved here, I brought his portrait with me." She glances at me and smiles. "Much to his disgust. But I think he's become used to living here. This cottage is around his vintage, the 1870s."

The elf chips in. "Fascinating. I ask because I wonder whether he can converse with other spirits. I'm thinking of the ghosts that haunt the library."

Fiona has never mentioned that the library is haunted. I wonder, why not?

The old lady continues. "Whether or not George can speak to them, if *we* could talk to Mrs. Wentworth, the ancestry research would make faster progress, I'm sure. Besides, I'd like to know that I'm not imagining those hauntings."

Fiona takes no time to formulate a reply. "I'm inclined to believe that you're not making it up. You clearly have a gift. Perhaps you should do what I did—practice talking to her."

Elaine shakes her head. "Easier said than done. There are always people about when the library's open. And if they see me talking to a painting, they'll assume I'm off with the fairies."

I stifle a laugh. The woman *is* a fairy.

Fiona thinks for a moment. "Why don't you come to my office after the next Ancestry Club meeting? We'll work something out."

"Agreed. I suppose I'd better get going now. Delightful to meet you, George."

I decide discretion is the better part of valor and say nothing.

"Elaine," says Fiona. "Please don't mention this to anyone."

"My lips are sealed."

Yet with the excitement in her eyes making her look ten years younger, I have my doubts. As I said—she might be trouble. So many women are.

CHAPTER 39

FIONA

After Elaine left, Fiona went back to the living room and picked up her cold cup of coffee. "Back in a minute, George." She returned from the kitchen with a fresh cup to find him lounging in the bergère chair by the fire.

"So—what do you make of the sprite?" he said. "Do you think she'll keep mum about me?"

Fiona arranged herself on the sofa with her feet tucked under her and gave a contented sigh as the aroma of coffee reached her. "Gosh, I hope so. The last thing I need is her giving people the impression I'm delusional."

"It sounds odd to be saying this—because I'm real, of course—but if she told people about me, wouldn't they think she was imagining things?"

"When you put it that way, George, I guess you're right. In any case, it's going to be a long time before I introduce you to anyone else."

"I imagine it will be. Precious few have the gift of sensing my presence."

Fiona looked up at him. "True. And, after all, no one else

here knows about you, so I'd prefer to keep your presence a secret."

He leaned back and crossed one elegant leg over the other. "That would be my choice as well. Were too many people to be aware of my presence, I might cause a riot."

Fiona laughed and succeeded in not spilling her coffee, though it was touch-and-go for a moment. "You have such a high opinion of yourself." Catching his expression, she made amends. "Not that it's not warranted, of course. You seem to make quite an impression on those you meet."

"Well, I suppose I'm something of a novelty." He stared thoughtfully at the back of his hand.

"And let's not forget your good looks, your charm, and your fancy clothes when you visit me..."

At that moment, the sound of a step in the hall suggested Fiona hadn't closed the door properly after Elaine left. It had started sticking right after the porch was damaged. Damn. Perhaps Elaine had forgotten something.

"You have to go," she whispered to George. She could almost hear him huffing in annoyance at being abandoned for someone else.

"Hello?" she called, rising to find out who it was. "Oh, Andrew." He'd brought a blast of cold air in with him. "You're here," she said unnecessarily, and groped for something to say. "Where's Newton?"

Andrew, dressed in a blue windbreaker that brought out the color of his eyes, gave no indication he was pleased to see her. "Good morning. I left him tied up outside. Hope that's okay. We were passing, on a walk."

"He can come in if he wants to—he's no problem."

Andrew shook his head. "He'll be fine out there."

"Why don't you come in and relax? I can make you some coffee." Part of her hoped he'd decline the offer. If he said yes, she'd have to drink something else. One more cup this morning, and she'd be bouncing off the walls.

Their rapport had been percolating slowly, at a speed that appeared comfortable for both of them. This seemed like an opportunity to move it along.

"No, thanks. I didn't mean to interrupt—I can come back another time."

She detected something odd in his voice, as if he were having trouble getting words out. She found his face hard to read. Had he overheard her talking to George? If so, it must only have been her side of the conversation.

"No, you're not interrupting. Not at all." She ushered him into the living room. "I was only talking to a friend on the phone." She wondered how much he'd heard, and felt an annoying blush rising in her cheeks.

Andrew stood with his back to the fire and George's portrait and gave her a piercing look, his eyes crinkled in...what? Puzzlement? Dismay? Annoyance? "Okay," he said. "Well, it's none of my business who your friends are."

Had he put particular stress on the word "friends"? Did he think she'd been talking to another man? Like Brian, for instance? Well, she had, of course. Only not the way Andrew thought. She struggled to remember what she'd said. Something about keeping George a secret.

She didn't owe Andrew an explanation, and it would be better not to try, surely. After all, what could she say? He would never understand, although, perhaps in the interests of honesty, she should give it a shot.

"This may sound a little strange, but the fact is..." She hesitated. Could she call it a fact? Her experience was real, she supposed, but as she contemplated saying it aloud, it sounded nonsensical, even to her.

"You don't need to explain." She thought she detected a hint of regret in his voice.

"I want to—but it's complicated." This was probably making things worse.

Andrew looked away—embarrassed, maybe, or annoyed. "If you were talking to your ex-husband, that's entirely your affair."

She couldn't disguise her surprise. "What?"

"I thought you might still, you know, have..."

So, this was what he'd assumed? At least this was a myth she could dispel if it really bothered him.

"What? Feelings for him?" She sighed and sat down, suddenly drained of energy. "No, it's not Brian. The only effect he has on me now is to irritate me. He's such a child."

Andrew seemed unconvinced. "Oh? Anyway, no matter who you were talking to, it's nothing to do with me."

Did the fleeting shadow passing across his face reflect disappointment? Fiona hoped that, if so, it was something to do with her. That he might even be a little jealous. But his eyes were still blue, not green. She changed the subject. "So, what brought you here?"

Andrew allowed a couple of seconds to pass, as if recalibrating. "Ironically, I came to talk to you about replacing the romance novels."

Really? His seeing irony in the situation seemed to hint at disappointment. Had he had a budding romantic interest in her? If so, she'd just poured weedkiller all over it. On the other hand, it wasn't her fault he'd walked in on her conversation with George. And if he weren't so uptight, she might have explained, and they might have laughed about it.

As for the books, they'd discussed the issue at the board meeting yesterday, so there was no need to go over it again. Still, if he'd chosen to use that as his excuse, she'd behave appropriately—the way the executive director, not a potential girlfriend, should. "Oh, right. You said Cece might be willing to help us out."

"Exactly. I've talked to her, and she's agreed to check with the publishers, but she doesn't think there'll be a problem.

Especially since Lucinda Parks is coming here to sign books." He might as well have been giving a lecture on mathematical formulae for all the enthusiasm she detected in his voice.

"Such a relief—thank you so much." She forced a thin-lipped smile as he walked out. A man who took umbrage at an imagined relationship, especially with a friendly ghost, must be very insecure indeed.

"Why is it every man you know is a jackass?" George clearly found this hilarious.

"Not now, George. I've had enough of all men—you included."

CHAPTER 40
FIONA

George was demanding a report on Fiona's progress, or lack of it, with the research into his ancestry. While she sipped her evening glass of wine and nibbled at some almonds, he sat across from her, wearing a new outfit—a gray three-piece suit with a velvet collar. A gold watch chain hung across his chest, and she wondered whether there was a watch at the end of it and, if so, whether it worked. And if it did, why? In a realm where time must be...

George interrupted her musings. He wasn't happy.

"So, you're telling me that you've done nothing in the past month?"

"That's right, George. You know perfectly well that I've been busy clearing up the aftermath of the storm you were kind enough to warn me about."

"You're welcome. In return, the least you could do is persevere on your typing machine to find out more." His voice took on a sarcastic edge that could have cut granite. "The information about the Wentworth family is fascinating—but it doesn't help me at all."

"Look, George. You've waited a century and a half to reunite with Rose, and a few days more won't matter too much."

"Not to you, maybe. But to me, it's the difference between being with my love forever and losing all hope. Having to face eternity alone."

Despite her irritation at his self-pity, Fiona felt a pang of remorse. "I know, George, and I'm sorry. Still, the next Ancestry Club meeting is tomorrow, so I'll begin checking the records to see what I can find out. Do you happen to remember the census of 1860 or '70 being taken?"

"Not really. I lived at home in the fifties and sixties. So, I must be listed there. How would that help, though?"

"Well, you married Rose in 1865. If we can follow you through the census, she and your two daughters should appear in 1870, and with any luck in 1880, after you...um...left. For eternity." She glanced at him to see how he was taking this.

George sat ramrod-straight, not moving a muscle. "Very well. I suppose you might find my parents too. My father may have made some small provision for my wife, although he was not overfond of her."

Fiona couldn't disguise her surprise. "Why on earth not? By your account, she seems to have been a wonderful person."

George's face took on a dreamy expression. "She was. A pearl beyond price."

"So, why...?"

His frown almost qualified as a scowl. "He was set on having a grandson to carry on the family name and the firm. When we had our two daughters, he denigrated her—as if she was to blame. And my mother, who adored the girls, had not the courage to withstand him." He leaned his head against his fingertips, closed his eyes as if in genuine pain, and sighed.

"How very sad."

He lifted his head and met Fiona's gaze. "It was. And,

worse, I treated my dear wife so ill."

He was certainly baring his soul today. "What can you mean? I thought you loved her to distraction."

"Indeed I did—still do." He paused to clear his throat. "But on the morning of my death, I fought with her over some trivial thing, and stormed out in a rage, to ride my horse and calm down." He gave a wry grin. "Apparently, I calmed down to the point of extinction. So, I never had a chance to apologize to her, and I fear that is why she has been avoiding me."

"Oh dear. I didn't realize you'd parted on such bad terms. You think she might not want to be found?"

George clapped a hand to his brow and looked away. "And if she doesn't, who could blame her? I was a brute. A beast. A cad."

The man could have made a living on the stage—in Victorian melodramas. He was always either stoic or overwrought. "George, calm down. There's no use in self-flagellation. It won't help us find her."

He heaved another sigh and composed himself. "You are right, of course. What I intended to say was that perhaps Rose went to live with my parents once I'd gone, so she may appear there."

"Let's hope you're correct. In the meantime, don't give up. We're going to pursue this until we discover her whereabouts."

"We?"

"You and I, George. And maybe the ancient fairy, too."

*

With the library problems taken care of for the time being, Fiona was ready to work on George's story and attended the next Ancestry Club meeting with more enthusiasm than she'd had in quite a while. She smiled and answered all the members who greeted her. Bill Hawley was a new addition, sitting next to Acacia. Bonnie, Tom Beresford's fiancée, had come to check on her Italian roots. Their wedding, postponed because of the storm damage to the conservatory, was now rescheduled until February.

Jane Kennedy had prepared a PowerPoint presentation to explain how to use the census data. Perfect topic.

"Today we're going to take a look at how official records can help us discover more about our families," said Jane. "We'll begin with the US census of 1860—the last one before the Civil War."

Fiona perked up at the mention of this date. This was exactly the period she wanted to explore.

Jane was still talking. "In looking at the city of Philadelphia, we see no trace of Abigail Prewitt, who would have been roughly fifteen years old at that time, and most likely living with her parents."

"So, the census was of no help?" Acacia asked, crestfallen.

"Not necessarily," said Jane, smugness radiating from her like a miasma. "In extending the search geographically, I came across a Prewitt family, a married couple with two daughters, residing in Warminster, about twenty-five miles outside Philly. And one of the girls is named Abigail, so I'm as sure as I can be that she's the one we want."

Elaine piped up. "But if her name was Prewitt before she married and had three daughters, how could it be the same person? Unless she married a cousin."

Jane drummed her fingers on the table, evidently displeased at being challenged. "This is one of the frustrations of studying one's ancestry—one often arrives at dead ends. But that doesn't negate the fact that, in other respects, this Abigail fits the bill. Though I have to admit, when I looked at the census of 1870, for Warminster and Philadelphia, I could find no trace of her or her parents. This could have been because they'd moved away, or even died." She scanned the room. "The important thing is not to quit."

She proceeded to show each member of the group how to pull the information up on their computers. "As a library, we have access to all the census data, but should you wish to pursue this at home, you might want to subscribe to Ancestry.com, which has the same information."

Silence reigned as they tapped and scrolled through scans of antique documents. Fiona opened the files and looked for the Manchesters at the address George had given her. There they were, along with a twenty-year-old student, George. Evidently, his parents had stayed in their original house and were still there in the 1870s, but George proved harder to find.

On checking the listings on Spring Street, a shiver of excitement ran through her when she discovered him and Rose in their own Philadelphia home. He would be so pleased to know she was making progress, although she was sure this wouldn't be enough for him. Because no offspring were listed there.

As they worked, an occasional elated "Here they are" caused the group to look up and listen, encouraged by another member's success.

By the time Fiona reached the records for 1880, though, the trail had gone cold. The Manchesters still lived in their home, with a long list of servants, but of Rose there was no trace. Disappointment threatened to make her give up. But if Jane wasn't quitting, then she mustn't either.

She pulled up a chair next to her. Perhaps she could help. "I'm having a problem doing some research for a friend of mine." Though it chafed to ask Jane for assistance, she'd do it for George. "The family I'm researching must have had children, or their descendants wouldn't exist today, but there's no sign of them on the 1870 census lists. How could that be if they were born before that?"

Startled at first, Jane apparently decided she liked the request for assistance. "A good question. Ladies, can you listen to this, please?" She repeated Fiona's request and went on to explain, "Remember, the census taker came door to door, filling out the forms. So, the most likely reason someone isn't registered is that they were away from home temporarily and listed at the place they were staying, rather than where they lived."

This made sense. Fiona would ask George about it. Meanwhile, she might as well get as many answers as she could while Jane was inclined to help.

"I have one last question," she said, and everyone except Elaine turned to look at her. No doubt she was annoyed at this distraction from looking for her Swedish ancestors. Fiona went ahead anyway. "A person on their family tree appears in the 1870 census, but not in the 1880 one. Is there another way I could try to find them?"

Jane looked up from the screen and smiled. "I'll help if I can. But you may be out of luck, if that's the case, unless they have an unusual surname, for example. Then you could look at the national census and hope there aren't too many other people of that name."

Fiona groaned inwardly. Manchester was hardly an uncommon last name. Just to be sure, she entered the name of George's father, Sebastian, into the national file for 1880. A lengthy list of possible candidates appeared. She was willing to help George, but she would never have time to check out all these people.

The last suggestion Jane had for finding his relatives was to search a website that listed all the graves in the country. After a while, Fiona sat back, stretching to release the tension in her shoulders. She'd discovered the Manchester mausoleum, an imposing edifice befitting the family's status. It bore out George's claim of their importance in the town.

Returning to the screen, she scanned the page again. Photos of the tomb indicated a square and compasses carved on the front. So, Sebastian had been a Freemason—another thing she would have to confirm with George. The dates could fit. On another wall she found the name of Martha Manchester, with birth and death dates that could have been those of his mother. And, on the last side of all, there he was.

George Manchester
beloved son
Born 1840
At rest with the Lord 1875

She gasped, and her fingers flew off the keyboard as if it were burning.

She'd talked to him, seen him as he was when alive. And though part of her knew he no longer existed in this mortal world, this stark confirmation of it suddenly made the fact that he was a spirit real.

No other person appeared to be entombed there—nor anywhere else. So, no Rose, no daughters. What could that mean? Had they not deserved to join the rest of the Manchesters? Or—and this might cause George some distress—had Rose remarried and been buried with her second—or, God forbid, third—husband? If her name was no longer Manchester, Fiona would never find her.

It would require all her tact to tell George what she'd discovered—and she was not looking forward to it. What would he do when he heard his quest was hopeless? Might he disappear from her life forever?

She found a tissue and surreptitiously wiped away a tear threatening to fall. She'd lost too much over the last two years. Her marriage, her hope of someday having a child. She couldn't lose George, too.

*

Fiona was as gentle as she could be when she told George. She'd found him sitting in his favorite chair, a pensive expression on his face. He looked up and smiled when she said hello, and then asked what had happened at the Ancestry Club meeting. She told him how the census had let them down.

"Is there no other record of them?" George's question was terse, as if he feared the worst.

How to put this? "Well, I did find your family mausoleum on my computer."

"It could not have belonged to our family. We had no such tomb. Could it have been constructed by one of my father's brothers? James or Thomas?"

Best to approach this obliquely. "Was your father a Mason?"

"Indeed, he was, head of his Lodge, as I recall, though, of course, he was not allowed to reveal anything substantial to us. I remember catching sight of his apron and other regalia laid out on his bed before he attended meetings."

"Then I believe this must have been built for your family. I found Sebastian and a Martha Manchester there too."

George's face twisted in sudden pain. "Ah, no. Not Mama." A tear leaked from his eye. "Did she at least have a long life? Please tell me she lived out her allotted span."

"Don't worry, George. She died at seventy-eight."

"And what of Rose? And the girls?" His voice was a trifle more optimistic now. How she hated to disappoint him.

"I'm afraid they weren't mentioned, George. And before you ask, I checked all the records that exist for the whole country but couldn't uncover any record of them." George's face registered anguish now, but she must not let that deter her. "There's one more thing I haven't told you." She wondered why the question hadn't occurred to him. "On the mausoleum...there's one more name."

"Oh?"

"It's your name, George."

The silence seemed to stretch on and on. Fiona felt compelled to break it.

"So, there it is, George. I'm so sorry."

George said nothing. He simply faded away before her eyes.

CHAPTER 41

FIONA

It had been a while since Fiona had spotted Andrew walking past the house with Newton. She knew that where he chose to take his exercise was not her concern, yet she needed to fight the urge to check every morning. She took it that his absence meant he was avoiding her. George, on the other hand, seemed to have gotten over the news of his own interment in the family mausoleum, and was prepared to speak to her again.

"Where's that man gone?" demanded George's voice. "The one who might not be as stupid as the rest."

"I don't know who you're referring to." Fiona bristled. "In any case, it's none of your business."

"Of course you know. The one with the dog."

The last thing she needed was George reminding her about Andrew. She ignored his remark. "I'm off to work. Have a nice day."

"If by nice you mean boring, I will. But if you can bring back some more information about Rose, I'd have something to look forward to."

Such a nag.

*

A couple of days later, she was enjoying her weekend cup of cappuccino in the living room when George spoke up again.
"Isn't that him?"
"What are you talking about?"
"The man with the dog—he's out there right now."
George's sightline from the mantelpiece gave him a view of the road, but until this moment, Fiona hadn't been aware that he actually kept an eye on what was going on. She forced herself to act as if she couldn't care less as she rose from the sofa and strolled over to the window.
"Hurry—you might miss him."
She almost did, because by the time she'd gotten there, all she glimpsed was Andrew's back disappearing around the bend. So, he was on his way out. Perhaps she'd catch him returning.
"You're right, George. That was Andrew Mackenzie."
"You like him, don't you?"
"He's a friend," she said, noncommittally.
"Oh, I think there's more to it than that, and on his part, too. I mean—he reacted like a simpleton when he thought I was your romantic interest."
"Don't remind me, George."
"But apart from that, he'd make quite a good husband, don't you think?"
"Are you nuts? I just got rid of one—I have no intention of ever marrying again."
"Suit yourself. If you want to be a spinster for the rest of your life, that's your affair. Well, not an affair as such. You know what I mean."
"Let's drop this, shall we? I'm not interested in Andrew as anything other than a friend."
George harrumphed and fell silent.

A FIELD GUIDE TO LIBRARY GHOSTS

*

Half an hour later, purely by chance and quite unplanned, Fiona, who'd been sitting by the window since he passed earlier, caught sight of Andrew on his way home. Newton trotted in his wake like a dinghy being towed behind a ship. It occurred to Fiona that she needed to check the front porch in case some winter hiking boots she'd ordered the day before had been delivered. One never knew.

"Hello, Andrew." She put as much surprise into her voice as she could. He stopped and looked around, as if trying to figure out where this greeting was coming from.

"Oh, hi."

She descended the porch steps and walked down the drive to the road. "Been for a walk?" Surely, she could have come up with something better than that.

"Just a quick one. I have lots to do today."

"I don't mean to detain you. I wondered if...you'd like to have dinner one evening." Where on earth had those unplanned words come from? As color flooded her cheeks, Fiona touched her face with chilly fingers in an unsuccessful attempt to cool off. "It was just an idea. As a way of apologizing for the disaster last time."

Perhaps she shouldn't have mentioned the time he'd been there for dinner and Brian had punched him on the nose. Referring to it made their friendship too complicated. Too late now. "Only if you were free some evening. You could come over here. We could compare our taste in books."

She was babbling and she knew it. They'd have nothing in common where books were concerned. He'd be all about math, while her own choice ran to historical fiction, preferably with a handsome protagonist. She hugged herself as a chilly breeze made itself felt.

Andrew's silence confirmed they had nothing at all to talk

about. She'd been crazy even to think of it.

"That would be nice."

What? He must have misunderstood her. Or possibly vice versa. "Do you mean you'd like to come over? Here?"

He frowned, and no wonder. "I thought that's what you meant. Did I get it wrong?"

Nothing ventured, nothing gained. "No, you didn't. Why don't you call me, and we can fix a date?"

He didn't hesitate this time. "No need to call. I can do any evening except Thursdays—I teach a late class that day."

So—no escape. "How about Tuesday?" she found herself asking.

"Seven?"

A weak sun made its way through the clouds overhead, illuminating the two of them.

"Why not?" Without stopping to think, she added, "I'll make sure there are no other men around."

Andrew's eyes, smiling until now, took on a different, dimmer light. What a stupid remark. Evidently, he remained somewhat sensitive about potential rivals, real or imaginary. Maybe it was only shyness. If so, fingers crossed, a quiet evening at home might reassure him.

He left Fiona with her heart beating faster than usual. She gave him an uncertain wave when he turned briefly, nodded at her, and disappeared around the corner. The invitation had been a terrible idea. But perhaps he'd be a no-show. Maybe she'd contract measles before Tuesday and wouldn't be able to see anyone.

She had to get a grip.

*

In the end, on Tuesday morning, Andrew texted her to confirm and arrived on time that evening. He stood at her front door with a bottle of Merlot, shifting from foot to foot. No knocking and entering unannounced this time.

Fiona led the way into the kitchen and poured him a drink before leading him into the living room. She had a sudden urge to turn George's portrait to the wall, but that might look a little eccentric. She hoped he wouldn't make any comments—at least not until Andrew had left.

Andrew walked up to the painting of George and stared at it intently for a moment, then moved away and back again. "This is an interesting face," he said. "You almost get the feeling the eyes are following you around, don't you?"

Oh dear. The last thing she needed was an irritable George. "I found it at an antique fair and it took my fancy." More or less true, if not exactly the answer to Andrew's question. How to explain that it wasn't only his ghostly eyes she saw sometimes?

After a pause, while they settled themselves on opposite sides of the room, they spoke simultaneously.

"About the last time you came for dinner—"

"I just wanted to—"

They laughed, and Fiona decided to say something before she lost her courage.

"You first," said Andrew.

Fiona breathed out and let her shoulders fall. They'd risen almost to her ears as she sat, leaning forward, both hands around her wine glass. Time to tell him.

"I'd like to apologize for Brian. And explain. He and I were married a long time."

Andrew shook his head as if to ward off her words. "You don't need to…"

Yet something compelled her to speak. She took a sip of her wine. "I want to. It was like this." She sipped again. Explaining was much harder than when she'd rehearsed it. "He and I wanted children but it just didn't happen. I always believed it was my fault. That's what Brian hinted at, anyway."

If she'd hoped for sympathy, she was disappointed.

"And was it?"

"No, as it turned out after our divorce." She went on to give him an edited version of the story, and the reason Brian had gatecrashed when she'd last invited Andrew.

"I see. Sounds like you had a lucky escape."

"I guess so." She hesitated. Did she need to explain her feelings about not having children? Or talk about the irrational guilt she'd felt for years, thinking she was somehow to blame?

Andrew regarded her with an expression of concern. "Children aren't all sunshine and roses, though."

Men. They never got it. He probably didn't even *have* children and thought this was comforting. "No," she said. "But I'd have liked the chance to find out for myself."

She wanted to ask him why he lived alone but felt awkward about it. So, she chose an easier topic. "I think the food must be ready. Are you hungry?"

*

Inviting Andrew to her house on his own hadn't provided any clues as to the status of their relationship. He didn't seem interested in her—not in the way she'd speculated about. Conversation was stilted, and not until they'd finished their after-dinner espressos did she begin to relax. He'd be leaving soon.

His question came out of nowhere. "Did you know there's a blue moon tonight?"

Fiona had heard the plaintive song, *Blue Moon*, and knew the phrase, once in a blue moon, but had never stopped to consider its meaning. She checked the window but couldn't make out any moon at all from where she sat. "I had no idea.

Can we see it from here?"

"We could go outside and find out. It's pretty warm considering the time of year."

She felt pretty warm herself as they found a place to sit on the porch steps and gazed at the sky.

"It's the second full moon in the same calendar month, and it only happens once every two or three years." He pointed upward. "That's it, coming out from behind that cloud. In fact, the cloud is moving, of course, not the moon."

Ah, yes. He understood physics, but she needed something more...personal. "Does it have any symbolic meaning? Like romance, for instance? I mean, the song is quite sad—all about someone lonely." She stole a glance at him to check on how he was taking this.

He stared resolutely at the sky. "Um...well...they say it's a sign of transformation, possibilities. Emotional release, even."

This was more like it. "You mean letting go of the past?"

"So some people say."

Interesting. She was willing to believe it even if he didn't. She rested a cautious hand on her knee, hoping he might notice.

Andrew cleared his throat. "I'm told this kind of moon is romantic," he said. He seemed to consider this before adding, "But I'm no good at romance myself."

What could one say to that? Was he warning her off? Was it true?

Fiona stared at the moon as she answered him. "I don't think it's so difficult. Though it's more chemistry than physics, I'd say."

If she waited for him to make a move, she'd wait all night. His fingers were tantalizingly close. She might cover them with her own or ignore him and see what resulted. Before she could decide, she felt his warm, dry hand settle on hers.

It had been years since she'd experienced that kind of tingling touch, and now it had happened, she wasn't sure what to say. She wanted to turn her hand over and hold his, but what if he rebuffed this mild advance? She hadn't felt this awkward and uncertain since she was a teenager.

"It's getting chilly. Perhaps we should go in," she said and regretted it immediately. She was running away again, anxious not to be rejected.

He removed his hand the moment she said it, leaving a waft of cool air to take its place. "Of course. I ought to get going. Newton's by himself, and I don't like to leave him alone too long." His voice sounded a little hoarse.

"I understand." She rose and stood facing him. In the moonlight, the expression in his eyes was hard to discern. Oh, well. It wasn't as though they'd had a passionate encounter, after all. He was probably just being sympathetic about her marriage.

He didn't bother to retrieve his jacket but thanked her for a lovely evening like a polite schoolboy eager to get away from a duty call to an aged aunt. She couldn't figure out what to make of the whole situation. She'd have to wait until the next time she saw him to gauge his reaction. Hopefully, it wouldn't be embarrassment.

She leaned forward to give him a polite kiss on his left cheek—the way anyone might. He leaned in too, aiming for her right cheek, and they collided. His lips brushed hers, sending another kind of fizz through her. If this was how Elaine felt in the presence of ghosts, no wonder she wanted more. This irrelevant thought was followed by a mixture of shock and guilt. Guilt because she'd enjoyed it, and shock because it had happened, even if by accident.

"Sorry," was all he said as he turned to go.

That was it? "No problem," she said, wondering why she couldn't come up with anything better.

She stared after him until he vanished into the dark, leaving his jacket behind. Perhaps he'd use it as an excuse to meet again. Or maybe she would.

CHAPTER 42
FIONA

"I'm glad you're here, dear. I need to ask you something." Elaine Johanssen approached noiselessly from behind, making Fiona spill the coffee she'd just poured. Elaine was allowed to enter the kitchen, of course, since she volunteered at the library, but did she really have to be so stealthy? Today she was dressed in one of her favorite cropped mohair sweaters, a pair of leather gaucho pants, and knee-high boots with a heel that looked far too high for safety.

Fiona recovered from her surprise at the ensemble the old lady was wearing. "Of course. How can I help?"

Elaine gave her a knowing look. "Is there somewhere private we could talk? I don't want people overhearing—you know what they're like."

Fiona wasn't quite sure she did, but to humor the old lady she invited her into her office, and they navigated their way downstairs.

Elaine made herself comfortable and looked up at Fiona with an expectant air. "It's like this, dear. The last time I saw you was when I came over and we were able to talk to the man in the portrait—George, I think you said his name was."

Fiona made a show of rummaging for something in a desk drawer while she decided on a reply, but eventually was forced to answer. She kept her voice as noncommittal as possible. "That's right. And?"

Elaine evidently considered this a feeble response. "You could sound more excited about it. It's not every day one gets to talk to someone beyond the grave."

The woman was not going to give up. Fiona had noticed her resolute chin before, but now it seemed more prominent than ever. "So, what is it you want me to do?"

Almost immediately, she wished she hadn't asked.

"A few things," Elaine said, and Fiona's heart sank. "The main one is, I need to be able to talk to George again. He's fascinating. And, better yet, to talk to the Wentworth portraits."

So, Elaine was under George's spell. Better to focus on the Wentworths.

"What? I don't see how I can help with that. I can't tell whom you can hear."

Elaine leaned forward, her gaze determined. "That's as may be, but I think if we were in the same place at the same time, I'd be able to hear Abigail Wentworth."

"And what makes you think she wants to be heard?"

"Let's start with first things first. Would you be able to meet me on the portrait landing sometime after the library closes?"

It began to occur to Fiona, who'd been trying to be as discouraging as possible, that the quickest way out of this gadfly's clutches would be to do what she wanted. With any luck, this would lead to an unsuccessful result and prevent further attempts to contact the dead. Enough was enough.

"Very well." She scrolled through the calendar on her phone. "Can you be here tomorrow at closing time?"

"I'll be here, rain or shine."
Time to put this whole ghostfest to bed.

*

The next evening, Elaine was waiting for her on the landing in front of the family portraits. She'd arrived for the event wearing a leather skirt so short that Fiona felt chilly just looking at it. The pink mohair sweater above it clashed with her hair, but despite that, the right lipstick color made it work somehow. Today's tights were a sedate navy, and Elaine's calf-length platform boots gave off a sixties vibe. The whole outfit was accessorized with a long string of (possibly imitation) pearls that reached almost to her knees.

"I thought I should dress up in honor of Abigail—in the hopes she's here. I wouldn't want her thinking that I haven't bothered." Elaine eyed Fiona's tailored pants and cashmere sweater without comment until she burst out, "You might have added some finishing touches, but I suppose it's too late now."

Fiona was taken by surprise. "I must admit, I hadn't considered what I wore. I hope Abigail will forgive me if I'm wearing the clothes I usually wear to work."

"Hmm," said Elaine without conviction.

"At least *you* look great. Let's hope that's enough."

Another voice broke through. "In what sense of the word does she look great? *Your* clothes are bad enough—trousers and sweaters, for heaven's sake. But this ancient person looks a fright."

Fiona's expression must have alerted Elaine to the fact that something strange was happening.

"She's here, isn't she?"

Fiona nodded at Elaine, but answered Abigail directly. "Hello, Mrs. Wentworth. Thank you for allowing us to talk to you."

Elaine waved both hands at her. "Fiona, I can't believe this is working. This is the most exciting thing ever. Do you think I might ask her something? If she could give us some answers, the ancestry research might go better."

Elaine had a point. If they gleaned some facts from Abigail, it would help a lot. She'd wait a while before she told Jane whatever they discovered.

Fiona imagined herself as an interpreter at some international conference—accuracy would be everything. So, the less translating she did, the better. She would ask Mrs. Wentworth how much she was able to hear.

"Did you catch that, Mrs. Wentworth?"

Elaine was agog. "What's she saying?"

"Nothing so far. I wonder if I was imagining it." Fiona had experienced this feeling at the beginning of her relationship with George—not sure what was real and what wasn't. He had turned out to be genuine, of course, so perhaps the prevarication and doubt were just the way connections were made from the other realm.

"I do not care to speak to people to whom I haven't been introduced." There it was—Abigail's voice. "And I never allow people to refer to me by my given name until I am a great deal better acquainted with them."

"Oh, dear. I'm so sorry, and I—we—perfectly understand, don't we, Elaine?"

"Understand what?" said Elaine, grasping at Fiona's arm. "What do we understand?"

Fiona turned to her. "It's like this. Mrs. Wentworth is a woman born in the nineteenth century, and modern informality doesn't suit her. She would like to know to whom she's speaking before she continues this conversation. Is that right?" she concluded, turning toward the portrait again.

"Precisely. I understand we have no mutual acquaintances to make the introductions, so you will have to introduce yourselves."

"Elaine, why don't you go first?" Fiona extended an arm toward the portrait as if Abigail were indeed in the room.

"How thrilling! Well, my name is Elaine Johanssen, and I'm almost ninety years old. I'm a volunteer at this wonderful library you gave us. I've often figured there was more to you than meets the eye, Mrs. Wentworth, so I asked Fiona if she would help me contact you. She has more experience with this sort of thing."

"What sort of thing?" interrupted Abigail.

Fiona gave her the abbreviated version. "I think she means that I have a friend who's passed on but resides in a portrait too, so she thought I might be able to converse with you."

"Shall I go on?" said Elaine.

"Yes, do. I was just explaining." This was complicated.

"Well, Mrs. Wentworth—and please call me Elaine—I've had certain feelings, a slight dizziness you might say, whenever I pass you on these stairs, so I've known for a while this place is haunted."

A sharp intake of breath from the direction of the portrait told Fiona that Abigail did not consider herself to be haunting anywhere.

"Shall we just skip that part? May I say, Mrs. Wentworth, that it's a pleasure to meet you. My name is Fiona Gordon, and I'm the new director of the library. I came here from Philadelphia. And a few weeks ago, I found a book on the stairs. I heard it fall, but I've no idea where it came from. It was the *Guide to the Philadelphia Centennial Exhibition of 1876*. I don't suppose you know anything about that?"

"Oh, well done!" Fiona thought she detected a smile in Abigail's voice as she said, "I wondered if anyone would notice it and speculate. And since you're from that dear old city, I imagine you put two and two together."

"Not exactly, no. But I was interested, because it made me think you might be from there too. And we found out you were."

"We? Who are 'we'?"

This was a longer story, and one Fiona wished she hadn't started.

"Mrs. Wentworth, almost a hundred years ago, you donated this building, your former home, to be a library for the people of Brentford."

"My, was it as long ago as that? I bequeathed it to the town, I recall, which means I must have died almost a hundred years ago, too." Abigail didn't sound too concerned, so Fiona kept going.

"Well, yes. The point is, we—the library and the town—want to celebrate your wonderful gift and your life on the centenary, which happens next year."

"I'm flattered, I suppose. But why should you need my help to do that?"

Elaine piped up. "We have been trying to find out more about your life so we can put together an exhibition—the Wentworth Story, if you like."

"And?"

Almost as though she'd heard Abigail's question, Elaine carried on. "And we found very little information about you and your life before you arrived here. So, if we could ask you about it, it would help a lot."

Fiona had the sudden sensation Elaine was speaking to dead air.

"What's she saying?" Elaine asked.

"Nothing, right now. Nothing at all."

CHAPTER 43
GEORGE

Fiona has avoided me for the last day or two. I suppose she feels she has failed me. It is not her fault, of course. I gave her only partial information on which to base her search.

It cannot be helped. I will have to tell her. Otherwise, Rose will continue to elude us. I'd hoped this would not be necessary, but I fear I have no choice.

"George, are you okay?" Fiona's voice summons me, and this time I will answer it.

I believe this conversation will have to take place eye-to-eye. I need to see how she reacts, and I suppose she deserves to be shown I am speaking the truth this time. The whole truth, as they say in the courts of justice.

I don't know why I didn't admit this before. She appears to be a woman with a strong constitution. I have never seen her faint when receiving bad news, unlike so many women in my time. The occasional tear is all she allows herself.

Yet her reaction to the dastardly Brian is enough to give one pause. She told him she never wanted to see him again, and I know she meant it. What if she abandons me too? Where shall I be then?

This will not do. I must face the music—no matter how strident. Although no one could ever describe me as a coward, I admit this makes me quake.

"Hello? George?"

Perhaps if I pretend I can't see or hear her, she will go away.

"George? Are you around?" Then, seemingly to herself, "Are all the ghosts ignoring me now?"

All the ghosts? What can she mean?

I shall ignore this because I need to confess. I have no other option.

"I'm here." I say this with little enthusiasm, and she hears it in my voice, I'm certain.

"Why can't I see you? There's no one else here. I seem to be having trouble all over the place today."

This piques my curiosity. "What are you trying to say, Fiona? Trouble with what?"

"Ah. I'm not sure I should tell you this," she says.

Now, naturally, I have to know. "What is it?" I say, beginning to become vexed.

"You remember Elaine? The sprite?"

"Of course. Has she been causing you trouble?"

"No. Yes. Indirectly. I think I mentioned she believes the library is haunted—something to do with the woman who bequeathed her home to the town to be used for that purpose."

"A Mrs. Wentworth, I believe you said."

"That's it. Elaine, guessing you and I communicated, was convinced I might be able to hear and speak to Mrs. Wentworth, so, to satisfy her curiosity, I said I would try, not expecting any result."

"But you made contact with this phantom? I told you—you have the gift."

Fiona takes a breath. "The thing is, her portrait hangs

halfway up the main staircase in the library. And I managed to connect with her because she seems to live in the painting, like you."

"So?"

"So, isn't that unusual? I mean, is living in portraits a common phenomenon? And even stranger—she's from Philadelphia. At least, she was."

This is fascinating. I wonder if this person knew Rose—or my parents. While an extensive city in many respects, our social circles are—were—selective. "Do you think she could tell you anything about me and my family?"

It's hard to judge Fiona's reaction to this. "It's remotely possible. She died shortly after the Great War. Have you heard of it? The one that ended in 1918? Never mind. It happened long after your time."

I am trying to follow this, but I do wish Fiona would stick to the point. She speaks again.

"She was married to Mr. Wentworth for a long time, and never remarried after his death. She had three daughters."

"If you had more to go on, I might be able to figure out whether Rose and I were acquainted with her. Could you ask her if she knew me or my parents? Wouldn't it be wonderful if she did?"

"Miraculous, I'd say. Because at the moment I don't believe she's prepared to talk to me."

Fiona does not make it easy for a man to bare his soul. Reluctantly, I make my presence visible.

"At last." She registers my expression, and her eyes widen. "What's the matter? You look like you've seen a…" She giggles. "Ghost."

Faintly amusing, I suppose.

"Fiona. I have something to tell you. I think you might find it easier to absorb if you had some gin in your hand and the rest of you on a seat."

"This sounds serious. Very well. Be right back."

She disappears for what feels like at least an hour, while I sit and stew.

"Okay, begin." She settles down with her gin and quinine water over an unconscionable amount of ice, ready to listen.

"It's like this. I was hoping you would discover where my Rose was with the information I gave you. But it appears you will require more to enable a satisfactory solution."

She frowns. "I see. So, what haven't you told me?"

I brace myself. "The fight Rose and I had, on the day I stormed out, never to see her again, was one of many over my parents and the way they treated her. She had been so patient with them, but I know I should have done more to insist on their respecting her."

"Why wouldn't they? She was the mother of your children, the love of your life. Didn't that give her some status?"

"Not in their eyes. My father insisted she had married me for my money—or, rather, my expectations. No matter what I said, he was adamant."

"Did you believe it too?"

The suggestion is monstrous. "Of course not. I fell in love with Rose practically the day I met her, and she with me. We were so enamored of each other that people called us 'the lovebirds.'"

I feel foolish admitting this, but if I am to tell the truth, it must be all of it.

"Where did you meet?"

"That was part of the problem. We met in Fairmount Park, where she was promenading with her sister Cora. I was with a friend who knew Cora and introduced us."

"It sounds romantic."

"In a way. The thing that made the connection unsuitable was that my friend was simply flirting with Cora, since the sisters were of a lower social order than we were. I believed he would discard her eventually, without making any serious offer. And, in fact, a few months later, he did so."

"Well, that wouldn't have been your fault, would it?"

"I tell you this to illustrate that marriages between wealthy families such as mine—and shopgirls—were not only frowned upon but could be downright hazardous."

Her expression indicates she has no idea what I mean.

"Financially hazardous. It was not uncommon in those days for fathers to disinherit disobedient sons and daughters."

"And is that what happened to you?"

"Let me go on. As I said, it's complicated. Rose and I were married in secret, and didn't tell my parents for three months. They suspected I had set some female up as my mistress, and Father turned a blind eye to what he felt was a normal rite of passage for any young man. But when Rose was in a delicate condition, I had no option but to tell them."

"Was she sick? What kind of delicate condition?"

Sometimes, Fiona can be extremely obtuse. I remain patient, however, since this is an important story. "No more sick than other women, she told me. No, I mean she was anticipating becoming a mother. I was delighted. I hoped this would reconcile my parents to our union. The prospect of a grandchild often does, I believe."

"And did it?"

"Up to a point. After the initial reaction caused by our secret marriage, my father, persuaded he would have a grandson to take over the family business, was reconciled to the idea, though he always considered Rose inferior in status."

"But you had a daughter, not a son. So, his happiness evaporated, and he rejected you all again. What a b—"

I interrupt before the word can pass her lips. "Exactly." I try to keep my features impassive, but I see concern on Fiona's face.

"What about your mother? Women generally love their grandchildren, don't they?"

"Oh, she did, but in front of my father she retained an equivocal stance. She was a dutiful spouse, and though she did her best to restore harmonious relations between us, her efforts were never entirely successful."

"I'm so sorry, George. But what does all this have to do with my finding her?"

"Hear me out. When we had our second daughter, seven years before I died, my father, though disappointed, offered me work in the firm, which I took because I had a wife and two children to support. But though he and I achieved some rapprochement, he never really took to Rose. And here is where I am culpable. I regret I didn't do more to make him accept her as someone good enough to marry me. More than good enough, when you consider her incredible patience.

"She'd been a little more irritable, sickly even, in the month or so before my accident, and I daresay I contributed to her unhappiness with my lack of backbone. I should have done more, as I said. Instead, on that fateful day, I had had enough of Rose's entreaties and my father's bullying, so I simply shouted at her and left the family home. I cannot spend eternity not knowing whether she has forgiven me for leaving her that way."

Fiona maintains an uncharacteristic silence for a moment. "Do you have any idea what might have happened to her after you died?"

"I believe I told you my parents took her in, but you say you can find no evidence of her in the census. When you suggested she might have remarried, I denied the possibility, but now I wonder. Is it possible to check the marriage records to see if she did so?"

I am trying to maintain a stiff upper lip, as the British are said to. It will not do for me to become sentimental over this.

But I admit the idea that my lamb has married someone else is heart-rending. Yet, I do not believe I left her adequately provided for, and if my parents refused to step up, she might have had no other choice.

"Could she have gone to live with Cora?"

"I doubt it. When I was alive, they only met during the winter holiday season, when we invited them to our home. Rose made overtures to her sister, but she told me Cora resented Rose's good fortune in marrying me. Misfortune, I'd call it!"

I am overcome by the feelings of guilt I have tried to suppress for so long, and have difficulty restraining the threatening tears.

"Come on, George. Stop feeling sorry for yourself. It's most unattractive."

I resent this comment. What can I say? How can I explain? I pull myself together.

"In any case, Cora lived with her husband and children over her parents' shop and had no room for anyone else. I imagine she thought Rose had come by her just desserts."

"Victorian manners seem to have caused no end of trouble, don't they? Today we women have some choice in whom we marry, at least in this country."

I sometimes think Fiona is only interested in herself.

CHAPTER 44

FIONA

Fiona was desperate to talk to someone about Andrew. She still couldn't decide where she was with him. Every step forward in their relationship seemed to result in a step back.

George had been no help at all as a confidant, simply laughing at her romantic aspirations. But thoughts of Andrew kept filling her head, and she was finding it difficult to concentrate on library business and the centenary celebrations while his intriguing eyes continued to appear in her dreams.

Andrew hadn't returned for his jacket, and she hadn't found the courage to take it back to him. After all, she couldn't make a habit of returning things—he might think she was stalking him. On the other hand, he ought not to be losing his dog or leaving his outerwear behind if he didn't want her to come over. Confusing didn't begin to cover it.

She understood that single women coming out of long relationships often had a hankering to replace the former lover with someone new, and told herself that she would not become one of them. Yet here she was, spending way too much time trying not to think about him—it was exhausting.

She stood abruptly and began to pace the worn oriental rug in her office. She would call Molly. When the phone on her desk rang a minute later, she was about to let it go to voicemail, but, after ignoring it for a few rings, picked it up.

"Hi there. I was literally about to call you. What's up?"

Molly didn't stop to ask why Fiona wanted to talk to her. "Fantastic news!" Fiona could almost hear the exclamation mark. "Lucinda Parks has offered to donate five hundred thousand dollars to the library. Not all at once, but over the next five years."

Fiona sank into one of the visitor chairs. "Half a million? That's incredible. Why would she...?"

"If you've got a minute, why don't you come over, and I'll tell you all about it."

*

Thirty minutes later, they were sitting at one of the small tables in a corner of the mezzanine at Books & Beans, nursing hot drinks. Fiona had chosen a cup of cocoa with whipped cream to celebrate—a rare treat. "Tell me exactly what happened."

Molly took a breath, but Fiona gave her no chance to speak. "Start at the beginning. The last thing we heard was that Cece had offered to arrange for the donation of some romance novels. Andrew confirmed she'd organized that, but never said anything about any money."

Molly glanced at her for a moment, her expression one of curiosity. Then her face cleared. "He's on the board, of course, so you've been keeping him updated on the financing front."

She'd have to explain about Andrew later. In the meantime, Fiona only nodded as Molly continued.

"Perhaps he told Cece that the library was having trouble raising money. After all, it's no secret."

"I suppose it's possible. And you think she mentioned it to Lucinda?"

"She must have. Anyway, Andrew was in here one day looking for a book to buy for his daughter."

A warning bell sounded in Fiona's head. Daughter? Never mind that now.

"And we were talking about the library's financial problems when he said he thought his sister might be able to help," said Molly.

"Cece?"

"Right. To cut a long story short, I called her."

"And she put you in touch with Lucinda?"

"Not directly. We went around the bushes for a while, and then finally I had an email from Lucinda with this amazing donation."

Fiona put her mug down on the table in front of her. "That's unbelievable."

"I assure you, that's precisely how it happened."

"I didn't mean I don't believe you. It's just hard to credit that she's giving us so much support. And you've never talked to Lucinda directly?"

"Well, no. I only connected with her via Cece. And then Lucinda emailed me. She said we'd have to put the details in writing, but there's no rush. And we can thank her in person when she comes in January."

Something nagged at the back of Fiona's mind. Something about Lucinda Parks in an odd location.

"Molly," she said as the mists cleared. "Do you have a photo of Lucinda?"

Molly reached back and pulled out one of the author's books from the shelves of romance novels behind her. "There should be one on the back cover," she said, turning it over. "Hmm. Not on this one. Let me check some of the others." She took out a couple more and handed them to Fiona.

"No pictures here," said Fiona, laying the books down on the table. "Is that usual?"

"It happens more than you'd think, usually when someone's publishing under a pseudonym. Some authors write in different genres and don't want to use the same name when they're doing horror, for example, if they're already writing romance. So, they leave the photo off. Funny, I never noticed before."

"You know," said Fiona slowly, "I have a suspicion that I know who Lucinda Parks might be."

Molly's eyebrows shot upward. "What? How do you mean?"

"I was at Andrew Mackenzie's house—" She broke off as she saw the interest flare on Molly's face. "Nothing weird. It was ages ago. He offered me a glass of water after I'd been running and got a bit dehydrated."

If Molly found this odd, she didn't say so. But a certain skepticism remained in her eyes. "Not sure what this has to do with anything," she said.

"Point is, while he was getting me the water, I happened to notice he had some books by Lucinda Parks on his shelves. In fact, it looked like he had all of them. He told me they were his sister's, and I assumed he meant they belonged to her." She took a sip of her cocoa and wiped some whipped cream from her upper lip. "But what if she wrote them—under another name?"

Molly's eyes nearly popped out of her head. "Oh, come on. That's ridiculous. I'd know if she had."

"Listen, though. He suggested you call her to get help from Lucinda, right? And she's called Cece. So, you know, Cece—Lucinda."

"Oh, come on. That's too much of a stretch. It's more likely to be short for Celia, Cecily, Celeste, or not short for anything. Just a name. What other proof have you got?" She made air quotes around the word "proof" to emphasize her point.

Fiona began to check off the clues on her fingers. "She's clearly connected in the publishing industry. I haven't found any photos of Lucinda online, which is odd, isn't it? She almost never does public appearances, so it's hard to know what she looks like. All her books are in his house. And she's been ridiculously helpful for an author who doesn't know us." She stopped to catch her breath. "What do you think?"

Molly was frowning as she thought it through. "It's way too far-fetched, surely?" she said, causing Fiona's excitement to subside. "Although, I suppose you might be right. Not that it helps us much. I mean, there's probably a reason why she wants to hide her identity, so we can't be the ones to violate her privacy. On the other hand, if she's coming in January, we can't look too surprised when Cece shows up."

"I can't wait to find out if I'm right. Either way, can you send me something to tell me about her gift? So I can thank her—and announce it at the board meeting next week." It occurred to her that this development wouldn't make it any easier to stop thinking about Andrew. And she hadn't been able to ask for Molly's advice. Too late now.

"Fiona—didn't you say you wanted to talk to me about something?"

Fiona could feel herself blushing. Dammit. "Oh, well. It was nothing."

Molly eyed her shrewdly. "Doesn't sound like it. Can I help?"

Perhaps it was worth asking, since Molly had mentioned it. Fiona's words came out in a rush. "Actually, it's about Andrew. Do you happen to know if he's involved with anyone?"

Molly sat back in her seat and clapped her hands. "I knew it!" she crowed. "You like him."

"Shh—not so loud. I don't want people to know."

Molly lowered her voice to a whisper. "Sorry, it's just that

I think he likes you too."

"You do?" She hadn't expected this.

"That's a definite yes—I can tell by the way he watches you in the board meetings. And to answer your question—he's divorced."

Fiona felt those butterflies again, but tried to appear cool—not easy when her cheeks were aflame. "Do you know why?"

"No, but it was a few years ago so far as I can tell, and there hasn't been anyone else since then." She smiled at Fiona. "So, give it a shot. Can't hurt."

"I'm not sure I'm up for a romantic relationship with anyone right now. I find him attractive, but—"

Molly interrupted her. "He's painfully shy, right? Well, take it slow. When he stops being frightened of single women, he'll realize you could be more than a friend."

Fiona wasn't sure she could manage any more conversation. Molly had given her plenty to think about. She stood. "I must go. In the meantime, I'm just grateful to him for persuading Cece to help. We need to think of a way to thank them both. And thank you, too, for listening."

"Any time."

As she walked back across the town green, Fiona pondered this unexpected turn of events. Andrew, Cece, Lucinda—they were all connected somehow. She made herself walk past the library gates and on toward Andrew's house. He wasn't likely to be in on a Friday morning, but she wanted to tell him how grateful they were before she had time to change her mind.

Disappointed when no one answered her knock, she turned back. She'd have to come up with a different way to reach him.

Another dinner invitation was out of the question. It was way too soon. There was only one solution—the jacket would have to serve as her excuse for getting in touch.

After some internal debate, she decided to keep an eye out

for him on his morning walk, and the following day, spotted him and Newton heading toward Brent Woods. Ignoring the cold, she ran out to the front porch and called, "Andrew!"

He turned his head and came to a stop. He crossed the road and approached her cottage, a look of inquiry on his face.

"You left your jacket here the other night."

Andrew's cheeks became a little pinker. "I wondered where it was."

"I have it here. You can pick it up after your walk, if you don't want to take it now."

"Okay, thanks."

He was giving off the vibe of a man being detained against his will. But she didn't want to let him leave yet.

"I want to thank you again for helping Molly connect with Lucinda Parks."

She waited for his reaction. Would he admit Cece was, in fact, the author?

He demurred. "I didn't do anything," he said. "I only put you in touch with Cece."

"About that," she said. "She's been so helpful, and gracious, and I'd love her to be here on the day itself. With Lucinda." Fiona had no doubt that she would be. If she *was* the author, she'd have to be there.

Andrew choked a little. Or it may have been a cough, Fiona wasn't certain. He took out a handkerchief and blew his nose. Then he stared at her and said, "I know she's intending to come."

Fiona beamed at him. "I'm sure she is." If he was going to pretend he knew nothing about Lucinda's true identity, she'd go along with it—for now. It appeared this was a game the Mackenzies played. "Perhaps you and she would like to join us for dinner after the event. I'm planning to ask you, Lucinda, Channing Madison, plus Molly and Nick."

If Cece and Lucinda were the same person, he'd surely say something now.

She glanced at him. Nothing.

"At the Black Horse. Not my place. I have a feeling that's jinxed."

He seemed unfazed, his face impassive. So, not about to confirm her suspicions. How maddening.

"Haunted by the ghosts of your past?" he said with an unexpected smile.

He'd put her on the defensive. "What do you mean? No. Not at all." Then she came to her senses. He wasn't talking about George. It was Brian who was on his mind. And the man he'd assumed was her lover when he heard her with George. Maybe this was the moment to tell him everything.

Newton had started straining at his leash, evidently bored with the conversation.

"If you're planning to keep walking, can I join you?" Perhaps if they were both staring ahead, it might be easier to explain than having to look him in the eye.

If Andrew was taken aback at this sudden change in subject, he didn't show it.

"Of course," he said. "But you'll need a coat."

"Be right back." Fiona ran up the steps and found her quilted jacket and a woolly green beanie hat. Emerging from the front door, she jammed the hat on so her bangs peeked out, and stood on the porch, ready to go.

She'd give him his jacket when they returned.

CHAPTER 45
FIONA

Fiona stopped staring at the financial reports on her desk and swiveled in her chair to stare out the window. November continued to be warmer than usual, and in the garden outside, Acacia and a team of volunteers were busy weeding the flowerbeds and putting in bulbs. The primroses they'd planted in the fall were wilting after a single ferocious frost, but would be back in the spring, heralding the new year along with the violets. Lavender and the other flowers would come later.

Her thoughts turned to the inspiration for these new flowerbeds. The plants had been chosen to honor Abigail Wentworth's daughters.

The afterlife seemed like a complicated place to be. Poor George, stymied in his quest for his wife. And Abigail, clearly unhappy, else why would she be hanging around the library? There was no sign her girls were still present—perhaps that was why she stayed. Was she hoping they'd return to visit from wherever they were?

A brisk knock at the door heralded the arrival of Elaine, who didn't wait to be invited in and made herself comfortable on her preferred chair, where the sun wouldn't be in her eyes.

"Good morning, Fiona. I came to remind you—the next Ancestry Club meeting is coming up. Shouldn't we try to find out more about Abigail in the meantime? We don't want her story minimized in the centenary exhibition."

This was a far cry from Elaine's initial complaint that too much time was being spent on researching the Wentworths. More recently, Fiona had hoped Elaine would lose interest in talking to Abigail, because it was taking time away from her efforts on George's behalf. She should have known better, but tried a distraction anyway. "I thought you wanted to research your own family tree, Elaine."

"I do, and I've learned a lot about my Swedish origins. But I'm not exactly in touch with my ancestors, whereas with Abigail, I'm beginning to forge a relationship. I believe she needs a friend or two—and you and I are destined to become them."

"I see." Fiona could foresee a lot of time wasted if she helped Elaine with her "relationship" with Abigail. Yet it was becoming clear that she did have a sixth sense that enabled her to communicate with the spirits of those who'd died.

Idly, Fiona wondered whether she might encourage Abigail to materialize. If George could do it, perhaps she could too. It had taken quite a lot of practice, of course, before he'd managed to be both seen and heard. So, perhaps being able to converse with Mrs. Wentworth was all she could expect.

Elaine's voice broke in on her thoughts. "Fiona?"

"Sorry, I was miles away. Okay, I'll give you a hand. Later today?"

Elaine beamed, revealing surprisingly white teeth for an octogenarian. She chuckled. "Wonderful. I'd love to find out more about her. Things the library doesn't know. I'd like to show Jane Kennedy she's not the only one who knows how to do this."

Fiona understood Elaine's point of view. But how would they explain how they'd discovered Abigail's story? Jane was unlikely to give credence to Elaine's source, no matter how authentic, but perhaps the librarian would find more conventional ways of confirming it. Meanwhile, she had more questions for the lady in the portrait.

*

Fiona and Elaine, who seemed to have learned or acquired the knack of encouraging Abigail to talk, returned to the painting on the landing at six o'clock.

"Abigail—Mrs. Wentworth, are you there?" Fiona began.

"Yes, *are* you? Do come and talk to us," said Elaine.

After a protracted silence, Abigail spoke. "Can you both hear me?"

"She's asking if you can hear her," said Fiona. "Can you?"

"Almost, I think, but she's quite faint. It's annoying, getting older. One's hearing isn't quite as good."

Fiona refrained from mentioning that any voice she might hear would be in her head. That was why Andrew hadn't heard George talking to her, only Fiona's side of the conversation. It had taken a while for Fiona to make out George's words, but Elaine did have some kind of psychic power, so maybe it wouldn't be long before she tuned into Abigail's wavelength.

"Did you hear that, Abigail?"

"I can hear her perfectly well," said Abigail, her voice that of a woman who'd been accused of being hard of hearing once too often. "If she talks sensibly, I might even answer her."

Oh, dear. This was going to be a trying conversation if Abigail's attitude was any indication. But at least Elaine had elicited an answer from the woman in the portrait. Best to start with something innocuous.

"Would you mind very much if we asked you some questions about how you came to be here in Brentford?"

"I suppose that would be acceptable." Abigail paused, as if accessing her memories. Presumably, she hadn't spoken of them for years.

Fiona glanced at Elaine, who was waving at her. "I can hear her much better now. It's like she's whispering."

Fiona gave Elaine a thumbs-up.

Abigail continued, "I was widowed young, and left with three daughters, as you know. I loved them all, of course, but my parents died not long after, and my husband's family was not inclined to offer me much support after he died. They were so unhelpful, and I was so incensed at my late husband..." Her voice trailed off.

"Why was that?" Elaine didn't hesitate to ask what Fiona considered intrusive questions, but was dying to know.

"I suppose I had no real reason to be angry, but he left me without any way of living independently. We didn't expect him to die so young, of course, but he was always somewhat irresponsible." She fell silent for a moment as if to gather her thoughts. "Enough of that. The result of all the frustration was that I abandoned my married name and returned to my maiden name, Prewitt."

"We discovered that through your wedding certificate," said Elaine. "The one from your marriage to Albert. Tell her, Fiona."

"I believe you heard, Abigail, didn't you?" Fiona didn't want to antagonize this fascinating woman—her story was too interesting to distract her from it. "I'm sorry—do continue."

The ghostly voice resumed. "Thank you, my dear. As I said, my in-laws were not willing to help me. Instead, in what they insisted was an act of goodwill but was merely a way to pass me off to someone else, they introduced me to a client of their firm, Albert Wentworth."

Elaine piped up again. "So, that's how you met. We wondered. Yet you lived in Philadelphia, and he lived here, is that right?"

"True. But he made trips to the city to inspect merchandise before buying it. He was always a careful man. In a way, I suppose he was inspecting me for the same reason—a lowering thought, to be sure."

Fiona thought she could detect a wry smile in the ghost's voice, and sought to reassure her. "I am sure he found you delightful."

"As to that, I cannot vouch for it. You have likely discovered that Albert had not married before, and to tell the truth, I don't believe he'd ever wanted to before. He said he was fond of children, but he showed no disposition to have any of his own. Gaining some through adoption was no doubt easier. And I think he saw a younger wife as a social asset—for entertaining and so on."

Fiona put a finger on her lips when she saw Elaine open her mouth to speak again. They needed to let Abigail talk now she was in the flow.

"In any case, Albert was willing to take me and the girls— even to adopt them, for which I was grateful. He was a kind man, though substantially older than I was. But affluent enough to support us, so, when he offered me marriage, I saw a solution to my difficulties."

Poor Abigail. Being a Victorian woman had its drawbacks, no matter how much money one had. "So, you made a marriage of convenience?"

"Yes, indeed. A common enough occurrence in those days, though by the time my own three girls were ready to wed, they wouldn't even have contemplated such a thing. Times had changed, and, on the whole, I think for the better."

Fiona interrupted this stream of words to ask Elaine if she'd been able to follow the conversation.

"Of course I have. Her voice is low, but clear. Ask her if she was happy with Wentworth."

Damn. This question had caused Abigail to clam up last

time Elaine had asked it, and apparently, Elaine had forgotten that Abigail could hear *her* too. Fiona was about to remind her when Abigail spoke up.

"An astute, if inappropriate, question. This woman plainly comes from an unsophisticated background."

Fine words from a woman with no background at all, but Fiona could hardly comment while Elaine stood next to her. "You don't need to tell us about your marriage," she said.

Elaine grimaced and mouthed the words "Why not?" but Abigail was still speaking.

"I am tired of answering you, enjoyable though it has been to confide in someone after all these years."

Fiona had one last question. "Just one more thing before you go, if you don't mind. Have you ever...managed to leave your portrait and appear in person?"

There was a pause before Abigail answered. "Only when there's no one around. It's not easy to do, and I can only manage it when I feel the need to explore my old home again—as I did after the recent storm. The damage is heartbreaking, isn't it?"

"Of course. We understand your feelings completely. Perhaps I can reassure you. We plan to rebuild everything exactly as it was. We have applied to have this place designated as a historic landmark, so it *has* to be perfect."

"Strange to hear it described as historic. To me, it's still the place I lived in for more than forty years. But I suppose if you add the time I've been stuck fast in this portrait, it's almost a century and a half."

"That's a long time," said Elaine, compassion in her voice.

But Abigail had gone.

*

Elaine should probably have left for home, since the hour was getting late. Instead, she was practically hopping with excitement as they discussed the conversation they'd had with Abigail. They sat in Fiona's office, where she should have been dealing with the dozens of emails that had accrued while she'd been preoccupied with the ghost and her story, but told herself this was research for the centenary celebrations.

"Of course, she's only confirming what we already know," said Elaine. "But it's wonderful to hear it from the horse's mouth, so to speak. Even though I didn't catch everything."

Fiona felt a pang of sympathy for the old lady. "Did you hear anything new?"

"Only very faintly. But I got that she married Albert for his money and protection. I guess that's how life was then. Even when I was a child, that still happened."

"Elaine, I don't believe it would have worked without you. Something about your presence there made Abigail willing to speak to us. I don't think she would have trusted me on my own."

"Well, thank you. By the way, I didn't quite get what she said when you asked her about manifesting. I'd love to see her in person—just once would be enough for me." Elaine's eyes sparkled at the prospect.

"I'm not sure we ever will. She says she can only do that when there's no one around."

"But I'll bet you can see your man George, can't you?"

Fiona wished Elaine had never come across her talking to an invisible George in her living room. Rather than confirm Elaine's suspicions, she prevaricated. "He told me he was practicing."

"Well then. It's only a matter of time, isn't it? He strikes me as a very determined man."

CHAPTER 46
FIONA

Fiona stood in her kitchen a few days later, waiting for a cappuccino to brew in her Italian coffeemaker. She wondered idly what George would make of a machine like this. He probably had no idea what a cappuccino was.

She dropped the teaspoon into the sink. She'd been trying to draw a heart in the foam with limited success, and decided a sprinkling of cocoa would make a good substitute.

She switched on the lamp in the living room to read through some papers she'd brought from the office, but Abigail's story circulated in her mind. What had the woman told her and Elaine exactly? She'd lived in Philadelphia, was widowed with three children, and had married Albert Wentworth because her in-laws were reluctant to help support her. And she'd gone back to her maiden name, Prewitt.

Meanwhile, Elaine had been so intent on *her* questions, they had spent almost all of their precious time talking about Albert. They never got to the most important question—the name of her first husband, if it wasn't Prewitt. Without it, they didn't have enough evidence to do follow-up research.

Fiona caught at wisps of ideas that floated, in a ghostly way, across the picture she was building up of life in Victorian Philadelphia. It wasn't impossible that Abigail and George might have been acquainted. Fiona needed more information, for sure.

*

She decided the next step was to talk to Abigail again—if she were willing. It would require great tact, though—something that wasn't Elaine's strong suit. The conversation might go any one of several ways.

Abigail had said she'd arrived with three girls.

If Abigail was, in fact, George's Rose, whose child was Violet? There was a three-year gap between his death and her marriage to Albert. Surely, Abigail wouldn't have strayed. Albert would never have married her if she had been that kind of woman. Unless the baby was his.

The questions were driving Fiona crazy, so one evening, when the library was empty, she walked up the staircase alone and stood studying Abigail's portrait.

It had been painted in 1903, when Abigail was sixty-ish, perhaps. The woman staring out at her must once have been pretty, and was still attractive, in the way that determined women who know what they want can be. The artist had doubtless made the best of her, yet, despite his efforts, she had a tired look.

She wore her somewhat faded brown hair swept into an extravagant bun atop her head, and her skin had the slightest of unfashionable tans—maybe from gardening. Her lips were set in a straight line. Maybe she had bad teeth. Lots of people did back then. Or maybe life had disappointed her.

She was dressed in typical Edwardian daywear, a high-necked pintucked blouse, and a navy A-line skirt that reached her ankles. She must have been wearing a corset too. That sloping bosom—there was no other word for it—the tiny waist and the emphasized hips definitely spoke of another, more conventional age. A garden basket filled with flowers stood on a shelf near her and she carried a wide-brimmed hat, trimmed with a blue ribbon and a profusion of scarlet poppies.

"Abigail?"

Silence.

"Abigail, are you there?"

Fiona thought she detected a voice coming from a great distance, so faint she couldn't make out what it was saying. When she'd told Elaine that she needed her presence in order to hear Abigail, she'd been trying to make her feel involved. But had she been right? Did it take both of them to connect with the library's ghost?

"I'll be back, Abigail, and I'll bring Ms. Johanssen with me."

She'd have to tell Elaine not to ask any questions, or Abigail might cut off their dialogue—perhaps for good.

*

It wasn't until a few days later that the opportunity arose for Fiona and Elaine to try again. This time, it appeared Elaine had made an effort to honor a young Abigail Wentworth by attempting to look like a twenty-year-old Victorian. She wore a full-skirted dress that might have been designed to end just above the ankle, but instead reached the floor on her diminutive form. It was set off by a flat-brimmed straw hat tied with a pink bow beneath her chin. She resembled nothing so much as an ancient Bo-Peep in search of her sheep, and what difference her clothing might make, Fiona couldn't guess.

"Nice, isn't it?" she asked, as Fiona took in this vision with one startled glance.

Fiona swallowed. "It's very...*fetching*, if that's the word I want."

In her head, she made out the faint echo of an exasperated female voice. "*Ridiculous* is the word you want."

Fiona stepped back, dangerously close to the top stair, but recovered herself before she tripped. "Did you say something?"

"No, dear. Why?" Elaine stared at Fiona, her face a question. Then excitement lit up her face. "Did Abigail speak? She *did*, didn't she? I thought I caught something. What did she say?"

"Tell her I think her costume is charming. I had no wish to offend her. I didn't realize anyone could hear me."

A chill ran through Fiona. Being doomed to conversations with portraits for the foreseeable future would make life impossible. But for now, she'd have to pass this message on to Elaine. "She says your costume is charming."

Elaine clasped her hands together in front of her chest, like an ingenue from a silent movie, and blushed. "Oh, madam—I mean Mrs. Wentworth—you are too kind." She was positively radiating delight.

"I considered ignoring you both, but I'm curious as to what more you want to know. And maybe you can help me too."

Fiona had so many questions that she hadn't given a thought to the order in which she'd pose them. "So, you don't mind if we ask you about a few things? We're so looking forward to being able to celebrate your life with an exhibition about you and your family."

"Ha. That's where things might become complicated. I daresay you've waded into those weeds already."

"I must confess that we were doing well until we found that what we thought was your previously married name—Prewitt—was, in fact, your maiden name."

Abigail let out a ladylike laugh. "Apparently, you misunderstood. Though I'm sure I told you that was my maiden name."

Fiona began to repeat what Abigail had said, but this time, Elaine didn't need her to. "It's you! How exciting! Your voice is just a whisper, but I'm so pleased to hear you at last. You have such a melodious tone."

"Well, thank you. I'm surprised it's not more rusty, since I haven't had a chance to use it for so long."

Elaine's face lit up and she nodded. "This is wonderful. You're coming through more strongly now. So, we were hoping to trace you through your first marriage if we could discover your whereabouts. The problem is that our archivist can find no records of your family in Philadelphia."

"I'm not surprised. My family came from a modest background. My father owned a shop in Warminster, one of Philadelphia's neighboring towns—an overgrown village, really. My sister and I worked there after we left school. I married up, you might say."

"Up?"

"Into a better class of family, though we weren't so different. And we thought love was everything."

Fiona wanted to cut to the chase without alienating Abigail. How to put this tactfully?

"And then your husband passed away?"

Abigail was irritated now—Fiona was sure of it when she said, "Enough of your namby-pamby euphemisms. He died when he was young and I was in the family way." Her voice was rising in pitch—and was that a snort? One might almost say she sounded angry.

Still, this was an important clue. So, Abigail's first husband died young, and she was pregnant. That's what "in the family way" meant, wasn't it? A thought drifted through Fiona's mind—when her husband died, she had only two daughters.

"Abigail," she said slowly. "Do you mean to say that your husband died before your third daughter was born?"

"I do. Violet arrived some seven months later. It was a terrible year altogether."

So that explained it.

Fiona could have sworn she heard a sob and almost regretted the interrogation she'd embarked on. Maybe Abigail wasn't as tough as she looked.

Elaine piped up. "It must have been so difficult for you."

Abigail sniffed. "Difficult? It wasn't difficult—it was catastrophic."

Fiona could feel the sorrow in Abigail's words and said, "I'm so sorry. My sincere condolences."

The waspishness returned. "It's a little late for that, wouldn't you say?"

Fiona allowed a moment to pass to give Abigail time to compose herself. She was itching to ask the follow-up questions, but didn't want to spook her. So to speak. When she could stand the silence no longer, she spoke, her voice low so as not to frighten the woman in the portrait. "Abigail, did you say your first husband's name was George?"

"I don't remember saying so. But what of it?"

This did not sound promising.

"Just wondering. So...what was his last name?" Fiona held her breath.

"I don't see why you need to know that," Abigail went on. "He became a shadow in my story long ago."

This was more difficult than Fiona had anticipated. Waiting for Abigail to reveal the truth required more patience than she could muster. She searched for an acceptable reason for her question. "It's only that...it would help make the records complete." She had a sudden inspiration. "We're trying to find out more about your great-great-granddaughter's history."

"What? I have a great-great-granddaughter? Why did you not reveal this before?"

At last. A show of genuine interest.

Fiona hastened to explain. "Yes, indeed. Violet was her

grandmother. Acacia is a wonderful woman who helps us run the library."

Abigail's voice became animated. "Might I have seen her here?"

"It's quite possible. She's a little older than you are in your portrait. Wears exotic, red-framed spectacles."

"Oh, my goodness." Abigail was verging on elated now. "I have seen her, I'm sure of it. Now I come to think of it, she has something of the look of my husband, you know. He was handsome, if I do say so."

"Yes, he was. I mean—I'm sure he was." Fiona had to give it one more try. "And what was his last name?"

"Manchester. George Manchester. May his name be cursed."

CHAPTER 47
FIONA

This made no sense. Abigail had just said she was married to George Manchester. And she was cursing his name? His wife was called Rose, not Abigail Prewitt. Could she have married one of George's cousins? Did he have cousins called George? Fiona wasn't sure how to respond to this wholly unexpected turn of events. Every new piece of information raised more questions.

If Abigail's George was the same man, what on earth had happened to "the lovebirds"? If it was something unforgivable, how would she tell George his lovely wife didn't want to see him? It would break his heart all over again. And what about the girls? George had two daughters; Rose had three. She needed answers.

"Abigail," she said, cautiously. "Did you just say you were married to George Manchester? George Manchester of Manchester and Son in Philadelphia?"

"I was, for my sins."

So—the same man. "But I thought his wife was named Rose."

Fiona waited, hoping Abigail wouldn't ask how she knew that, but no reply came.

"Rose?" Fiona prompted.

"That's what he used to call me. I never allowed anyone else to. 'My darling Rose.'" She sighed. "My single name was Abigail Rosemary Prewitt. George never liked Abigail, so he called me Rose. He thought it was more romantic. And it was."

So that was it. Abigail—Rose—had gone back to her full maiden name after George died. No wonder the connection had been so hard to trace. But there was one other matter to sort out.

"You didn't seem to think so a minute ago. You seemed unhappy with him. Why should George's name be cursed?"

"Perhaps *cursed* is too strong a word, though I must admit my anger at his leaving has been buried for so long that it threatens to overwhelm me now I'm talking about him again. After all, this happened more than a century ago." She didn't seem inclined to expand further.

"Did he do something to upset you?" He must have, but maybe a little gentle probing would elicit the information she needed.

"I don't wish to talk about it. Mr. Wentworth never allowed me to mention his name, so this is the first time I've uttered it aloud since I left Philadelphia."

Perhaps a more neutral question would be easier to answer. "Can you tell me *anything* about him?"

Elaine, who'd been restraining herself until now, chipped in. "You said he was handsome? I'm sure he must have been. You were so beautiful and the two of you must have been a striking pair."

Fiona turned to Elaine, ready to tell her to be quiet, but the comment seemed to be the key that unlocked a more positive memory.

Abigail sighed wistfully and answered. "Oh, he was.

Everyone said so—including him."

Fiona stifled a laugh. That was her George, all right.

"He was only thirty-five when he died, you know, so his looks hadn't had time to fade. Seeing him lying there, in his coffin, not a mark on him, I could scarcely believe he had gone. As for his hair, I had them cut some of it off to be made into a brooch that I kept by me until the day I passed on too." She broke off to muse. "Ought I to say I've passed on if I'm still here?"

"As for passing on, it doesn't matter," Elaine said in a comforting way. "We understand what you mean."

"I'm sure you do. It won't be long before you, too—" Abigail broke off as if realizing this might not be tactful now Elaine could hear her. "In any case, yes, he was handsome with remarkably fine eyes. A girl could drown in them. And I was a girl—only twenty when I met him and fell in love."

Fiona needed to cut to the chase and ask Rose about her girls. "Tell us about your daughters," she said.

"They were beautiful girls if I do say so myself. I named them after flowers, you know. Well, of course you do. Their portraits are labeled, aren't they?"

"What prompted the flower names?" Elaine was going off topic again. Fiona would have to drag it back, but Abigail was already answering her.

"I always loved gardens. I planted a lovely one here. People often remarked on it. Is it still blooming?"

Fiona didn't have the heart to disillusion her and was glad Acacia had begun to replant it. "We're restoring it to the garden you once planted, and we're adding some new plants to represent you and your daughters."

She could almost hear the smile in Abigail's voice when the woman said, "That's wonderful. We named our first Lavender, hoping she'd have the traits of peace and tranquility that the flower represents. And did she? Not a bit of it. A more headstrong girl would be hard to find. But we loved her anyway."

"What about Primrose?" Elaine asked—she was fascinated, Fiona could tell.

"Ah, Primrose." Abigail gave a sentimental sigh. "Her name meant femininity, youth, and new beginnings. And it proved to be exactly the right one for her. A lovely girl."

Now for the big one. Fiona had one more vital question that needed answering. Who was Violet? Abigail must be persuaded to talk more about her third daughter. "And Violet?"

"Poor Violet." This was said with a hint of regret.

"Why poor?" Elaine was agog.

"Well, she was named for remembrance, of course. Modesty and humility, too."

Now they were getting somewhere. "In memory of someone special, you mean?" said Fiona.

"Of course. I told you, she was born seven months after George died. I didn't realize I was expecting, so he never knew about her. I hope he would have been pleased, even if his father wasn't."

"Oh, I think he'll be delighted." Fiona clamped a hand to her mouth, wishing the words unsaid. What had possessed her to say them aloud?

"What do you mean, *will* be?" Even Rose's painted face appeared confused.

Elaine took a step back, and Fiona could see something dawning in her eyes. "You mean…"

Fiona nodded, a finger to her lips. She'd have to be tactful. "I wanted to say he *would* have been delighted." A comforting idea suggested itself. "Perhaps he's aware of her, in the afterlife, you know." After all, why not?

Rose was skeptical. "Hmm. You may be right. But I've never met anyone here, including my girls. It is a trial to me."

"You gave the girls such enchanting names." Elaine couldn't resist. "So, you and George were happy while he lived?"

"Blissfully—except for one thing."

"Oh, no." Elaine was clearly disappointed at this fly in the romantic ointment.

"Every rose has its thorn—that's what George would say when we had a tiff. But the real problem was George's family and their attitude. As I told you, they never took to me, because my parents were 'trade' and therefore beneath their notice." She snorted. "It's not as though they were so fine, mind you. Only they traded on a bigger scale and made more money than we Prewitts did."

Fiona remembered the advertisement in the exhibition catalog. "Ah, yes. The wool and textile import company."

Apparently, this was a step too far. Abigail's voice took on a sharpness in stark contrast to her previous nostalgic note. "How do you know that? I never mentioned it."

Damn. She hadn't meant to let it slip. "The guide," Fiona said at last. "The one for the centennial exhibition. It mentions the Manchester family, so I thought it might be the same one."

"Odd you should remember that particular piece of information. Still, you are correct."

"It sounds like you had a difficult relationship with them," Elaine ventured. "Not all smooth sailing."

"No, indeed. If I hadn't loved George so much, I wouldn't have been able to stand it."

She had loved him. Did that mean she could be persuaded to be reunited with him?

Fiona had to phrase this tactfully and keep her fingers crossed for a positive response. "Do you ever wonder what it might be like to meet him again?"

"I have avoided thinking about him for years. I haven't come across him in this in-between realm yet, and I'm not expecting to now."

"Could it be because you're stuck in your portrait that you can't meet anyone?"

"And that's another thing. How do I come to be here? It certainly wasn't my idea. I expected to be somewhere in heaven, sitting on a cloud with a harp. But the universe is inexplicable, don't you think?"

Elaine, now practically quivering with excitement, said, "But if you could, would you like to see him again?"

"I might. But I doubt it will happen, now. It's been too long. What if we had nothing to say to each other?"

Fiona didn't want to leave it like this. "I'm sure you'd have a lot to talk about if—"

Rose interrupted. "There's no point in speculating, is there? So, I'm not going to. This conversation has tired me. I will bid you good night."

*

It was clear Elaine could hardly wait to talk over this new information. But Fiona shook her head at the suggestion that they should both return to her cottage.

"I don't want to discuss this at my house, in front of George, so come into my office. If anyone sees the lights on, they'll assume I'm working late," she said and opened the door.

Elaine made a beeline for her favorite chair. Before she'd even managed to sit, she began, "You see what this means?"

Fiona couldn't help but smile. Elaine's enthusiasm was infectious. "Yes, I do believe she is George's Rose. Strange how their portraits have ended up in such close proximity, but—"

Elaine interrupted her. "I know. We cannot understand these things—we can only witness them. But why didn't you tell her we know where he is? We have to reunite them. We simply must, Fiona."

If they were to bring two sundered hearts together, they needed to be very sure the reunion would be successful. A happy ending, in fact, like the last page of a romance novel.

So, planning would be paramount, and Fiona suspected Elaine hadn't thought this through.

"There are some things we have to consider," she said. "She's sixty-something in her portrait—he's only thirty-five. So, she'd be like an old woman to him."

Elaine bristled. "Not necessarily. Sixty-something isn't exactly ancient." She remained, as ever, an optimist.

"True," said Fiona, belatedly recognizing she might have been less than tactful. "Maybe they'd see each other as the young lovers they once were."

Elaine clapped her hands together, her eyes wide with anxiety. "Something's just occurred to me, Fiona. What if they meet and she's still mad at him?"

"That would be awful, of course, but the fact is, we can't do anything about it. But at least George will know we did what he wanted. We found her, but it will be up to him to make their reunion work."

Elaine pushed herself up from her seat. Her body exuded tiredness, but anticipation made her face look decades younger. "I can't wait to tell him."

Fiona hadn't banked on that. Perhaps a little advance warning for George would be in order. "I know. Let me sound him out to make sure he's still interested in meeting Rose, and then perhaps we can break the news together."

CHAPTER 48
FIONA

The whole revelation had gone better than Fiona could have expected, although, in the end, Elaine hadn't been there when she broke the news to George. Fiona, who'd planned only to ensure he was prepared to hear it, soon found herself telling him everything.

To start with, George had been impossible. Overexcited didn't begin to describe his reaction as he sat in one of his more dashing suits—the coffee-colored one with the lapels and pockets edged with navy-blue braid. All he needed was a straw hat, and he'd have been ready to go boating—although, this close to Thanksgiving, he'd freeze if he tried.

He leaped to his feet and began pacing the room. "What? Rose? My Rose? She's here? In Connecticut? She can't be. Can she? Really? You haven't made a mistake?"

"George, you must calm down." It felt good to say this to a man. If there was one thing Fiona hated, it was being told by some self-important misogynist to calm down when she was simply trying to get a point across.

He stopped in his tracks. "You're not sure, are you? This

is just some cosmic jest designed to raise my hopes—only to dash them. Fiona, this is cruel."

The man was *so* demanding. "Look, George. So far as I can tell, the woman who gave us her house as a library was Abigail Wentworth, nee Prewitt, widow of George Manchester."

The blood drained from George's face. Fiona waited, fingers crossed that his yearning for Rose would overcome his outrage at the thought of her with another man. He clasped his hands together and then released them. He resumed pacing the living room carpet, as if there were nowhere else for his energy to go.

"Why did she go by Abigail? And why Prewitt? And why here?"

"We had no way of knowing that she returned to her maiden name when you died, and your family was so mean to her."

"Yet she did. Disowned the Manchester name."

"That's true. But it wasn't because of you, it was because of your father's attitude. And she didn't want anyone else to call her Rose. You were the only one."

George harrumphed, but it seemed to Fiona that there might be a tear in his eye. She continued.

"Remember? We thought the reason we couldn't find her was that she might have remarried, which she did, to a man called Wentworth. A client of your father's firm, in fact. Your parents introduced them."

"Did you say Wentworth? The name sounds familiar. Was it..." He frowned, and then his face cleared. "Not Albert Wentworth, surely. He was at least fifteen years older than Rose."

"I'm afraid so. But at least you know it was only a marriage of convenience."

He snorted. "Now I see. It was doubtless a way to get her off their hands. Scandalous!"

Fiona watched him and said nothing. He would come to terms with the situation in his own time.

After taking a breath, he turned back to face Fiona, and the color returned to his cheeks. His face cleared and took on the expression of someone who suddenly sees salvation and can't quite credit it.

"You're certain she's still there? In the house?"

"She is, I believe. I haven't seen her, so I can't confirm this one hundred percent, but I have faith the woman I've spoken to is truly your wife." She refrained from telling him that Rose had distinctly ambivalent feelings about meeting him again. Best not to overload his circuits, as it were.

George began to walk again, occasionally running a hand through his hair before he stopped. "Wait, though. You told me this woman already had three children when she agreed to marry this buffoon. That can't be right."

"To begin with, Albert Wentworth wasn't a buffoon, George. He was a kind man who took pity on Rose, married her, and provided well for her and the three girls."

"Three. Exactly."

"That's right. Lavender, Primrose, and Violet."

He frowned. "Lavender and Primrose must be mine, I grant you. But Violet?"

Before he could speculate as to Violet's origins, and thankful she had positive news to give him, Fiona said, "She was born seven months after you died. Even Rose didn't know she was expecting, the last time she saw you."

George's furrowed brow smoothed out, and he took a little leap in the air, like some vaudeville dancer. "She's mine? Violet is mine?"

Fiona couldn't help smiling. It was wonderful to see him so elated. "That's not all. Violet's descendants are still living near here, and very active in running the library." Acacia would likely be thrilled as well to discover her great-grandfather's portrait had been found. As for Channing, she imagined he'd pour cold water over the whole idea. Best not to mention that to George, who was bubbling with enthusiasm.

"So, they're my descendants too? Well, I'm not at all surprised that my progeny should occupy such prominent places in the community. It's only fitting, after all."

And the old George was back, making it all about himself, as usual, exactly the way his great-great-grandson, Channing, did. He stood there, hands grasping his lapels like a small-town politician about to make a speech. He would never change, which made sense, of course. How could a person alter if they were no longer alive? Although he'd become more tolerant of today's peccadillos since he'd known her. Occasionally a little less self-absorbed.

Which reminded her.

"There is one thing, before we take this any further."

George returned his gaze to her. "Nothing bad, I hope."

"It depends on how you look at it—literally. Sit down, George, you're making me giddy moving around like that."

"I'm sorry." He perched on the edge of the armchair and leaned forward. "Well?"

"You were thirty-five when you died." He nodded. "But when Rose did, she was...much older."

"So, she lived a good, long life. I'm glad."

A lovely sentiment, but he'd missed the point. "Here's the thing. She might not look the way you remember her."

"Oh. I suppose not." For a moment, he looked downcast, but it didn't last. He sat up straighter. "Never mind. It's Rose I fell in love with, not her looks. She'll always be my beautiful bride inside, if not outwardly."

Fiona blinked away a tear that threatened to fall. Just when she least expected it, George turned out to be a prince. She only hoped he'd react the same way when he saw his love.

Now to tell Rose. If she didn't want to see George again... Fiona would have to talk her around—there was no other way.

*

Elaine sulked for several minutes after she discovered she hadn't been present when Fiona explained things to George.

"I thought we were going to do that together."

"We were, of course, but obviously, when he asked me, I had to tell him. The main thing, though, is that he agreed with us—Abigail is his Rose."

Elaine had to sit down as she took the information in. "Is this true? Can it be?"

"I think it must be. And so now we have to break the news to Rose."

Elaine beamed, her delight evident. "I can't wait. Let's do it this evening."

At six o'clock, they headed up to talk to Rose. Elaine's excitement was almost at fever pitch by now—which might not be a plus.

"Rose?" said Fiona as they reached the top stair.

Silence.

"Try her again," said Elaine in a stage whisper. "We can't lose touch with her now."

A sudden doubt assailed Fiona. "You and I are the only people who can talk to these two ghosts. What if we're both imagining it? Like a joint illusion?"

Elaine's penciled eyebrows practically reached her hairline. "How can you, Fiona? This is not the time to lose faith. We've come so far." The reproachful tone made Fiona squirm.

"But we have no real proof, do we? Don't you think that sometimes wanting something to be true can make it appear so?" Fiona said.

They startled as Rose's voice interrupted them, making her outrage clear. "A fine time to have doubts, I must say."

Oh, dear. They'd forgotten Rose could hear them.

"We're sorry, Rose," said Fiona, staring at Elaine and indicating the portrait with a tilt of the head.

"Fiona is sorry. I have nothing to apologize for. I never doubted for a second. Although it would be lovely to actually meet you—in the flesh." She hesitated. "You know what I mean, don't you?"

"I'd need a better reason to manifest than two inquisitive women like you."

"Like meeting another spirit—someone you know?"

"Unlikely in the extreme, I'd say. I'd have met them before now if that had been a possibility. I would like to see my girls again, though. I fully expected to, but they've never appeared here. Nor has anyone else."

This would require careful handling. The last thing Fiona wanted was for a reunion to go horribly wrong. George and Rose might not fall into each other's arms. What if they carried on with their painful unfinished fight? Would that doom them to be apart forever?

Elaine clearly had no qualms. "What if we could introduce you to someone special?"

"I can't imagine anyone important enough to tempt me out of my frame. It takes a lot of effort, you know," said Rose, unconsciously echoing George's comments on materializing. "I don't think I could manage to appear in front of real people."

George was now so adept at manifesting that he appeared as a matter of course. But it had taken quite some practice.

Fiona persevered. "Still, would you object if we tried to help you?"

"I suppose I can't stop you." Rose sounded as though she couldn't care less. "However, if I don't like them, I'm leaving—I'm certainly not going to bother making an appearance."

"We wouldn't dream of making you do anything you didn't want to."

"Very well. When would you like to attempt this introduction?"

Fiona considered the logistics. She'd have to lower George's expectations, for a start. In this seemingly indifferent frame of mind, Rose might be a horrible disappointment to him. Oh, well. He couldn't say she hadn't tried.

"Rose, may we get back to you with a solid plan? Then you'll know what to expect."

"I don't see what *I* have to say to it. You're going to, whether I like it or not."

She was as grumpy as George used to be, only *he'd* improved as soon as he knew he might see Rose again. Never mind. Nothing ventured, nothing gained.

"We think you'll be glad once you've met him."

Elaine added, "Yes, we're sure you will. Definitely. Not a doubt."

"I shall reserve judgment."

At least Rose hadn't said no.

CHAPTER 49
FIONA

When she ran into Andrew a week later, Fiona found him sitting in Platform 1, the town diner, sipping at a mug of coffee and reading the latest edition of the *Brentford Bee*, a stack of which lay on the counter for the benefit of patrons. The place was located in the now-obsolete station waiting room, and beyond the windows, the overgrown rails disappeared in both directions.

Someday, Channing had told her, they were going to turn the track into a trail for walkers and bikers. In the meantime, the diner did a brisk business, partly because they served breakfast from seven in the morning until closing.

And Fiona was starving. She'd been for a long run that morning and was ready for something substantial. She scanned the cozy café. Only a few seats remained vacant. But Andrew sat alone—taking up a whole booth, no less. He ought to be sharing. She would be performing a public service by offering to join him.

"Do you mind if I sit here?" she asked.

He raised his head and smiled at her. "Sure. I've just given my order, so if you know what you want, go ahead and tell the waitress."

Their orders arrived almost simultaneously, perhaps because he'd asked for the full and completely unhealthy breakfast, with two fried eggs, bacon, sausages, and hash browns almost spilling over the edge of the heavy white plate. A toasted blueberry muffin with extra butter rounded it out.

Fiona's more modest meal included scrambled eggs with smoked salmon and a couple of slices of wholewheat toast. Truth to tell, the sausages looked enticing, but she didn't have time to change her mind now.

While they ate, they discussed the latest local news and commented on the weather and their holiday plans. The clatter of plates and chatter of other diners created enough of a sound barrier around them that Fiona decided they wouldn't be overheard.

She waited until he'd taken his last piece of sausage before she said, "Andrew, I have something to ask you." She wasn't going to mention the blue-moon evening. Was she? "The other night, you told me you weren't very romantic, and since you're something of a physicist, I wondered if..." This was probably too strange for a breakfast conversation in public, but what the hell. "...if you believe in ghosts...or other psychic phenomena."

Andrew, who'd taken a sip of his coffee, almost choked as he set it down on the table with care. "Wow. I certainly wasn't expecting that question."

Fiona mopped up some of the spill with a paper napkin, concentrating on the table's surface. "I didn't mean to startle you. It's related to a situation I have going on in my life, and since we're friends, I thought I'd tell you. Clear the air, if you like."

"I didn't realize we needed to." The troubled expression on his face belied his words.

"It concerns you, in a way. You mentioned my preoccupation the other day, and you wondered whether I had a man in my life. It's to do with that."

"I see." He leaned back and put down his fork, as if his breakfast had caught fire without warning.

"Let me explain. My question about the supernatural is relevant. If you don't mind answering it, I'll know whether or not I need to explain anything."

He glanced at her before answering, perhaps to ensure she wasn't mocking him. "Well, that's a complicated issue. I don't believe there are other worlds like ours. The chances of that are billions, maybe trillions to one. But given that time and space might not be immutable, perhaps there's room for something else."

Fiona pondered his answer. If she told him the truth about George, he might think she was a fantasist. Or, worse, a liar. But she didn't want to have him believe she was acting strangely for no reason.

If she spent too much time considering this, she'd never decide. Best to get it out of the way.

"You know the day you heard me talking to someone in my living room, and figured I was on the phone with a man?"

He nodded.

"I was—in one sense." Now that the moment had come, her hands felt clammy. She needed to dive in. "There's a ghost living in the gatehouse, and I was talking to *him*."

She stole a glance at Andrew, checking his reaction.

A stunned silence on his part was followed by a peal of laughter. "You have to be kidding. That's literally unbelievable. But you really didn't need to invent an outrageous story to explain things."

Fiona tried to smile but couldn't manage it. She'd assumed he'd have misgivings about this. She hadn't predicted he'd laugh.

She turned away from him, not sure what to make of his response.

"No, wait. I'm sorry I laughed. I can see you believe it, so are you willing to tell me more about him? About everything?"

No going back now. "He's looking for his wife in the afterlife. He's named George Manchester and he's around a hundred and fifty years old."

She could tell Andrew was trying to keep a straight face. "And he's haunting the cottage?"

"Not exactly. I brought him with me from Philadelphia."

Andrew leaned back, his face wary and puzzled to equal degrees, so she went on.

"He's the man in the portrait in my living room. The one whose eyes follow you around."

Now she read complete skepticism in his face. "You can't mean..."

"I didn't believe he was real, to begin with, but over time, he and I became friends, and I said I'd help him find out more about his widow."

"This is incredible. Literally. You must be imagining it. Even if it were true, how could you possibly become friends?"

If he didn't believe her, there probably wasn't anything she could say to convince him, but she would give it one last shot. "The fact is, I can hear him when he speaks to me, and he hears me when I reply."

"Seriously?" Andrew was definitely trying to suppress a smile.

"I know it's hard to believe, and that's why I haven't told anyone, except Ms. Johanssen."

"Elaine? Why her?"

"She has a psychic gift too. Listen, I'd like you to believe me, even if you find it implausible. But if you can't—or won't—I guess there's nothing more to be said."

Although there was one more thing. Since it concerned the library, she might as well mention it.

"I should tell you this, too. I was researching George, and the library was looking for information about Mrs. Wentworth. What Elaine and I found convinced us there's a connection between them." She fell silent, trying to gauge his reaction. "We have to find a way to share the information without saying how we found it. That way we can include that part of Abigail's life in the centenary exhibit."

"I don't know what to say." He stared at her with concern, perhaps trying to gauge whether this could possibly be true. "Um...It does sound like a plot from a romance novel, don't you think?"

Fiona laughed. "Really? And what would you know about romance novels?" Granted, he might have some idea if his sister was Lucinda Parks.

The color in Andrew's cheeks was turning a dull red. She must have hit a nerve. Perhaps now she'd told him about George, he'd reciprocate with information about Cece. Maybe even confess he'd read some of her books.

"Doesn't everyone know the basics of those books?"

"Not men. Not usually. Especially when they've gone to the trouble of explaining that they're no good with romance. Unless, perhaps, they have a sister who writes them." She stared pointedly at him, waiting for a confession.

Andrew was gazing at the railway track outside the window. "I said I was no good at the practical side of romance. That doesn't mean I don't understand the theory."

Talking to him about this was like rearranging furniture in a dark room and hoping the new layout would prove more comfortable.

She'd give it one last try—and lay her cards on the table. "I get it. I noticed Cece's books—that's to say Lucinda Parks' novels—on your bookshelves. The complete set, I'd say. And everything I've learned about Lucinda simply makes her more of an enigma. So, Molly and I—"

"You and Molly have been discussing me?"

Well, yes, but not in connection with Cece's books."

"Of course not. This is about Lucinda Parks. We have to start promoting her visit for the centenary, and we can't find a photo of her anywhere. So, naturally, we began to wonder. And Cece makes perfect sense as the author."

"Let me stop you right there. I'm sure it's not her. She would have said. But she does enjoy the books, and I told her she could store some at my place." He glanced at Fiona as if to check how she was taking this. "So she has something to read when she comes to visit. And so does my daughter."

This reminded Fiona of Molly's passing comment about Andrew's daughter the other day. "You have a daughter? You never mentioned her."

"I thought I had. When you were telling me about Brian, and not having children. And I said children weren't all sunshine, or something like that."

"You did, but how could I deduce from that remark that you had a child yourself?"

Andrew gave a good imitation of a kitten trapped up a tree. "Well, the topic never came up, did it? Anyway, yes, I have a daughter, Ellie. She's at a difficult age, but I'm hoping she'll be around over the holidays. If she is, I'll introduce you." He breathed out heavily, like a criminal relieved he'd finally confessed to the crime.

She sought to reassure him. "I'm guessing you don't feel comfortable telling people about yourself, am I right? Perhaps you need more practice. Keeping secrets puts a barrier between people, I find. It's one reason I told you about George, even though I don't think you were convinced."

"I don't know what to believe."

Okay—that was up to him.

"If you prefer to think I'm imagining things, that's your choice."

She'd done what she could to clear the air, and her conscience was clear. In exchange, he'd given her Ellie. But he hadn't answered the question about Cece. Those barriers he put up must still be there. Or perhaps it wasn't his secret to tell.

"Well, this has been lovely." She rose and left, forgetting to pay for her share of the bill.

CHAPTER 50

GEORGE

I don't know whether I am on my head or my heels. Fiona tells me Rose does want to see me. Of course she does. I was confident she would. Fairly confident.

Fiona's exact words were "Rose has agreed to see you." I expected nothing less. She must long to be reconciled at last. Although "agreed" does not convey the enthusiasm I was hoping for, I am overjoyed. Shouldn't Rose at least be pleased?

Never mind that now.

I must look my best. What should I wear? Something that reminds my bride only of a time when we were happy. Perhaps my summer suit with the straw boater? No. Too frivolous. The smoking jacket suggests an intimacy I doubt she is ready for—at least not yet. She may be skittish, so I have to be circumspect.

So, it is my morning suit—Rose always told me I looked elegant in it. They didn't bury me in it, did they? I would hate to see her faint at the sight of me. Is she able to faint? Maybe not.

Do concentrate, man. This is going to be the biggest day

of your life. Not life, exactly. But the concept is correct. The greatest day of my afterlife, for sure.

"George, are you ready?"

It's Fiona. She's appeared in the doorway, in the dress she sometimes wears when she thinks she might meet Andrew. It brings out the stormy sea color of her eyes. She may think I don't notice these things, but I do.

"What do you think? Will she like it?" I pop out of the picture frame and turn about so she can check my attire. "Do I need a hat?"

"Of course she will, George. You're wearing timelessly classic clothing, though I think the hat might be a bit much—a bit too formal. And you look so handsome."

The last thing sounds like an afterthought, but never mind. So long as Rose agrees with her, that's all I desire. I asked Fiona to bring me a photograph of Rose's portrait, but for some reason, she hasn't. It matters not. Tonight is the night.

"George—I need you back in the painting. Otherwise you won't be going anywhere."

She reminds me of the nurse I had when I was a child. Always telling me to do things. Back then, I would deliberately disobey, but today I am full of the joys of spring, albeit we are coming up to Thanksgiving. I will have much to be thankful for if I am with my Rose again.

I return to my place and wait for Fiona to transport me to my destiny.

She picks me up and we leave the cottage. My heart is hammering in my chest. A strange feeling, since it must be formed of a memory, yet it is as real as though my heart were still beating. I believe we're inside another building now, and mounting a staircase, if I'm not mistaken. I hope I'll be the right way up again quickly. This buffeting is confusing me.

We must have arrived at the library. Fiona sets me down and tells me to hold my tongue unless asked directly, which

I always do, so I have no idea why she feels the necessity to mention it again. I sense my painting is leaning up against the banisters on a landing of some kind. Looking down the stairs, which swoop away from me to my right, I can tell I'm in a substantial mansion. And on my left...

I think I'm going to pass out.

There she is. My darling, my only, my precious Rose.

"Fiona! Look!"

"I know, George, but have a little patience. I need to ask her if she's ready to see you."

"Look at her beautiful hazel eyes, that soft and shiny chestnut hair, the lilac dress. She hasn't changed at all."

"Lilac dress?" Fiona scans the paintings on the landing. "Oh, no. George, wait."

I ignore this. Why should I prevaricate? "Rose, my lovely—"

Fiona interrupts. Has she learned no manners from her acquaintance with me? "That's not Rose."

"Of course it is. You never met her, so how would you know? Rose, my sweet—"

Fiona breaks in again. This is intolerable.

"It's...Violet. The daughter you never met."

She has silenced me at last.

CHAPTER 51
FIONA

George stared at Violet's painting, a dazed expression on his face.

Fiona had never considered this scenario.

What had made her imagine she could create a straightforward happily-ever-after ending for George and Rose? Seeing Violet's picture had knocked him sideways. It seemed she and Elaine had found the right people, but here they were, you might say, and neither Rose nor George was talking to the other. The whole endeavor was probably a mistake. No doubt Rose was wondering how he'd feel about meeting a much older version of her than he'd ever known.

Oh well. Here went nothing.

"Rose? Are you there, Rose? I have someone here I'm convinced you'll want to meet." That might be an exaggeration, but she'd let George handle it.

The silence dragged on. And on.

"George," Fiona hissed. "Why don't you ask Rose if she'd be willing to at least talk to you? I'm going to show her your portrait now. I'm sure she'll find you irresistible."

A quiet huff greeted this remark, but as she picked up the painting and turned it to face Rose, George gave a little gasp and finally spoke.

"Rose, my darling. With your picture before me now, I recognize you. You are unmistakable. Your outer appearance may have changed—a little," he added hastily. "But your eyes haven't—they're still that beautiful hazel color. You look so brave, so strong. I entreat you, won't you please at least greet me somehow? Despite the decades we've been apart, I love you still."

A heartbeat, and then, "George? Can it really be you?"

"It is I, dearest. Can you see me?" He materialized in his morning suit, looking as attractive as Fiona had ever seen him. Anxiety gave his face a humility she'd not noticed before. Rose wouldn't be able to resist him, surely.

"Oh, George." Rose's voice broke on a tiny sob. The minutes stretched by.

George glanced at Fiona as if asking what he should do. She nodded and pointed at Rose's picture until he said, "Rose?" He sounded more tentative now. "Sweetheart?"

And then she was stepping forward from her frame on the wall.

This would be the moment of truth. How would this meeting of May-December lovers go?

"My love, I'm so sorry. Sorry for everything. Please forgive me." George's face was suffused with contrition. He had never looked more endearing. This was the real George. The one behind the bluster and bombast.

Fiona watched Rose's stern visage crumple, and sighed when she saw a teardrop trickle down the widow's cheek.

She swiped the back of her hand across her own eyes. The tears she was trying to hold back must be impeding her vision. They both looked hazy.

As Fiona gazed at them, awestruck, Rose's skin smoothed

out, and her figure became more slender. Her hair darkened to a beautiful russet, and her neat hairstyle was softened by ringlets cascading from above her ears. A full-skirted white muslin dress embroidered with tiny rosebuds was on the verge of revealing an ankle—but not quite. No wonder George loved her.

Now the resemblance to Violet was uncanny, though perhaps their daughter's eyes had a touch of George about them. Well, it was no longer her affair. Rose would explain.

Yet, she still hadn't responded to his request for forgiveness.

George took a step forward, his hands reaching for Rose's. She spoke.

"I forgive *you*? How could I not? I need your pardon too. For trying so hard to forget you."

He stepped back. The ardent lover had been replaced by a man who was visibly struggling to rise above an insult. "What? You tried to forget me? How could you?"

Fiona felt the urge to intervene. She did not resist it. "Come now, George. You were gone. Poor Rose was left in dire straits and needed to make a new start."

"You stay out of this, madam," said Rose, turning to Fiona. "George and I will work this out—because we love each other." She smiled at George. "Soon he'll tell me every rose has its thorn—won't you, dearest? That's what you always said after a tiff."

The library almost felt warmer.

"Ah, you remember. I knew you hadn't forgotten me."

Any minute now, he would tell her she too was unforgettable.

But he didn't need to. Seeing Rose reach out to him, Fiona backed silently away. They should have time and privacy to mend their fences. She'd decide what to do with George's picture later.

She couldn't leave him on the landing. People would be bound to notice, and when they asked, she'd have no ready explanation. She would have to take him home until she'd broken the news to the Ancestry Club and Jane had found some evidence. After all, the only proof of their relationship was the couple's presence in front of her.

In the meantime, she would offer to carry messages between them. She could only imagine George's response to that, but it was the best she could do.

CHAPTER 52
GEORGE

I am elated, exhausted, and aggrieved because I have found my Rose at last, and she has found me too. Ecstatic, because we are reunited, and our love has endured. I feared it might not have, so my relief is inexpressible. Fatigued, because I was able to express the emotions I have had to bury for so long. I'm not sure why that should be tiring, but it has proved to be so. As for being irritated, I'm maddened by Fiona's decision to separate us again.

I can hardly bear to leave my sweetheart in the library, but Fiona has forced my hand, in her usual high-handed way. Rose's picture cannot be moved, and Fiona tells me mine may not reside there without comment from passersby. Does this mean we can only be together when *she* judges it expedient?

She carries me home, a most undignified procedure because I am the wrong way up again. Once we get there, and I have been righted and placed on the mantelpiece, I refuse to manifest. Frankly, in addition to my annoyance with her, manifesting is arduous work, and I am depleted of resources— for today at least.

Fiona seems oblivious to this and says something innocuous. "George, I'm thrilled your reunion went so well."

As am I. She has reunited me with Rose at last—that I cannot deny. "And why should it not?"

She hesitates. "You remember, I wondered about the age difference," she says, refusing to look me in the eye. Such poppycock.

"What age difference?" I cannot help but close my eyes to relive that moment. "She materialized exactly as I remembered her. A person is more than their portrait, you know. Her spirit hasn't changed one whit."

"I'm so pleased you feel that way. And I'm so glad Rose wanted to see you too."

What nonsense. "Ridiculous. Why would my love not want to be with me again? In fact, she wants us to be together every minute, as do I. What do you propose to do about that?"

"I know you want to be with Rose all the time, now that you've seen her again. But I couldn't let you stay there yet. People would notice your portrait leaning against the banister and would require an explanation."

"And?"

"I'm not prepared to explain your presence to other people right now, but I *am* working on a solution."

I consider this. The idea of being jostled by the locals is somewhat daunting, to be sure. It would not improve my frame of mind. Or, conceivably, my picture frame either. Oh, what a witty fellow I am.

"Very well."

"My proposal is that you should be in an honored place, next to Rose, to be the star attraction of our centenary exhibit."

This is more like it. I ought to be honored—as the head of a dynasty that stretches down to the present day—if nothing else. "I agree to your suggestion."

Fiona rolls her eyes for some unaccountable reason.

"Having you there will allow you to reside in the library permanently. But in the meantime, I can carry messages from you to Rose and vice versa."

"I reckon this method of staying in touch will have to do. I will dictate my missives to you, and you may bring me Rose's in return. It's not perfect, but I daresay we'll manage. How long do you think this might continue?"

Fiona tilts her head to one side, presumably considering. After a moment, she says, "I'm not sure, but not long, I hope. Once I've explained things to the Ancestry Club—or, rather, the reference librarian who's doing all the research—I should be able to take you back there, and place you somewhere near Rose."

At last. "And then we'll never be parted again."

I am composing my first love letter to Rose in my head as we end our conversation.

"I'll have a message ready for you in about an hour" are my parting words.

Come to think of it, I might handwrite a note—the way I did when I first tried to communicate with Fiona. I shall experiment and see.

CHAPTER 53
FIONA

Hanging George's painting next to Rose's would require concrete evidence that Abigail's first husband was George Manchester. As for explaining to Jane how Fiona came to have George's portrait...she would have to come up with something. Coincidence only went so far.

When Fiona walked into the Ancestry Club meeting a couple of days later, she took a second to register what she was seeing. This was unexpected. Among the other members sitting around the big table sat Andrew Mackenzie.

"Hello. What brings you here?" she asked without preamble.

Elaine had followed her in, determined to support her. "Yes. Why are you here?"

If he was surprised at Elaine's joining the conversation, he gave no sign of it. "I'm interested in the exhibition we're putting on for the centenary," he said, "and as a board member, I thought I'd check in to see how things were going."

As if. He was likely here to find out whether Fiona's suppositions were correct. No doubt he'd feel vindicated in his skepticism if Jane couldn't prove the relationship.

The librarian spoke up. "Thank you, Andrew. It's kind of you to take an interest. And now let's settle down, everyone. Fiona, I believe you have an announcement to make."

Fiona had given the matter a great deal of thought. She'd warned Jane that she and Elaine would be able to reveal newly discovered information that would materially influence the direction the research was currently taking—that was to say, rotating in circles. It ought to provide a forward path.

After thanking Jane, Fiona began. "I've been doing some work on my own account. That's to say, I've been tracing the family of a man whose portrait hangs in my cottage."

Murmurs of curiosity and surprise came from the club members, but they settled down as Fiona continued.

"I simply used him for practice, never expecting to find out anything relevant to the library."

Elaine interrupted. "Tell them where he came from." Without a pause, she added, "Philadelphia."

The response from the group was a little less interested this time, so Fiona hastened to clarify.

"That's right, and as some of you know, that's where I worked before I came here. I used to live in a converted warehouse once owned by his family, so I was always curious about him."

Jane was frowning, as though considering whether to dismiss the information as a distracting waste of time. But evidently, her interest had been piqued. "So, did you discover something useful?"

This was the point at which Fiona would have to prevaricate. Okay, lie. She certainly couldn't say that she and Elaine had been talking to George and Rose.

She took a breath and let it out with a whoosh. "It was hard to find evidence, because, of course," she said, glancing at Jane, "I'm not as experienced as you. But I believe he married a certain Abigail Prewitt."

Jane radiated skepticism, but the avid silence from the group indicated they were intrigued, either by the news or this battle of wills. "And what is that assumption based on?"

"It's just a hunch. Because George, *my* George, died about three years before Abigail moved here."

"Who?"

"Sorry, did I not say? The man in my painting. His name is George Manchester, and I found an advertisement for his family business in the Philadelphia Centennial Exhibition guide that appeared on the library staircase."

"You talk about him as if he were still alive." Jane smirked at the club members, but they remained silent—unresponsive to her witticism.

"Just a slip of the tongue," said Fiona, and glanced at Andrew, whose eyes widened as he listened to this. Best to concentrate on Jane and work on persuading her to help. "Let's suppose she was married to him. Could you try and trace Abigail's history backward? If we could find their marriage certificate, it ought to prove it."

Jane was giving off the air of a woman who has heard one ridiculous lie too many. Before she could say so, Fiona continued.

"Elaine can tell you. Can't you? She has a psychic gift, as you know." At this point Fiona stared fiercely at Jane, daring her to contradict her. "She has a definite feeling about this, right, Elaine?"

Taken aback by this unexpected option to contribute to the discussion, Elaine rallied. "I do. You may think I'm a muddled old lady"—she stood a little straighter, her mascaraed eyes scanning the room—"but I know what I know. There's a relationship between George Manchester and Abigail Wentworth. We have to prove it, or we won't have any information about Abigail's life before she came here, which means we can't help Acacia find her antecedents."

"Which," said Acacia with a steely look in her eyes, "will be very disappointing. And the exhibition will be a failure."

This aspect of the situation had evidently not occurred to Jane. Her forehead furrowed. "If your guess turns out to be correct, you make a good point," she said to Fiona, her tone reluctant.

"Exactly. I'm thrilled to hear this wonderful news, Elaine," Acacia said, having turned toward her. "Thank you. Assuming you're right, you've given me a real chance of finding out who my ancestors were." She scanned the other members of the club. "Until today, all I knew was that my grandmother Violet was Abigail's daughter. Now I may be able to trace my family even further back. I know Channing and my granddaughters will be excited too."

The faces around her reflected their elation at this major discovery. No one expressed any doubt, though Jane urged caution. "Of course, we can't make any assumptions. We must find the documentation to prove it." Then she seemed to relent. "I'll get onto it right away. It will be such a coup for the library if we can fill in these gaps."

Even Andrew nodded at this. Fiona caught him doing it, and relief flooded her. He believed her, at last. Or at least he didn't discount her relationship with George completely.

*

It took Jane a couple of days of solid work to track down the evidence she needed. She waved a printout of the marriage certificate as she leaned across Fiona's desk. "I'm hoping to get a facsimile of the original record to add to the exhibits."

"That's fantastic, Jane—well done. Only you could have managed it." For once, Fiona felt she was speaking the truth, rather than saying something to pacify an indignant employee.

Jane blushed. "It wasn't only me. I had to call an expert I

know—a friend who understands the more obscure methods of researching ancestry."

This was quite an admission coming from her—admitting somebody might be more experienced than she was. So long as her work brought results, though, Fiona didn't care.

"Knowing a person like that is almost as valuable as knowing it yourself. The important thing is, we can go ahead with that part of the exhibit."

And now she'd be able to return George to Rose. She felt a pang at the thought of losing him. He'd become a friend, someone she could talk to. Someone who exasperated her and made her laugh. Perhaps she'd still have the connection that would allow her to contact him via his portrait, no matter where it ended up.

"So, you'll let us have your painting to include with the other artifacts?"

Fiona took a breath. She knew what this would mean to George. "Of course. Under one condition."

"What's that?" Jane bristled.

"He has to be next to his wife and daughters. I want them to be reunited at last."

Jane's puzzlement was obvious. "Well, okay. But what do we do with Albert?"

Good point. "Well. His portrait never hung near Rose's, because he wasn't the benefactor, even though his money allowed Rose to do what she did. Also, I think she and George deserve to be together again."

Without actually saying so, Jane conveyed her disapproval of this blatant sentimentality.

Fiona needed a reason that would appeal to Jane's sense of propriety. "Besides, I know Acacia and Channing would want their great-grandparents hanging on the same wall."

"Hanging out, I suppose you mean."

Had Jane just made a joke? Fiona laughed, and the answering wry smile from Jane told her she was right.

"That's exactly what I mean."

CHAPTER 54
FIONA

Fiona invited Jane to her cottage to view George's portrait for herself.

"I suppose I ought to check him out," she said. Not exactly gracious, and her accompanying expression was skeptical. But her next comment made Fiona think she was changing her mind. "I'll bring photos of his daughters with me."

Fiona couldn't quite understand why that was necessary, but Jane's ways were mysterious. "Do whatever you think might help."

*

Standing in front of George's picture, Jane glanced between it and the photo she held.

"You know," she said finally, "I think I detect a resemblance between him and his girls, Violet in particular."

"I suppose that's something, at any rate," George commented in Fiona's head. "Though Violet is much more like Rose than me."

She tried to ignore it. "I'm so glad. I was sure they were related and knew I could rely on you to prove it."

Jane smiled, a rare occurrence, and one that changed her appearance completely. "I'm going to work on the project over Thanksgiving so that the exhibit is ready to go by the end of the year. We can launch it to the public in January."

Fiona felt a moment of sympathy for this woman who had time over the holiday to ensure the centenary would be a success. Most people would be with family, but Jane was devoted to the library. "That's wonderful, Jane, and I appreciate everything you're doing to complete this. Let's settle on a date, and I'll have people start to plan the opening reception."

Once she was certain the project was in safe hands, Fiona traveled back to Philadelphia to see her mother, leaving George fuming at being left behind. His longing to be with Rose again seemed to make him irrational.

"Why do you need to travel back there for this new-fangled holiday? It's hardly worth it, is it?"

"George, Thanksgiving is a family holiday nowadays—a chance for everyone to be together. I must visit my mother and some of my cousins. I wouldn't dream of ignoring them."

He snorted. "Huh. I suppose you're going back for the goose with oyster stuffing. And the mince pie. I always found that too sweet, myself."

A moue of distaste crossed her lips. "If that's what you ate back then, I feel kind of sorry for you. These days, it's turkey and pumpkin pie here in New England. But that's neither here nor there. I'm going. I'll be back on Saturday, so you'll only be alone for three nights. You'll be fine."

His silence prompted her to add, "Don't forget, Jane Kennedy is working on preparing the exhibit about you and your descendants. You'll be with Rose at last. And you'll be a sensation."

"Very well. But don't leave me here by myself for too long."

*

Driving back from the Philadelphia suburbs, Fiona considered the holiday season ahead and wondered whether Andrew meant it when he said he'd introduce her to his daughter. That would be a milestone in their relationship—as friends, of course.

Library functions didn't offer much scope for getting together, since Andrew tended to be reclusive, if anything. It was amazing he was a board member, when she came to think of it. He was obviously interested in the Wentworth, but one wouldn't have known it from his input—or lack thereof—in meetings.

Perhaps she should try to organize a dinner for Andrew and Cece, and Molly and Nick again. Something festive.

When she rang Molly, her friend apologized.

"I'm so sorry, we can't make it. It's my busy season. And as for Nick—he's Bob Cratchit."

"Sorry?" said Fiona, not sure she'd heard right.

"In *A Christmas Carol.* It's in three weeks' time. You must have noticed. The Brentford Players do it at this time every year in the Wentworth ballroom. We're fortunate the room is back in decent shape after the storm damage."

"I remember now." Of course, even though she'd been preoccupied with George and Rose, she knew about it. How could she forget when the various unusual noises she'd been hearing kept reminding her? A week before, the sound of voices declaiming and songs being rehearsed made a mockery of the usual quiet ambiance.

"I can understand why they have Nick playing Bob Cratchit," she said. "He's perfect." Tall and lean, with those horn-rimmed glasses, he would embody Scrooge's clerk to perfection. Whether he had any acting talent was a matter of conjecture.

Molly laughed. "I think so. The performance is a bit of a dog's dinner, really, but everyone enjoys it. Most are only too happy to get a free chance to listen to the familiar show tunes."

That made sense. Fiona began to feel some excitement at being part of this community in her library.

"So, how long is the run, again?"

"It's the two Fridays, Saturdays, and Sundays before Christmas, and tickets sell out fast. I've bought mine, and a couple for my dad, Tom Beresford, and his soon-to-be bride."

To guarantee the conservatory would be fully restored, Tom and Bonnie had settled on Valentine's Day as their wedding date. Everyone applauded this decision. The venue would be ready, and it was the most romantic day of the year. Plus, it would come three weeks after the opening night of the exhibition and Lucinda Parks' visit, so nothing would distract from the wedding.

"The play sounds like fun. I'll check out the ticket availability. With any luck, they'll manage to find me a seat."

"I imagine they've saved you one already. By the way, I think Andrew's coming, with his daughter."

Fiona wished they were on a video call so she could see Molly's face—then she'd know if this was just a casual observation or whether she was to interpret it as something more meaningful.

Andrew had said he'd introduce them if the chance presented itself. Fiona wasn't at all certain she wanted to meet someone at "a difficult age." Oh, well. Never mind that now.

She kept her reply neutral. "I'm sure they'll enjoy it."

*

Bill Hawley was playing Scrooge this year. Sticking her head into the ballroom to take a peek at the dress rehearsal, Fiona recognized his high cheekbones and twinkling eyes. In truth, he resembled Santa Claus rather than Scrooge, but she wasn't going to argue. Neither, apparently, was Acacia, who was standing in the wings, nodding at him encouragingly.

Fiona noticed Elaine adjusting some of the costumes, giving them a little tweak here and helping with a hard-to-reach zipper there. The woman was full of surprises.

It dawned on Fiona that now she was part of the Brentford community, even if she were offered a position elsewhere, she wouldn't accept it, no matter how lucrative the deal was.

The day of the performance arrived. Ticket sales had been brisk, and the ballroom was filled to capacity. Having stood before the audience to thank them for coming and for their contribution to the life of the Wentworth, Fiona relaxed in her front-row seat. Further along the row, she spotted Andrew, looking uncomfortable in this conspicuous position.

Next to him sat a blond woman staring into a phone, her head bent, her long hair obscuring her face, making it hard to guess at her age. As if sensing someone's gaze on her, she glanced up and straight at Fiona. She would have been attractive had it not been for the sulky pout of her bright red lips. She clearly didn't want to be there.

Fiona had the impression, as the girl shook her head, that she looked a lot like Cece, Andrew's sister. Oh. She must be—his daughter. Not wishing to be caught staring, Fiona turned her head away.

The five-piece band from the high school struck up a somewhat wonky overture, the house lights went down, and she fixed her gaze on the stage. The play was performed by enthusiastic amateurs, and Fiona found the spirit of the audience catching as they clapped and cheered at every opportunity. She even had to fight back a tear or two as Tiny Tim blessed everyone. And when Scrooge woke up on Christmas morning and realized he was still alive, with time to change his ways and live a better life, she blew her nose very hard.

*

At the cocoa and cookie party afterward, Fiona wondered when she'd be able to escape the friendly inquiries from the people present. They wanted to know about the progress of the repairs, the upcoming celebrations, and the Lucinda Parks event, all of which she'd covered in her speech already. She wished they'd provided stronger drinks for people and not just hot chocolate, but since so many children would be in the audience, and people would be driving home, they'd decided not to.

She could have used a drink in her hand now, as she registered Andrew walking toward her. The sullen blond girl trailed behind him.

"Ellie, I'd like you to meet Ms. Gordon, our executive director. She's responsible for all the great things going on here these days."

Fiona's eyebrows shot up. Andrew had never commented on her work, and she colored at the unexpected praise.

"Fiona, this is my daughter, Eleanor—Ellie, say hello."

"Hello." This was more of a grumble than a greeting, but Fiona remembered her own teenage years and allowed the girl some leeway.

Back then, taller than her high-school classmates, and with a troublesome complexion, Fiona hadn't thought of herself as pretty. It was only at college, when the freshman fifteen had given her a few curves and her skin had taken on a rosy glow, that it occurred to her she might be moderately attractive. Still too tall, though. She wore heels anyway.

"It's nice to meet you. Are you here over the vacation?" She was finding it difficult to judge the girl's age. Was she in high school? University?

Ellie refused to look her in the eye, her gaze instead straying around the ballroom, like a drowning woman searching for a lifebelt in a stormy sea. "I'm at my father's this weekend. I take it in turns."

Fiona didn't need to hear more to understand that this child was likely still in high school, and therefore her parents shared her. It was hard on a teenager, as she remembered from her own childhood. She wondered whether Andrew was anything like Fiona's father, who always bought her something when he came to visit, instead of paying attention to her.

"Well, I expect he's delighted you're here." Though, to be frank, she'd find it difficult to be thrilled if her weekend companion was as surly as this one. She glanced at Andrew as she spoke, and thought she read defeat on his face.

"Can we go now, Dad?" Ellie was making no effort to converse.

"Sure, honey." Andrew gave Fiona an apologetic tilt of the head. "Good to see you, Fiona. Merry Christmas."

He turned to leave, giving Ellie a chance to say something. As if Ellie had read her mind, she leaned into Fiona and hissed, "You need to back off following my dad around. He's got enough female fans already, so if I were you, I wouldn't bother trying to catch him."

Female fans? What did that mean? Fiona, too stunned to reply, plastered a fake smile on her face as she watched the girl follow her father out. Did he have any idea what his daughter was saying about him?

CHAPTER 55
FIONA

Looking into her fridge the following morning, Fiona found nothing to satisfy the particular hunger she was feeling. What she really craved was an almond croissant, with lots of butter on it. The roads were dry, so she would go for a run to work off the calories in advance—and make sure her return route took her past Barb's Bakery, where she could buy one if she still wanted to.

Pleased with her plan, she stepped out into a misty morning and began her run. She checked the surface as her feet pounded the road, looking for ice that might cause a fall. Chilly to begin with, she felt the blood coursing through her veins as she warmed up, her mind mulling over the encounter the previous evening.

Last night, her shock at being accused of chasing Andrew had made her angry. She ought to have been able to brush the comment off, but somehow, Ellie had touched a nerve. She and Andrew were friends. If she'd considered anything more, she certainly had no desire to be more than that now—particularly if it involved dealing with a hostile teenager.

He was interesting, of course, and solicitous. He'd guided her home when she'd lost her way in the woods. That seemed like an age ago. He'd come to check on her after the storm. He'd helped connect the library with Lucinda Parks. He appeared to have forgiven her for Brian's punching him. And Newton was a sweetheart of a dog.

But the memory of her marriage still made it hard for her to have confidence in her judgment in matters of the heart. Or to open up to a man who hadn't believed her when it came to George. Lack of trust was a serious obstacle. It wasn't as though he didn't have secrets of his own. His daughter, for instance. He'd only introduced them when there was no avoiding it.

She slowed her pace to a walk as she spotted the shop sign for the bakery hanging out over the street, the painting of a loaf and a cupcake enticing buyers to enter. Swinging the bright pink door open, she stepped inside, where the cheerful hubbub of a Sunday morning clientele greeted her.

People stood in line, waiting for the freshly baked rolls and donuts whose fragrance hung in the air. Fiona inhaled deeply. She'd earned this croissant. As she waited, she did a few surreptitious calf stretches. Behind the counter, Barb was busy ringing up the customers, while her young assistants filled paper bags with goodies.

Fiona succumbed to two croissants, telling herself she'd eat the second one tomorrow. As she turned to go, clutching them in her hand, she almost ran into someone entering the shop. Ellie Mackenzie.

Fiona stopped dead. She could either ignore her or take the high road and try to connect somehow.

"Good morning," she said, deciding to act as if nothing had happened at the play. "Here to find some breakfast?"

Ellie looked surprised to be addressed in this innocuous fashion. "Hello. Yeah. Dad's gone off for his stupid walk with

Newton, so I thought I'd buy something."

Not sure what made her say it, Fiona said, "I've got a couple of croissants here. They're still warm. Want one?" She opened the bag and held it somewhere near Ellie's nose.

The girl hesitated and then sniffed. "Okay," she said as if she grudged even this single word.

"We could sit on one of the benches on the Common, if you like. It's getting warmer now the sun's out."

She shrugged. "I suppose so."

This was going to be a one-sided conversation, Fiona could tell. Served her right for beginning it. Why had she done so, anyway? She regarded Ellie, who, lacking her father's height, was almost jogging to keep up with Fiona's long stride. They sat on the bench, and Fiona held out the bag, waiting for the girl to help herself.

"You're right about me liking your dad," she began. "But not in the way you think."

Ellie took a huge bite of the still slightly warm croissant and then looked at her.

"He's on the board of the library, you know. And he's been very supportive in helping me get things done. And we're neighbors."

"Oh, sure." Apparently, Ellie wasn't convinced, because there was that cynicism again.

Fiona suddenly had a flashback to the conversations she'd had with her mother about her mother's suitors. As a teenager, there'd been several of them, and none had lasted. At the time, she thought that was because her mother had managed to scare them off. Now she wondered whether her mother had abandoned them because her daughter wasn't happy.

"I understand what it's like to grow up with a single parent. I never got enough attention, because my mother was preoccupied with finding a man to marry."

Ellie stared out across the Common. "What about your dad?"

Her dad. More of a father than a dad. And not an active one, at that. She would see him some weekends, but often it was just for lunch, or some other activity that took a bit of time but wasn't necessarily interesting.

"Well, unlike your father, mine wasn't much of a presence in my life," Fiona said. "I don't know whether it was his or my mother's fault. He disappeared one day when I was little, and it was a while before I saw him again."

"That must have been upsetting for you."

So, Ellie was capable of empathy. That, at least, was a positive sign.

"It was sad. How about you? Is it hard for you to deal with?"

"Not exactly. But perhaps it would be easier if I'd had siblings, someone for company. I don't know."

"Don't you like hanging out with your father?"

A little breeze had sprung up, and Ellie pulled her oversized scarf tighter around her neck. "It's okay, I guess. But it's boring."

"How do you mean?"

Ellie's answer sounded almost rehearsed, as if she'd said or thought it many times before. "We never do anything interesting. We go for walks on the beach, or maybe to a museum if it's raining. Or like the stupid Christmas show last night."

"What do you talk about?"

"Talk?" She thought for a minute. "Well, he always wants to know how I'm doing at school. Of course. Especially with math."

Fiona swallowed the bite of croissant she'd taken. "Well, that's his special subject, so I suppose it's not surprising. Does he ever help you with your homework?"

It was Ellie's turn to look surprised. "No, why would he? I hate math, in any case. I'm no good at it."

Fiona said nothing to this. Father and daughter clearly had different interests.

Ellie snorted. "And you must have noticed he's not very good at conversation. He's a teacher, so I guess he doesn't have to listen that much."

She wondered whether Andrew realized this was how his daughter felt. She had the sense that a relationship with Ellie was important to him. And this girl needed someone to hear her, perhaps precisely because she was at a "difficult age."

"So, what is it you'd rather he did differently?"

A look at Ellie's face told her she'd hit a nerve. Maybe if she confided in her, the girl would find it helpful. "I wanted my dad to myself when I got to see him, but there was always some woman around. At least for the first few years." Honesty forced her to tell the truth. "He married one eventually."

"So, you had a wicked stepmother?"

Fiona laughed. "I thought so at first. But I got used to her, and she turned out to be nice. They live in Florida now, so we're not close, but we're in touch sometimes." Not enough, though. She made a silent resolution to call more often. Her father was pushing eighty, and one never knew.

Ellie was scowling now. "Well, I don't want a replacement mother."

Fiona, briefly picturing herself in charge of a recalcitrant teenager like Ellie, agreed. "I get that. I had a stepfather, too, kind of. In fact, several of them. My mother is one of those people who thinks she can't manage without a man."

Ellie's eyebrows rose. "That's stupid."

"Well, it's definitely an old-fashioned way of looking at the world. When she was young, all women wanted was to be married and have children. The feminist movement passed her by completely."

"Do you have kids?"

Something tugged at Fiona's chest. "No. I never had the chance. It just didn't happen for me," she said, trying to forestall the next question.

Ellie was silent for a moment. "So, you did have a husband?"

Fiona's momentary regrets vanished. "I'm divorced, and I prefer it this way. Men do complicate one's life." At least, Brian and Andrew certainly did. So did George, come to that.

"You like living by yourself?" Ellie had relaxed, seemingly relieved to hear that Fiona wasn't interested in settling down with her father.

The conversation meandered after that, with Fiona listening more than talking. A teenager's concerns weren't so different today than they were when she was young, and she found herself reliving some aspects of her younger years. As they strolled back in the direction of Fiona's house, it was as though the floodgates of Ellie's life had opened, and she was soon sharing about her mother, her father, her boyfriend, and her best friend.

All Fiona needed to do was listen.

CHAPTER 56

FIONA

The exhibit was ready at last. Jane had done an amazing job, and the ballroom walls were covered with the family documents, all the photos Acacia had managed to find, and a couple of letters from Rose to her daughters that had surfaced too. A modern photo of George and Rose's home on Spring Street hung next to a map of Philadelphia in 1860.

In a glass display case against one wall, *The Official Guide to the Great Philadelphia Centennial Exhibition of 1876* lay open to the page with the advertisement for Sebastian Manchester and Son. Other antique photographs of the exhibition, magazines showing the kind of clothes that might have been produced with the imported wool and silk fabrics, and additional background information rounded out the offerings.

The family portraits took pride of place, of course. George's picture hung to the left of Rose's. Violet's, Lavender's, and Primrose's were grouped alongside them. Surveying them now, Fiona almost believed that Rose looked younger and less severe, the faintest uptilt to her lips softening her face and minimizing the discrepancy in their ages. George appeared a little more mature, and the laughter lines around his eyes gave the impression he was smiling too.

*

The exhibition marking the beginning of the centenary year was scheduled to open just after New Year's with the hope that bad weather wouldn't discourage people from attending. Bill Hawley had run two articles about it already, without any direct prompting from the library, though Fiona suspected Acacia had persuaded him to do so. One of them was an interview with the Manchester descendant about her ancestors. With a view to encouraging people to attend, Acacia talked up the thrilling revelations to be made at the opening.

It seemed to have worked. Almost two hundred people were registered to come, so they'd organized a video feed into the reading room to handle the overflow. Joanie had arranged hors d'oeuvres and drinks to accompany the celebration. At the last minute, Channing had donated two cases of prosecco, perhaps feeling his family deserved to be celebrated in style— though not in champagne style.

Acacia opened the exhibit, and Channing stood beside her, allowing her the spotlight.

"We're so grateful for the incredible good fortune that our director, Fiona Gordon, came to Brentford with a portrait of my great-grandfather." She scanned the room and her eyes fell on Elaine. She was hard to miss in her trademark mini and flowered tights. "And to Elaine Johanssen, whose instincts about Abigail and her history proved to be correct. We're not quite sure how she figured it out, but she did. Thank you, Elaine."

The old lady blushed, and a faint voice in Fiona's head murmured, "The elf has come into her own, I see."

"Shh," said Fiona, eliciting surprised glances from some of

the silent patrons around her. "Sorry," she said.

Members of the Ancestry Club gazed intently at the portraits, and Acacia pointed out the trace resemblance of George in his daughters. When Fiona glanced back at his portrait, she was convinced she could sense his satisfaction.

The rest of the evening passed without a hitch, and toward the end, Fiona reminded those present that Lucinda Parks would be visiting the Wentworth in two weeks' time to launch her new novel and sign copies. Registrations to meet the famous author exceeded anything the library had ever seen, and the event already promised to be a huge success.

*

Lucinda Parks' books arrived the day after the exhibit opening, and the final details were being firmed up. Molly would sell the novels, while Lucinda sat and signed them. They'd hired a car service to bring Lucinda from New York.

Fiona and Molly could barely conceal their excitement as the black limo pulled up under the porte-cochère an hour ahead of time. Some members of the board were already assembled, keen to have a chance to meet the bestselling author before the celebration began. Among them was Andrew, which only made Fiona more positive that Lucinda would turn out to be Cece.

The two women hurried outside to greet her, almost certain they knew who would emerge from the car.

"I told you so," whispered Molly, as the chauffeur ran around to open the back door and an elegant woman with long blond tresses stepped out. Despite the change in hair color, there was no mistaking her.

"*I* was the one who figured it out," said Fiona out of the side of her mouth, but there was no time to resolve the issue.

"Hello, Cece. Or should I refer to you as Lucinda?" she said.

Cece blushed. "Just for today." She took a breath. "Before

we go in, I want to apologize. I ought to have told you who Lucinda really was."

Fiona and Molly eyed each other. "We guessed it was you. You can't keep a secret around here, right, Fiona?"

Cece glanced at her brother, who'd followed Fiona and Molly out to the driveway. Fiona wondered whether she suspected Andrew of spilling the beans.

"It wasn't him," she said, to clarify. "Molly and I worked it out ourselves. And we understand why you'd want privacy. Your fans are many and very determined. Don't worry, we'll keep them in check," she added, seeing a flash of concern on Cece's face.

"Okay. On we go."

*

An hour later, Andrew stood at the back of the fully restored ballroom, watching as his sister gave a talk about her book and answered questions. Afterward, lines of fans queued up to get their books signed.

Fiona joined him. "I guessed it was Cece all along," she said, her expression smug. "But I think, as a friend, you might have told me. Friends don't keep secrets like that from each other."

Andrew looked away. "The publishers didn't want anyone to know—I've no idea why. So, I wasn't free to say anything." He turned to her again. "Sorry."

There was no time to pursue the topic before it was time to leave for dinner.

The event had continued long past its scheduled time, and the group heading over to the Black Horse arrived almost an hour after their reservation. The maître d' didn't seem at all perturbed. "When I heard about the lines at the library, I figured you'd be late, so I kept your table. And then Ms. Kennedy called to confirm my suspicions."

Fiona felt a twinge of guilt that she hadn't invited Jane. The woman was always on top of everything requiring organization. She'd make it up to her somehow.

Champagne was the order of the day, and the inn concocted a special cocktail they named "Romance Rush," with a champagne base, cranberry juice with other flavors, and a sprig of rosemary garnish in honor of Abigail's middle name. They toasted Cece, the library, and themselves for the work they'd put in to make it all happen.

"I have one more toast," said Channing, to Fiona's surprise. "To George Manchester and his wife, Mrs. Abigail Rose Wentworth. But for them, I wouldn't be here."

He appeared to have embraced the idea of his ancestors, after his initial reluctance. How typical of Channing. He could make anything about him, the way his great-grandfather did. Though perhaps he was right, in a way. None of them would have been there without George, because then Rose wouldn't have had three daughters, she wouldn't have married Albert Wentworth, and the library wouldn't exist.

The butternut and sage soup was followed by braised short ribs in red wine, served with a wild rice pilaf and honey-roasted vegetables. The spiced pear and almond tart was only surpassed by the maple bread pudding with ginger ice cream.

Surfeited by their dinner, they rose reluctantly to leave. Fiona was glad she'd gotten a ride to the restaurant with Molly, because now she felt like some fresh air and decided to walk home. She emerged from the front door, where she stood in the shadows, waiting for the others. She could hear a woman's voice—Cece's, she thought—saying, "I can't keep doing this, Andrew. It's one thing with strangers, but these people are my friends, and yours. It's just not right."

CHAPTER 57
FIONA

What could Cece mean? Remembering the dinner conversation, Fiona had sensed a certain tension between Andrew and his sister. It wasn't anything spoken aloud, only a slight rigidity to Cece's shoulders, and—come to think of it—the way she'd avoided looking at her brother.

Now, Andrew's low murmur answered her, but Fiona couldn't make out the words.

Cece spoke again. "It's not just that. The questions are getting harder, and I feel like I'm making mistakes. It's only a matter of time before I mess something up."

She shouldn't have been eavesdropping. Fiona moved out of range, and when, a second later, Channing and Acacia walked out of the restaurant, she said good night more loudly than she needed to. Perhaps Andrew and Cece would realize they could be overheard.

Fiona found herself preoccupied as she set out for home. What did Cece mean when she talked about messing things up? Was this about her authorship of the books, or some unrelated family matter that had nothing to do with it?

She mused on this as she kept an eye on the road, grateful for the full moon illuminating the surface through the bare winter branches of the trees. She could come up with nothing that satisfactorily explained the conversation. It wasn't any of her business, of course, but an inexplicable sense of having been misled—perhaps intentionally by Cece, Andrew, or both—accompanied her until she reached her house.

And George wasn't there to talk it over with. Truth be told, she missed him now that he was hanging in his rightful place alongside Rose. A couple of times, after a long day, she'd gone to the ballroom to run something by him. But his portrait remained silent, as did Rose's. It had not occurred to her that when George accomplished his mission, he might no longer need her. Fiona felt a pang of loneliness as she slipped into bed and turned off the light.

*

At the library the next morning, staff were busy clearing up the remaining evidence of Lucinda's visit. The extra chairs they'd ordered for the occasion went back to the rental company. The caterers arrived to collect their crockery and glassware. Slowly, things returned to normal.

Fiona took a detour to reach her office and stopped in the ballroom to say hello to George and Rose. "Good morning, you two. How is it, being back together?"

"I'm sure they're much happier now," came a voice from behind her, and, turning, she saw Andrew standing in the doorway.

"Oh, it's you." Fiona knew her tone was ungracious, but she wasn't in the mood to be teased about her ghostly friends.

Andrew took a few steps toward her. "Listen, can we talk? There's something I need to say to you."

"Do you want to discuss it here? I don't think we'll be disturbed." She indicated the conservatory, where two Victorian loveseats upholstered in green velvet stood—ready for guests who'd be attending Tom and Bonnie's wedding in a couple of weeks. She headed through the archway that led there from the ballroom and made herself comfortable on one of the sofas.

To her surprise, Andrew sat down next to her, though in his case, comfort seemed to have eluded him completely. He shifted in his seat, as if unable to find a restful spot.

"So, what's this about?" said Fiona, still a little brusque.

Andrew gave a good imitation of a man who'd swallowed too much ice cream and was now dealing with brain freeze. He took a breath and sat up straighter.

"Look—it's about Lucinda Parks—and Cece."

She hadn't expected this. "Her visit was a triumph," she said. "And the fact that your sister turned out to be the author was a bonus. Her being an honorary local, so to speak. I do think you might have told me earlier, though. Didn't you trust me to keep the secret?"

Andrew looked away and said nothing for a moment. Then he cleared his throat. "It's not about Cece—at least, not exactly. It's about me."

Now Fiona was totally confused. "Sorry?"

"I'm the romance author."

This was too much. The surprise of it caused Fiona to laugh out loud. "What are you talking about? Cece wrote them. She said so—and she signed the books."

"Cece is wonderful. She's been helping me out all these years, but I think yesterday she realized she doesn't like deceiving people, especially not her friends here."

He wasn't joking. He was telling the truth.

Fiona's confusion grew, accompanied by a sense of outrage. He'd deliberately deceived her. She kept her voice level as she said, "I think you need to explain."

"All right. Here goes. I started writing the first romance to find out if I could do it. After my marriage fell apart, I needed to figure out where I'd gone wrong, so I decided to write about it. I chose fiction. It seemed easier than writing about me."

"Okay. But why romance?"

"I bought some books on the subject, took a couple of online courses, found a good editor—a woman—to show me where I'd made mistakes or misunderstood the emotional responses."

Well, that was logical in a weird way, even if he hadn't quite gotten the hang of translating the fictional relationships into real life.

She nodded. "Go on."

"You know Cece works for a big publisher. She showed it to them as a manuscript by an anonymous author, and they loved it. Gave me a two-book contract, meaning I had to write another. I still wasn't sure what I was doing and thought working on a second novel might help me."

"What do you mean, 'help you'?"

"The first book was a sort of therapy for me, I suppose, and it helped me understand the theory, but true romance eluded me. And I knew I could be anonymous, at least to the reading public. The publishers didn't want to spoil the success I'd had with the pen name, so they asked Cece to front appearances for me."

Perhaps the deception hadn't been all his fault. It sounded as though he'd fallen into it without negative repercussions and just carried on.

"Is that why she was wearing that blond wig?" She didn't wait for an answer. "So that's what you were talking about last night."

Andrew's eyebrows rose in surprise. Apparently, he hadn't realized they'd been overheard.

Fiona explained. "I heard her telling you she was fed up with it."

"Oh. Well, as a result, I've promised her I'm going to stop writing romance novels, so she won't ever need to appear as me again."

Fiona wasn't convinced. "Are you sure you can give it up? Won't you miss it? What about your fans? Won't they want you to keep writing?"

"The novel I'm working on now is going to be my last. And if the publishers come clean, Cece tells me readers might even be intrigued by the idea that their favorite romances were written by a man."

He might be right, though the picture of this reticent man dealing with hordes of Lucinda Parks fans almost made her laugh.

Andrew was still talking. For a man who was usually so shy, he had a lot to say. "I don't need to write any more novels, but I've decided to do something in this one I haven't done before." He smiled at her. "I'm including a new character—a friendly ghost who needs a happy ending too."

"Are you mocking me?"

"No. Not at all. I realize not everything can be explained rationally, and I've become convinced you may be able to sense things others can't. Like dogs can tell when there's an earthquake coming."

It wasn't a perfect analogy, but nothing was ever perfect. She'd take it. "I appreciate that, despite being compared to a dog. Thank you for telling me."

"Can you forgive me for not confessing before?" He took her hands in his and, when she tried to take them back, gripped them more firmly.

"Would you help me not to be so afraid of...getting close to someone?"

She'd told Ellie she wasn't interested in a new relationship, but judging by the way her heart was racing, that might not be true. If she said yes, the two of them would be feeling their way in a changed world. They'd both have to overcome their anxiety, but at least they would understand each other.

"Let's give it a try," she said.

"Oh, there you are." Joanie Yazbeck's voice bounced back from the glass walls of the conservatory. "Hello, Andrew."

They dropped each other's hands and leaned back, startled.

Joanie gave him a shrewd look, perhaps noting his pink cheeks. "Fiona, I need to talk to you about the Beresford wedding. It's the first one since this was rebuilt, so it's got to be perfect."

"Indeed, it has. How can I help?"

Andrew smiled ruefully at Fiona as he rose and said goodbye. "See you soon."

"Do we have a board meeting coming up?" Joanie's query sounded innocent, but Fiona couldn't be certain.

"Hmmm," she said, noncommittal. Some kind of get-together seemed to be in their future, for sure.

CHAPTER 58
FIONA

Valentine's Day finally arrived. To her surprise and delight, an arrangement of pink roses had been delivered to Fiona's front door before she left for the library. Andrew was getting the hang of real-life romance, apparently.

And romance would be the order of the day when Tom Beresford married his sweetheart in the conservatory.

She stuck her head into the ballroom for a last inspection and surveyed the tables positioned around it, sparkling with the gleam of silver and the glint of reflected light from the old chandeliers.

Molly was walking through the room, adding the finishing touch—pale pink paper hearts that Bonnie had requested be strewn on the tabletops.

"I'm about to do a last-minute check of the conservatory—I want everything to be as perfect as possible for my dad and Bonnie."

"May I take a look?" said Fiona, following her. The place appeared ready, but Molly wandered the newly restored ballroom, straightening a flower here, a seat there.

Acacia had taken charge of the floral decorations, claiming her right as a member of the flower-obsessed family who'd built the conservatory a century ago. She'd decked it out with seasonal plants in pots—cream-colored hellebores, pink-and-white-striped amaryllis, poinsettia, and some winter-flowering jasmine that released its sweet fragrance over the room. Beyond the glass walls, the garden lay under a light dusting of snow, adding a fairy-tale backdrop to the scene. Everything was ready.

"What a lovely background for a wedding," said Fiona, walking up to Molly. "I'm so glad your father is the first to marry here since we restored it."

Molly smiled. "Me, too. He and Bonnie have waited long enough for this day. Even though they moved in together a while ago, having the ceremony makes a difference. We're expecting a contingent from Maple Corners, where they live, to celebrate with them. And my daughters, of course. Heather and Jackie wouldn't miss their grandfather's wedding. I'm so looking forward to it."

"I'm sure you are. I am, too, and I thank you for the invitation. It should be a wonderful day."

Molly beamed. "Listen, I have to run and get changed. People will start arriving before we know it." She retrieved her coat from where she'd dropped it on one of the loveseats, now pushed against the wall to make space for the guests' chairs. She shrugged into it.

"Of course," said Fiona. "Don't worry, I'll keep an eye on things here. Text if you need me to do anything."

Two hours later, the conservatory was as full as the fire laws allowed. Fiona waited in the second row, just behind Molly and Nick, for the *Wedding March* to signal the beginning of the ceremony.

When the first notes boomed out, she stood and turned along with the other guests and took in a breath. Walking arm-in-arm, Tom, elegant in a formal suit, glanced at Bonnie, wearing a dress and jacket in the palest of her signature pinks. As their eyes met, Fiona saw the love they shared and silently wished them well.

She listened to the couple taking their vows and wondered whether there was an echo in the conservatory—a faint repetition of the words following those of the bride and groom. In an instant, she realized, and scanned the space, hoping to be sure.

There they were. George in a gray tailcoat, a white vest, and a bow tie, Rose in the white muslin gown with the pink rosebuds that she'd worn when they met again. They stood near the windows, invisible to all but her. Or perhaps not. Elaine, who'd been sitting nearby, was staring in the same direction as Fiona, eyes wide, her smile as broad as she could manage.

So, it seemed Elaine's wish had come true. At last, it appeared she could see her ghostly heroes. Warmth spread through Fiona's chest as she absorbed the joyful energy in the room. When the justice said, "You may kiss the bride," George bent his head to leave a lingering kiss on Rose's lips. Then, as the moments passed, they faded from view.

A moment's sadness was dispelled by the applause that broke out in celebration of Tom and Bonnie. This was no time for melancholy, as George might have said. He'd certainly had an impact on Fiona's life. She followed the others into the ballroom for a late lunch and allowed herself to join the celebration.

Andrew arrived at the library after the reception was over, not being an invited guest. The conservatory didn't have enough room for too many people, so it could only handle relatively small weddings.

"Are you ready to head out?" he asked.

"More or less," she said. Some irrational feeling urged her to take one last survey of the ballroom, to scan it one more time before she turned out the lights and locked up the building. "Wait here. I'll be right back."

"Okay. Don't be too long. I managed to book us a dinner reservation. No mean feat on Valentine's Day."

She stood in the doorway of the ballroom and gazed at the remains of the wedding party. A few trampled streamers rested on the dance floor, and the tables around it looked desolate without their linen and sparkle.

As she lingered, she could make out the faint strains of a Strauss waltz. She must be imagining it, or maybe Andrew was listening to something on his phone. She reached to turn off the nearest light, and as the room darkened, she gazed in astonishment at a couple dancing slowly in time to the music.

George and Rose. They looked so in love that she couldn't bear to disturb them by saying anything. She felt bereft—this was their goodbye to her, she was certain, and she'd never see nor speak to them again. She tried to hold back the tears forming in her eyes.

CHAPTER 59
FIONA

"Is everything okay? You seem upset." Andrew was standing behind Fiona. She hadn't heard him approach.

She kept her eyes on the happily reunited pair as she answered. "I'm not upset. I'm happy for the married couple."

"Tom and Bonnie will love being married, I'm sure of it. At their age, they know what a marriage is. I think most people who've been married before have some idea of the mistakes they shouldn't make, don't you?"

"I don't mean them. Can't you see?" Fiona pointed toward the center of the room, where a beam of sunlight traced the waltzing lovers' steps.

"What?"

"George and Rose. My George and Mrs. Wentworth. They're here."

A silence followed before Andrew said, "I'm sorry, I believe you, but I can't make them out."

"They're dancing to the music."

"I can't hear any music."

He would never be able to see them, but the fact that he

was prepared to believe her meant a lot. "It's a waltz—the *Blue Danube*, I think."

While they whispered, George and Rose began to fade, as though through a mist that appeared to be undulating across the ballroom floor, until they dematerialized before vanishing.

Tears began rolling down Fiona's cheeks. She couldn't tell whether they were prompted by happiness because the Manchesters had found each other again, or sadness because of her sense that they wouldn't be back. George's quest was over, and they could be happy—now and always.

"Nothing to cry about," Andrew said as he handed her a clean napkin left behind on one of the tables encircling the dance floor. He took her into his arms. "I know how to waltz. One-two-three, one-two-three..."

Fiona smiled despite herself as they followed in the Manchesters' footsteps.

"A mathematician should know how to waltz," he said. "It's only counting, after all. Someone once told me that math was physics." He clasped her closer to him. "But romance was chemistry."

THE END

Author's Note

My thanks go to Stephanie Coakley and Christine Catallo of the delightful Pequot Library in Southport, who encouraged me from the start and offered advice on library protocol, some of which I ignored in order to make the plot work. I don't know of any haunted libraries, so I needed to have my characters do things no self-respecting librarian would do! They fact-checked the final manuscript, but any mistakes are purely mine. The Pequot Library was the inspiration for the book, but I invented the characters, the building, and the location. Because this is a work of fiction, names, characters, places, and incidents are either products of my imagination or are used fictitiously. Any resemblance to actual events, or locales, or persons, living or dead, is entirely coincidental. This applies to the ghosts, too.

ACKNOWLEDGMENTS

If you're the kind of person who reads the acknowledgments at the back of the book, you probably know that no book is written by the author alone. Not even the best-sellers. Especially not the bestsellers. So, I want to thank the people who helped me realize my dream of publishing a second book set in the fictional town of Brentford, Connecticut.

First, thanks to my critique group, who, as they always do, gave me helpful suggestions, as well as all the encouragement a writer needs. Liz Morten, C. Lee McKenzie, and Gillian Foster believed in this book and fell in love with George the minute he appeared, making me produce new pages every week until I was done.

The writers at the Women's Fiction Writers Association continue to be my friends and supporters. Their daily write-in sessions made me sit and write every day. Without them and their humor, support, and encouragement, I might never have finished this book.

Among them are Katherine Williams, Linda Rosen, Lorraine Norwood, Julie Coder, Linda Avellar, Joan Fernandez, and Stephanie Claypool, who read the book and liked it enough to review it before it was published. Thank you!

The team of people at Atmosphere Press includes editors, artists and designers, formatters, proofreaders, and production and distribution experts. Any typos should probably be laid at my door, since I signed off on the final version! Thanks in particular to Megan Turner, Alex Kale, Erin Larsen, and Ronaldo Alves for delivering the book and always being there to answer any concerns I might have had.

And thank you to my family and friends, who encouraged me and believed I could do it, even when I had doubts.

About the Author

Award-winning writer **GABI COATSWORTH** was born in Britain but has spent most of her life trying to figure out how America works by living there. So, if you find a British flavor in her books, don't be surprised. Her first Brentford novel, *A Beginner's Guide to Starting Over*, was published in April 2023 by Atmosphere Press, who also published her memoir *Love's Journey Home* (2022).

Unlike many writers, she can't write in coffee shops because they're too distracting, and she only drinks coffee as a last resort. She lives in Connecticut in a cottage that's American on the outside, and English inside. If she's not reading, writing, or traveling, you'll find her relaxing in her flower garden with a cup of her preferred beverage, strong English tea.

To learn more or to sign up for her newsletter with special bonus materials, start here, https://linktr.ee/gabicoatsworth, or on her website www.GabiCoatsworth.com.

MORE FROM GABI COATSWORTH

Thank you so much for reading *A Field Guide to Library Ghosts*. If you enjoyed it, I'd be grateful if you'd tell your friends. And if you could take a minute to write a review on Goodreads, Amazon, or BookBub, I'd be very grateful. Reviews mean a lot to authors because they get our books noticed by new readers. It doesn't have to be long. Just a star rating and a sentence or two is perfect!

About Atmosphere Press

Founded in 2015, Atmosphere Press was built on the principles of Honesty, Transparency, Professionalism, Kindness, and Making Your Book Awesome. As an ethical and author-friendly hybrid press, we stay true to that founding mission today.

If you're a reader, enter our giveaway for a free book here:

SCAN TO ENTER
BOOK GIVEAWAY

And always feel free to visit Atmosphere Press and our authors online at atmospherepress.com. See you there soon!

www.ingramcontent.com/pod-product-compliance
Ingram Content Group UK Ltd.
Pitfield, Milton Keynes, MK11 3LW, UK
UKHW010738291025
8653UKWH00030B/324